LONELY TRAIL

Rob Morgan is young, bold, and burning with ambition as the lonely leader of his footloose friends. They witness a stage-coach robbery, and Morgan vows to find the silver-hatted bandit for the rich Wells-Fargo reward.

He also covets the Fontana Rancho and hacienda, and by chance befriends the Señor Fontana's son Benito. In the valley town of Twenty Mile, Morgan's quest becomes complicated: a number of men sport silver hats, he acquires a vicious enemy in Steve Question, the main suspect and gang leader, and a mysterious girl who the locals call Golden Tiger Lily, appears—and disappears—in the moonlit Rancho garden where Question and Morgan are guests. She wears gold coins from Question's hidden cache; he is furious. Each man trails the Lily, and soon the lives of everyone involved are in danger.

Jackson Gregory was born in Salinas, California. He graduated from the University of California at Berkeley in 1906. His early career was in journalism in the East, primarily for the New York City News Association. By 1913 he was writing Western and adventure fiction for the magazine market. *The Outlaw* (1916) was his first Western novel, published by Dodd, Mead. "Silver Slippers", an early story appearing in Adventure Magazine, was filmed as *The Man From Painted Post* (Artcraft, 1917), starring Douglas Fairbanks, a story later expanded to form *The Man From Painted Rock* (1943). *Six Feet Four* (Pathé, 1919) was the first of Gregory's novels to be brought to the screen, directed by Henry King. *Judith Of Blue Lake Ranch* (1919) was the first of his Western romances published by Charles Scribner's Sons where Gregory's editor was Maxwell Perkins. The style and types of stories he told appeared to be a combination of Zane Grey and F. Scott Fitzgerald, the latter another noted author edited by Perkins. *The Bells Of San Juan* (1919) was serialized in four parts in Adventure Magazine in 1918 and, following book publication, was filmed in 1922 by Fox, starring Buck Jones, a popular movie cowboy of the time. Buck Jones particularly liked Gregory's stories and often used them for his film vehicles, including *Hearts And Spurs* (Fox, 1925) based on *The Outlaw*, *Timber Wolf* (Fox, 1925), *Desert Valley* (Fox, 1926), and Sudden Bill Dorn (Universal, 1937). Tom Mix starred in the screen adaptation of *The Everlasting Whisper* (Fox, 1925). Beginning with *Redwood and Gold* (1928), Gregory returned to Dodd, Mead as his book publisher, and for the next decade and a half would publish one and sometimes two Western novels a year. His best novels would certainly include *The Shadow On The Mesa* (1933), *Into The Sunset* (1936), and *Secret Valley* (1939). Perhaps the New York Times said it best about a Western story by Jackson Gregory: "It is the sort of book that, once started, one gallops eagerly and absorbedly through, hating to put it down until the final page."

LONELY TRAIL

Jackson Gregory

GUNSMOKE

First published in the UK by Collins

This hardback edition 2007
by BBC Audiobooks Ltd
by arrangement with
Golden West Literary Agency

ISBN 978 1 405 68177 3

British Library Cataloguing in Publication Data available.

Printed and bound in Great Britain by
Antony Rowe Ltd., Chippenham, Wiltshire

CHAPTER ONE

THEY won through.

Small, slight words if you can say them fast, but one has to realise what can lie behind them.

They won through.

They came from the East and the South to the West. They battled through drought and blizzard and starvation, through every day's perils, through Indian attacks, through burning thirst and privation of every sort. But——

They won through.

Some of them died. Died fighting, and had their scalps lifted while they could still feel knife and hatchet, or died otherwise and lay in shallow graves, or no graves at all. Well, they had lived their lives, young though so many of them were. They had killed as many Indians as the Indians had killed of them. And they won through, either in themselves or in their children.

It was nearly dusk out on the prairie. A little girl, a pretty and delicately dainty, fairylike little thing, about five or six years old, was picking flowers along the creek. She was singing a little wordless song; she was all lighted up with happiness and springtime, and the candles of her own young youth.

Then, like an explosion, the whole world, for her, crashed all to pieces about her. She heard the screaming, the wild Indian yells, the gunshots. She cowered down in the willows. She went down on her knees and prayed to the Good God as she had neved known how to pray before. She said, " Oh, dear God, don't let this happen to my mamma! Don't let it happen to papa and Dickie and Jess! Please, God *don't*!"

But it did happen. And she saw it. She tried not to peek between her fingers, tightly pressed on her eyelids, but she saw the stark horror of the thing.

And she ran and ran, and kept on running. . . .

And so it started with little Golden Tiger Lily, then five or six years old.

She saw her father, her mother, her brother and sister slaughtered, like beef cut down. She even saw her own mother's hair lifted. . . .

At five or six years old.

She ran away, frightened nearly to death. She ran and hid in the willows. She lay down, her small, slight body pressed tight to the mother earth, the only mother she had left to her, and sobbed her heart out. She had been so happy, a little girl of five or six, with a great big wonderful daddy with fine black whiskers, and a lovely mamma who was like a flower in your dreams, and a brother and sister—and now—all of a sudden, she was without anything in the world. Just a little girl sobbing her heart out. And afraid. Afraid of everything. Nothing to do but run and hide.

And that is the way it started.

It was early springtime, else she would have died, and there would be nothing to say of the Golden Tiger Lily. But springtime leads on to summer.

I don't know, I who am trying to tell you about this thing, all that happened, and you couldn't know of your own knowledge either, because neither of us lived then. We have to begin with, a little frightened girl, hardly more than a baby, running away from a scene of sheer, stark horror. But we both do know that there is something indomitable in all of us that clings on to life and to all life's promises, be they lies or verities.

She didn't even know her own name. They had called her Pet, Dolly, Baby; mostly they called her Honey. She didn't know her mamma's name, her papa's. Just mamma and papa they were. She was too young to read or write. She did know some Mother Goose rhymes and fairy tales, and something of Adam and Eve, and Jonah and the whale.

She was just a little girl, all alone in a terrifyingly enormous world, afraid of Indians, even afraid of white men. For there had been that white man, a laughing devil, who stood with his hands on his hips, his lean face bronzed in the firelight, while her whole world was cut down.

She ran and she hid. She hid from everything. And she slept in the heart of the bushes, for warmth and for refuge. And she ate what she could find to eat. Springtime brought a few crude berries; she ate grass and she nibbled at roots and green stems of growing things.

And the mountains towered about and above her, and were as tall as the high heavens, and the forests were armies of grim giants, and there was no end to the plains that ran out east and west. She saw the sun come up and saw shadows shift stealthily across the face of the world; she saw the stars come out, and the moon. And she sobbed morning and noon and night until, exhausted in spirit and tiny body, she fell asleep.

And even dreams seemed to come and catch her by the hair and drag her back, again and again, through all that had happened.

There were the times, a few times only, when she saw the lights of camp-fires. She crept, in silence and fascinated fright, as soft-padded as a wildcat, to the edge of a thicket and peered out at them. But she would not go close to them. They might be Indians—they might be bad white men.

Five or six years old. With all that horror stamped on her plastic brain.

The days, with summer on the way, grew warmer and more generous, and saved her.

Out of her there grew a tradition and a legend. It is still remembered throughout the Middle West and the Far West. The story of the Golden Tiger Lily.

CHAPTER TWO

THEN, some ten years later, there were an even dozen men squatting on their heels about a camp-fire. They were men from Kentucky, Georgia, Tennessee, and one man from Virginia.

The man from Virginia was the youngest of the lot, nineteen or twenty years old, he didn't exactly know. But already he had a small moustache and a bit of a beard like Robert E. Lees', and there were fitful fires in his dark eyes. He thought being young, that he knew what he wanted and where he was going. Life to him was very simple: Go out, young man, go West, my boy, and fill your hands with all that you crave to have. It's there and it's yours. All you've got to do is go out and get it. Never mind the other man.

That was Rob Roy Morgan.

Ringed as they were about the fire, the twelve men were much alike. To be sure, the flickering firelight, half smoke, brought out a sameness; it showed lean, brown, hungry faces and watchful eyes. They didn't know what was going to happen next, or how soon; they suspected the world into which they had entered, and they had ample grounds, one and another, to suspect one another.

Big Mouth spoke up, gnawing a bone. They called him Big Mouth because it exactly described him: He was always talking. He knew about everything.

" Two days from now," said Big Mouth, " we'll hit a town. It's the town of Twenty Mile. I know because Kit Carson and Dan'l Boone——"

Luke Brady guffawed. He had no respect for names. He said:

" Kit Carson was his uncle and Dan Boone was his sister's grandpa! Haw!"

" Shet your mouth," said Big Mouth. " I'm a-telling you."

And he told them.

Big Mouth's name, if names count, was Leicester Altoona Jackson. None but Big Mouth himself knew the full name, and he was by way of forgetting it. But he told them.

And he could tell a story, wrapping his tongue round it.

" I went out last afternoon and brung home a fat deer, didn't I?" said Big Mouth.

Charlie Duff had to speak up. He was almost as bad as Big Mouth when it came to spilling out empty words. He said squeakily, Charlie's voice being like that:

" You brung us a deer, feller. I couldn't say it was a fat one. Haw!"

" How much meat did you bring into camp?" Altoona asked him. And then he went on, " Like I'm telling you boys, I brung in a nice fat deer. While doing so I met up with a stranger. We squatted over a fire and cooked us some meat, and we talked awhile——"

The other men laughed. They said, " Who talked? Just you, while he swallowed his deer meat?"

" Leave me alone," said Altoona, and sounded disgusted.
" There was something I was going to tell you. Now, I've
changed my mind."

Buck Braddock spoke up, and Buck as a usual thing kept
his lips locked. He said:

" Let's have it, Al. We'll listen, and if you don't tell it
quickly you'll just nacherly swell up and bust. Here we go,
huh, Big Mouth?"

Big Mouth, Leicester Altoona Jackson, heaved himself up.

" Take it away or just leave it on the table," said Big
Mouth. " Here's what."

And he told them, while they picked their teeth, what he
had learned from the stranger. It was the story about the
Tiger Lily girl.

They laughed; being young, all but two of them, and,
boisterous and without any deep thought, it sounded to them
like a fairy tale. Because, the way he told it, the way it was
being told all across the western country, the Tiger Lily girl did
sound like something you had dreamed, like something that
had never had any actual existence.

Rob Roy Morgan laughed loudest and longest of them all.

" If there was a real girl like that," he said, " if I could
find a girl like that, why, I'd just naturally go out and rope
her. I'd keep her for a house pet."

"If you only had a house first," chirped up Red Barbee.
And they all laughed.

" Tell us some more, Big Mouth," said Smoke Keena. He
spat freely, being a truly great tobacco chewer. " Sounds
good."

" We-el," said Big Mouth, taking his time, " this here
stranger, he told me some more things. Like this: Two more
days and with lucky going we land up in Twenty Mile. He
just come from there. There's an old man, and he's got a wife
along with him, and he's got a daughter, name of Barbara,
that's nicer to look at than a young moon in a summer sky."

They yowled at him, young Rob Roy Morgan's laughter
being louder than the rest.

" You fellers is all crazy," grumbled Big Mouth Altoona.
" You make me kind of sick. Here all I says is that there's
a pretty girl inside two days' travel from here, and you yip
like coyotes. How long since any man of you has let his eyes

creep over a good-looking young female? Like I says, you make me sick.''

'' Where are we going from here?'' said young Morgan, and stood up, his thumbs hitched into his belt. '' And what are we looking for anyhow?''

Obviously he meant to make something of the moment. His companions caught the altered inflection of his voice and looked at him curiously—all but the Blind Man, who could feel where the fire was through his eyelids, and the Old Man, who kept on toothlessly sucking a bone.

'' Make us a speech, Virginia,'' said Buck Braddock. '' Let's pretend we are back down in Georgia, and they's a camp meeting, and you're Senator Bills that they've paid ten dollars to come down and shout. Go 'head, Virginia.''

Young Morgan scowled at him. '' You're a damn fool, Buck, and ever will be,'' he said morosely.

The young half-breed, Tony they called him, in a dreamy mood and not listening, had rolled his cigarette and began plucking sentimentally on his guitar. Rob Roy Morgan kicked the instrument out of Tony's hands and sent it flying in splinters. Tony sprang to his feet with all the fury of a spitting wildcat and whipped out six inches of slim, shiny steel. But Morgan was watchful and was as quick or even a thought quicker. His hands were close to the guns at his hips, and of the odd mixture of a dozen men there was no other as quick and as accurate with pistol or rifle. His eyes were as hard and cold as shoe buttons as he fired the one shot that broke Tony's wrist and disposed of the knife.

Men came surging up, all but the Old Man and the Blind Man. The others, seeing Tony, whom they rather liked in an off-hand sort of way, shot and cruelly hurt, and all for nothing, were ready like a pack of wolves to pile on to the man from Virginia and make an end to him and his overbearing ways. Or if not quite ready, almost.

But '' almost '' has a way of falling short of getting anywhere. There was no almost about Rob Roy Morgan, no taint of it in any fibre of his being. He brushed his big, black, battered old broad-brimmed hat back and regarded them balefully, a gun in each hand.

'' We're a party, a party of twelve men, and we're headed west, all the way west to California,'' he told them. '' If we get anywhere and do anything, someday this party will get to be known as Rob Roy Morgan's party. I'm the only man of the lot that's got brains and gumption and a sort of habit of coming out on top. And you'll keep your damn mouths shut when I've got anything to say, or else you'll get what Tony got or more of it. Now hunker down and I'll make you that speech like Buck Braddock says, like a senator paid ten dollars to shout in your ears. Do like the Old Man does and like the Blind Man does, or get the hell out of here and leave me alone to have as big a hunk of the world as I'm craving. Any leavings, you boys can have."

They had never seen him fire up like that, him or any other man. Before their puzzled eyes he seemed to swell to a greater stature. His eyes lashed at them like fire-tipped whips. They saw that he was in the mood to kill—they knew how deadly he could be with his two guns—they kept thinking of how swiftly he had meted out Tony's punishment.

Altoona Jackson said, " Let's hunker down, fellers, and listen to the kid blow his top off."

Not a man of them had even drawn a gun; not a man who wasn't afraid to. They muttered, and some of them laughed and some sneered, but they again squatted on their heels.

Morgan slid his weapons back into their holsters. He even rolled a cigarette. In both gestures there was braggadocio, but a braggart he was, and not yet twenty. He took his time with them; he took time enough for it to dawn on even the most stupid of them that he was defying them all, that he held them in no fear, that it was he who meant to dominate them from this moment on. He licked and lighted his cigarette.

Then he spoke to Tony. He said, sounding amused, " I could have shot you plumb square through the gizzard, Tony, and you know it as well as I do. This time, you get a lesson in manners. Next time, so help me, if there is a next time, I'll kill you."

Tony did not answer. He clasped his broken, bleeding wrist and looked wildly, his eyes like a mad dog's, at the fallen knife.

Young Morgan saw the look and stepped quickly to where the knife lay, bright in the firelight. He picked it up and flipped it to Tony's feet.

" If you still feel grouchy, kid, and want to fight," he

said jeeringly, " just pick up your dagger and get started.
Me, I'll give you a break; I'll use my bowie knife against you,
and in my left hand, too."

Hotter than ever flickered the fires of rage in Tony's eyes,
but his glance dropped to his shattered wrist. He was in dire
pain, and the blood was dropping steadily to the ground.

Young Morgan laughed at him.

" You've got more sense than I thought you had, Tony,"
he said. " I reckon you've learned your lesson good and
plenty; just keep off me after this." Then he called to Altoona
Jackson, saying curtly, with the ring of command in his voice,
" You, Big Mouth, you know how to take care of a wound
like that as good as any of us. Well, fix up Tony's crippled
wing for him."

Perhaps Big Mouth was already on the verge of doing just
this, for he liked the young half-breed. It is equally likely
that the new note of a dictator in young Morgan's tone was
all that was needed to set him about the humane business. At
any rate, without a word, he rose again and went to minister
as best he could, crudely yet efficiently and with a certain
gentleness, to the wounded man.

" What I was going to say was this," continued the young
Virginian: " Like I said already, we're a party of men
headed for California. We're getting almost in shooting distance of the land of gold. Now, we got to make up our minds
what we want when we get there. And most of all, how we're
going to come at it. You boys haven't thought much about
that, have you? Me, I have. That's why I'm making you an
oration like a senator to-night. Either you boys do what I
say, figuring me as captain of this party, or I boot the lot of
you out to hell, and I go ahead alone. And I aim to know
right now!"

Some of them laughed at him, but it was noteworthy that
the laughter of the few was short-lived and that there was
small spontaneity in it. For the greater part their lips were
locked tight; nothing about them moved except their eyes,
and they shifted only from his lean, hard face to the faces of
their companions, then back again to him. Yes, of a sudden
they were afraid of him. Give them a chance, some of them
later might shoot him in the back, but now they were con-
strained to squat silently and listen.

Swiftly, in some queer fashion, his mood changed. His voice, too, took on a new quality. His eyes were just as bright, but even they seemed to glow with a new sort of brightness; they weren't so hard, they were like the eyes of a man on vast distances, dreaming great dreams. He spoke to them slowly, thoughtfully. He should have had a long white beard then, and a tall staff to lean on; his attitude was that of a patriarch.

" Every man who heads for California," he said, " has his mind set on gold. Even the Old Man and the Blind Man, that's what they're thinking about. So are all the rest of us. But now, I've talked with a sight of men we've met up with, going and coming. There's more gold in California that would choke up the Rapidan River—only, where is it and how do you get it? It's in the ground and you got to dig it out. Some days, being lucky, maybe you dig out ten dollars, maybe a hundred, say you even hit on a lump that's worth a thousand! But first you get a pick and a shovel, and you go to work. You work like niggers in a cotton field; you work until your muscles cramp and your back aches and you get blisters. You drown yourself in sweat. How many of you boys figure it would be a lot of fun, working like that? You just think a minute, any of you that can think, and speak up."

Again they looked at each other, then back at him.

" Hell," said Red Barbee, I've worked since I was five or six. I've hoed in the corn, and I've chopped wood and toted it. Hell, I can work if I've got to."

" You'd work. Pick and shovel. You'd make your ten dollars, or your hundred, or your thousand. Then what?"

Red Barbee had a prompt answer to that one.

" Wheee! I'd throw my hat over the highest tree and burn the trail for town! I'd buy the damn place! I'd get me a pair of boots and a hat, and man, would I eat! I'd strike for the nearest dance hall and, oh man, would I break in them new boots! I'd——"

" You'd have yourself a hot old time, Barbee, and it would last you about ten hours. Then you'd go back to your pick and shovel and sweat and blisters and sore back. And it wouldn't be any fun working the day after a jamboree like that one you've got in your mind."

" It ain't no senator making us a speech," said Charlie Duff. " It's a damn preacher! "

That elicited a small ripple of laughter, but still men watched young Morgan and listened to him.

" Here's what I'm going to do," he told them. " Me, I'm going to live like a king the rest of my born days, and I don't aim to do a single lick of work. I aim to have me a fine place, a big warm house come winter, servants all over the place, so much gold that when I go to town I'll take an Injun boy along to carry it for me, and I don't hanker for any sore back and sweat and blisters on my hands. Not me. If you boys want to stride along with me and do like I tell you, I'll see you're all well fixed; that you've got plenty to eat, good clothes to wear, warm beds to sleep in, licker by the barrel, plenty of gold in your pockets—and no pick and shovels within a day's journey! "

He talked now like a pirate captain, and that was just about what he was in his heart. He had his dream, and there was poetry in it; there was the unbridled spirit of piracy, too. And he had their attention riveted.

He cast a spell over them. He didn't promise, " We'll all live like kings." He meant to live like a king and they might share in overbrimming measure with him. He talked on and on; he fascinated them. Even the half-breed, Tony, listened to him with eyes that grew big and bright.

Thus that night Rob Roy Morgan elected himself their leader. And when he went to sleep, slightly drawn apart from the others, there was a gun in his hand and a contemptuous smile upon his lips.

CHAPTER THREE

THE next morning they were a sober crowd. There was little talk among them as they built their fires and made their breakfast. The sun was red and genially warm above the tall mountains behind them, a purple, flinty barrier which they had surmounted, and there extended a land of fair and dimpled loveliness before them. The land of promise it was— the young Virginian's promise!

Their cavalcade made, in its small way, a splendid showing. The twelve men were well mounted; their horses had been acquired in various ways, some even having been bought and paid for. For the twelve there were twenty-seven horses. Each man, besides the mount he bestrode, had a led horse, and there were three pack animals. At the fore, taking his place and keeping it, no matter what the terrain, some twenty to fifty feet ahead, rode Rob Roy Morgan. He wore his hat with the broad brim well tilted back, and this morning he had a red-hawk feather for a plume of sorts in his hat band. He didn't mind dramatising himself. The horse he rode was ink-black, and he had named it Jet. The one he led was flawlessly white, a slim and graceful yet swift and tireless thing he named Snow White. There was not a horse in the lot for any man to be ashamed of.

At times they were strung out in a long line, following the leader. At other times they rode three and four abreast. Coming down into a broad, undulating valley, they scattered out on a wide front. But when they had crossed the valley, riding swiftly with smooth going underfoot, they came again into the hills, then into another range of mountains, and here again they were forced to ride single file. And still their new captain of adventure kept well to the fore. They followed him and the long feather dropped from a red hawk's wing.

Always, bringing up the rear, were the Old Man and the Blind Man. It was their custom to keep in the background. They didn't talk much, even to each other. But they understood each other, so not many words were needed. On every day's ride the Old Man put one end of his rope into the Blind Man's hand; they by now could signal each other along the short length of rope. And it was their job to lead the three pack horses.

One dropped into routine. Thus, like the two old men, Smoke Keena and Buck Braddock had got into the habit of riding together most of the time; more than half the time, anyhow. So this gala morning their horses nuzzled each other, as did their led horses.

" Listen to him sing," said Smoke Keena.

The boy from Virginia was in fine fettle this morning. And he did have a voice that rang out as fine and clear as anybody's bugle. And he had been to school. Of all incomprehensible things, he knew his Browning! He sang lustily:

> " Fifty score strong,
>   Marching along,
>   Great-hearted gentlemen,
>   Singing this song——"

and from then on, forgetting the words, he improvised. A
dozen great-hearted gentlemen headed into California. The
feather in his hat stood high.

> " Riding along,
>   One dozen strong,
>   Old Man and Blind Man
>   And some that's done wrong,
>   Young men and old,
>   Both cowards and bold,
>   Ain't you glad you've been born, you are!
>   So open your arms, California!
>   Beat the drum! Here we come!
>   *Here we come !* "

" He's drunk," said Buck Braddock.

" Like hell he is," said Smoke Keena. " He's just got fire
under his bonnet. Watch me ride up with him. Right alongside."

And Keena spurred up ahead. And when the Captain of
Adventure had to stop to take a breath, Keena said:

" Me, I'm with you, kid. And, if you'll listen to me,
you're going to need somebody you can tie to. How about
it?"

The Captain of Adventure grinned at him. He said:

" Can you sing, Smoke?"

The king of tobacco-juice marksmen, Smoke Keena shot
out a long amber stream at a hurrying lizard—and hit it.

" Sing? Just you listen!"

" But what songs can you sing?"

" Church hymns? I'm good at them. Then there's
' Susanna.' If you hadn't broke Tony's arm, and he had his
banjo——"

" ' Roll, Jordan, roll '?"

" Just you spread your ears and listen!" said Smoke Keena.

They sang together, and all the small crowd rolled along with them. And so, over a hilltop, they came down into a lovely California valley.

" It won't be long now," said the boy from Virginia. Then he half swung round in his saddle to look Smoke Keena straight in the eyes. " You're sticking with me, Keena? Whether she blows hot or cold? We'll have some tough days; we'll have a lot of fat days. You got to take 'em as they roll, both high and low. Want it like that?"

Smoke Keena hadn't been sure until now. Now he shoved out his hand.

" Shake, kid," he said.

They shook. And with that simple ceremony they cemented an enduring partnership. Rob Roy Morgan, Captain of a handful of nondescript ruffians; Smoke Keena, first lieutenant; two young fellows born to go places. Two young men to be heard from and to be remembered in one way and another. Two staunch friends, except when hot blood and cross-purposes shook them to their, as yet, uncertain foundations. For both of them were still groping for the true. They loved each other, they hated each other; they tried to kill each other, and they risked their lives for each other. In the end, their friendship endured.

" Where'd you come from, anyhow, Keena?" asked Rob Roy Morgan. " Tennessee, wasn't it!"

" Nawp. Nary Tennessee. Me, I'm from No'th Ca'lina. It's a right good place to be and a right good place to come from."

" Hm," said Morgan. " North Carolina, Huh? Initials, N.C." he laughed. " You sort of like to call me Virginia, don't you? Sounds sort of girly, calling a man Virginia. Now, you. North Carolina, N.C.—and that sounds sort of like Nancy! Here we go, Nancy."

He smote Keena on the back and the two rode on laughing.

" I'll bet a man," said Smoke Keena, newly dubbed Nancy, " that, your name being Robert, they call you Rob or Robbie when you was a kid. Short of robber!"

And playfully he knocked Morgan's tall hat off.

" Who scoops it up first gets a dollar!" said Morgan. " Riding at a gallop!"

They played fair. Their following cavalcade watched them with mild, humorous interest. They two pulled back and circled and swooped down upon the fallen hat, leaning from their saddles. And it was the hat's owner, Morgan himself, who snatched up the fallen headgear. He put it on, its feather still cockily in place, and extended a hand. Smoke Keena dug down for a dollar and the two rode on, still laughing.

" There's a game they got out here in California," said Morgan. " Turkey pulling you might call it. You dig a hole in the ground and plant a live turkey, just his neck and head sticking out. Then you swoop down on him on horseback, riding hell for leather, and you grab. He dodges and you take your chance. Pull his head off and he's yours, and five dollars along with it. A man I was talking with back yonder was telling me."

" Let's go!" said Smoke Keena.

It was the following afternoon with dusk not far off and small gusts of rain blowing into their faces that they witnessed a happening which held them rigid in their saddles. They had just come to the crest of a long line of live-oak-clad hills! Off to the south they saw a white road winding. It was a couple of miles away, yet despite the shafts of rain there was a sun shining, and the lumbering red stagecoach with its four lean, racing horses was as clear in their vision as a picture done by an artist who challenged the eye.

That white road snaked windingly up into the hills, hidden here and there by groves of pine and oak intermingled. What caught their attention was a small body of horsemen, some half-dozen of them, bursting out of the timber into the road and stopping the stage. They saw a tangle of flailing horses; they saw the stage lurch and all but turn over. Too far for any accurate vision. But they knew what it was all about and fancied, rather than saw clearly, unmounted men swarming like ants over the ambushed vehicle.

" Stage robbers!" said Smoke Keena.

" See how it goes, Nancy?" grinned Rob Roy Morgan. He sat loosely in the saddle, one knee caught up over his saddle-horn, resting himself. " There's a Wells Fargo box on that stage; it's got plenty money in it. Well, somebody worked for that money, huh? Pick and shovel, huh? And now these easy gents pick it off. Like what I was already talking to you about."

" Meaning we're turning road agents?" asked Keena.

Morgan laughed at him.

" Let's ride along," he said.

So they rode, turning down into another valley, paying no further attention to a stage hold-up, which was certainly no affair of theirs and which, also, was at too long range to bother about. But what they had seen stuck in their minds.

" You see," said Morgan, " it's like I told you. Now, if you and me overhauled those road agents and lifted the gold money off them, whose money would it be? And who would have done all the hard work? And what could we do with it?"

" I got you, Virginia," said Smoke Keena. " Only we can't ever come up with 'em. They're too far off and going hell-bent."

" We might see them later, Nancy. Or some more like 'em. And I'll tell you something: Maybe you didn't notice, but I was using my spy-glass while the fracas was on." He tapped the spy-glass which he carried at his hip in a slender buckskin scabbard he had made for it. " And I'll know their head man unless he changes himself a whole lot. He wears a high white sombrero, and he's got silver spangles all over him that shine like broken glass in the sunlight, and he's got a certain sort of way of riding, loose in the saddle and at the same time like a snake standing straight up on its tail. And you can tell, far as you can see him, how he'd take the middle of any man's sidewalk and would bust his way into a bar-room and damn the man whose toes he stepped on. We'll likely meet up with him some day, Smoke, as I can feel it in my bones. And you can just figure that from now on he is working for me!"

Their trail, while generally trending westward, wound sinuously among the hills, brought them into a steep-walled ravine, turned them briefly southward, and from a slight eminence they came again in sight of the spot where the stage had been held up and robbed.

" All we've got to do is ride out of our way half a mile and look things over," said Smoke Keena. " Why not? We ain't hurrying to anybody's wedding or funeral, and maybe in their rush they dropped a few gold pieces."

All they found was one man dead and another dying, and a woman's bonnet. The dying man tried to sit up and talk; he did manage to say, " Silver Hat, he done it." Then, his duty done, one would say, very promptly he settled down and died.

Silver Hat? A name easy to remember.

" Funny the stage went on and left these two dead men, ain't it?" suggested Smoke Keena.

" Yes, it's kind of funny. Maybe they were a couple of Silver Hat's gang. Anyhow, let's travel."

" And they left a lady's Sunday-go-to-meeting bonnet," said Red Barbee. He stooped from the saddle and caught it up. " Say, look at the glad ribbons!" He removed his hat and put on the bonnet, and they laughed and rode on.

Now, of all this, of course, the Blind Man had seen nothing, but the Old Man had told him all about everything so that it was as though he had seen. Even the detail of Red Barbee wearing the bonnet with its streaming ribbons. The Blind Man laughed with the others.

An hour later their self-appointed leader checked them upon a hilltop; his roving and alert eyes had picked out three things worthy of notice—anyhow, of his notice. One was a rolling cloud of dust puffing up from the road ahead. One was the glint of the setting sun upon the windows, making them glitter like diamonds. The third was the long, sinuous valley down into which they were headed, with a group of whitewashed buildings the size of doll houses in the far southern distance.

" There goes the stage, I reckon," he said. " And yonder is a town; must be Twenty Mile, and the stage is headed for it. And this valley—Well, it looks like home to me! It's a valley like a man's dream, long and winding, rich and shady. And talk about silver! Look at that crooked little river winding along. The grass is high and green, and in the hills there'll be deer and bear and all sorts of small game, and in the river trout as thick as the scales on their own hides. And there are the houses with the white walls to live in! This here is my place! I can feel it in my bones. The folks down there have just been getting it ready and waiting for me!"

The Old Man said whisperingly to the Blind Man, " He's awful damn young, he is."

Tony, with his arm in a sling, spoke up. He said, " That's a nice place you got waitin' for you, Virginia, sure for sure. But that leetle town, she looks good to me. Maybe they got a doctor there to feex me up, no? And from the leetle town to the hacienda is maybe ten, fifteen mile."

There was a clamour of voices. The big rancho would wait, men decided, but a town was what they wanted right now.

" And remember," shouted Big Mouth, " that that old gent and his old lady and a pretty young girl name of Barbara is in Twenty Mile! With Twenty Mile not over three-four miles away, and the sun still a-shining!"

Red Barbee waved his bonnet with its bright, flaunting ribbons.

" A present for Miss Barbara!" he called out, and for once, and for a few minutes he spurred into the lead. But that " awful damn young " man from Virginia overhauled him and swept by him and led the way into town just as the sun, going down, left bright banners of gold and crimson in the western sky.

CHAPTER FOUR

IT WAS a town like other towns along the old Mother Lode. It was a town very much like towns still are along the slopes of the Sierra Nevada, like Hang Town and Yankee Jim's, like Columbia and Jackson and Sutter Creek and Columbia and Sonora. A man's town, since not many women had arrived as yet, and those negligible; a young man's town for the most part, though there were a few white-beards, as witness the Old Man and the Blind Man. On the slopes back of the one street were cabins where, after a fashion, men lived; anyhow, dens in which they slept. On the street there were saloons. A store or two, and a false-fronted hotel, barber shop and lunch counter and stable, at the bend in the road, and black-smith shop. Mostly saloons and dance halls. And at this early hour the air throbbed with music.

Music, if rightly it could be called that. Anyhow two or

three old pianos tinkled tinnily, and there were accordions and a fiddle or two, and a great wheel into whose slot you could drop a coin, the quarter of a dollar, and get " Home Sweet Home," or " When the Roses Bloom Again."

And the restless feet of young men made quick spurting clouds of dust up and down the main street. For it wasn't every day, and it wasn't every week or month, and it wasn't even every year, that a young lady like Barbara McWilliams came to town! Word of her coming had travelled ahead of her; miners had dropped their picks a score of miles away and were here in their gala best before her arrival. Rumour sped as fast as a horse could gallop, and seemed mysteriously to speed even faster. It was known that her father was a cousin of sorts to old Abner McKinnon, who owned and operated the General Merchandise Store; that old Abner, in failing health, was planning to return to Kentucky; that Mr. McWilliams had bought him out and had come to take over. And somehow it was also known that Mr. and Mrs. McWilliams had left their gay little daughter with friends, the Bayberrys of Little Run, and that she was coming on to-day by stage.

She was as pretty as a picture when she allowed her slim, slight self to be lifted down from the stage, but she was a tragic sight, too. Her cheeks, were usually pink roses bloomed, were white, and there was a smudge of dust on one of them, and there were traces of tears from her great, swimming blue eyes. If a man had jumped at her and said " Scat!" she was all set to keel over and faint.

The old red stage, rocking crazily on its leather straps, pulled up in front of the hotel just as a small cavalcade of strangers, twelve men with their extra horses, came pounding into town. It had been a neck-and-neck race at the last; they had seen the stage ahead and meant to be on hand when it got to town; the stage driver had seen them, had thought that maybe here came another gang of highwaymen—and he wasn't far wrong!—and used his long whip so that it cracked like a string of pistol shots.

Little Miss Barbara—recently she had heard it announced that she was just arrived at marriageable age, sixteen, to be exact—caught and held the eyes of the young men, good and bad. She had a pair of big eyes that were as blue as California skies at their best, she had a wealth of sunny-gold hair which the wind had blown all about her piquant face—and she had lost her bonnet.

She did have a parasol, but it was a small, futile ruin, and her summery blue dress was all in disorder.

A stalwart man, just about old enough to be the girl's father, wearing high shiny boots, a battered old hat and a luxuriant pair of whiskers nicely parted in the middle under a square chin, was the first at the stage door to lift her down.

" Barbie!" he said. " What is it, Barbie? What's happened?"

She threw her arms around him and hugged him tight.

" Oh!" said Barbara. And again she said " Oh!" Then, still clutching him, she said, " It was terrible! Terrible! Why did we ever come out to this horrible country? I want to go back home, daddy! Take us back home."

He patted her on the back with a big, awkward, yet very gentle hand.

Red Barbee was already on foot and pressed forward throught the crowd, elbowing right and left. In his hand, held high, was a bonnet with gay streamers of ribbons.

" I brought you your bonnet, Miss Barbara," he said politely.

Barbara looked at him with truly enormous eyes; she looked at the bonnet and gasped.

" Oh!" she said again. It was very nearly all she could say to-day. Then with a second gasp as she accepted his offering, she said, " Thank you, sir," And her big eyes took him all in from top to toe—and even smiled faintly at him.

" You're right welcome, Miss," said Red Barbee, and his eager eyes held hers for a moment so that she flushed up—and so did Red Barbee. He hurried back to his horse.

Men were holding the stage horses' bits. The stage driver sat high up on his seat like a king on his throne; he had to drive on yet to the crooked bend in the road where the livery stable was. He said, as many began asking questions:

" It was a hold-up. Up near Fiddler's Gulch. Yep, they got the strong box. And they shot Tom Stukey; he's inside; better get him out; he's bad hurt. But Tom got two of them, anyhow. Silver Hat's gang."

They got Tom Stukey, the guard, out and carried him into the hotel and to a bed while a boy ran for the doctor. The stage unloaded and went rocking and swaying away, down to the stable.

"Barbie!" yipped a shrill voice, a voice that cut through the uproar like an old, rusty knife blade through leather. "Barbie! Be that you?"

The Old Man and the Blind Man had shoved their horses to the fore; they had left the pack horses and their antiquated jackass, Maxwelton, in charge of Charlie Duff and Buck Braddock. It was the Blind Man, who so seldom spoke at all and whose voice had rather gone rusty, who shrilled his words in a thin, piping bugle.

Barbara gripped her father's arms. She said in a small voice stifled with astonishment:

"Daddy! Look! it's Gran'pa Jonathan and Luke Christmas!" She waved her bonnet wildly. "Hallo, Gran'pa Jonathan! Hallo, Mr. Luke Christmas! Oh, this place is just like heaven now!"

The Old Man, to wit, Luke Christmas, got down and gave a hand to the Blind Man, none other than "Gran'pa Jonathan," and led him forward through a crowd which, having ears and eyes and a modicum of understanding, split wide open for the two old men to pass through. In another moment little Miss Barbara, thrusting parasol and bonnet into her father's care, had her plump arms around first the Blind Man, then the Old Man. She laughed and she cried.

The two old fellows grinned but altogether looked sheepish, with so many eyeing what went on. Red Barbee stared and stirred restlessly in the saddle into which he had just eased himself.

Then McWilliams put out his brawny hand to the Old Man and groped for the hand of the Blind Man, and he and his little daughter and the two old men went together into the hotel.

"Get an eyeful of all that, Virginia?" said Smoke Keena. "Funny, huh?"

"What about it?" said Morgan, never more crisp and curt. "Just a fool girl, with Barbee making himself another fool over her, and the two old boys happening somehow and some place to know her and her old gent. No money in our pockets, Nancy. Let's move along to the stable, and bed our horses down."

So the small cavalcade moved along in the wake of the stage, with Buck Braddock and Charlie Duff leading the pack animals, Maxwelton included. They unsaddled and pulled off pack-saddles and sketchily cleaned themselves at the watering trough. Two or three of them had combs or relics of combs, and made a stab at tidying their uncut hair; they adjusted the bandanas about their brown throats, cocked their hats at various angles, and stepped along back up the street towards the centre of things.

The town regarded them with interest, ten of them, strangers all, stepping along almost like a squad of soldiers. All hardy young men, now that Luke Christmas and Gran'pa Jonathan had temporarily deserted them, they had the air of constituting an invasion of Twenty Mile.

" She's an awful cute girl," said Red Barbee to Big Mouth, walking alongside him on the narrow board sidewalk.

" Say, Red, how'n hell did you know it was her bonnet?"

" It's funny," went on Red Barbee dreamily. " Here my name's Barbee—and did you hear the Blind Man call her Barbie? Almost just the same, huh, Big Mouth?"

" Your girl-crazy," grunted Big Mouth. " Let's go get a drink."

" Wonder where the Old Man and the Blind Man got to know her and her dad?"

" Maybe some place between here and the other side the Mississippi," said Big Mouth. " Who cares? Here Hawk Feather is turning into the Pay Dirt Saloon, him and Smoke Keena. Step it up; kid, maybe Hawk Feather's buying the drinks, he's that proudlike lately."

With Rob Roy Morgan and Smoke Keena leading the way, they trooped into the Pay Dirt. They lined up at the bar, where already a dozen men were telling the two bartenders what their tastes were.

" I bet you a dollar Morgan don't buy nobody a drink," said Red Barbee to Big Mouth.

" Take you. Bet a dollar he does," said Big Mouth.

Morgan, being first at the bar, was served first.

" I want to fight wildcats," he said to the bartender. " Give me the right medicine." And he plunked down his round silver dollar.

They all ordered. Every man paid for his own. Red Barbee jabbed an elbow into Big Mouth's middle.

" You lose, I win," he grinned. " Dig, feller."

Standing next to Big Mouth a tall, booted, cowboy-looking sort of man said drawlingly, " Usual thing, me, I don't butt into strangers' affairs. But I heard your bet. Seems as though there's two sides to it." He looked straight into Red Barbee's eyes. " Your bet was that he wouldn't buy nobody a drink, wasn't it?"

" If it's any of your damn business, yes," said Barbee rather pleasantly.

The stranger lifted his high, bony shoulders.

" Seems as though he's just bought himself a drink," he said.

Barbee scratched his head. Big Mouth guffawed, and it was his turn to jab Red Barbee in the ribs with a forceful elbow.

" You lose, kid," he said. And to the man standing with them he said with a broad grin, " Thanks, stranger. Have one with us."

The stranger pulled thoughtfully at a lower lip.

" Then there's this to think about," he said judicially. " The bet was that he wouldn't buy nobody a drink. Well, he bought himself a drink. So the question is, is he nobody? Like I said there's generally two sides to a thing."

And right there he had both Big Mouth and Red Barbee stuck. They stared at each other, they stared with kindled interest at the stranger. For the first time they noted his hat. A high, wide Stetson it was, silver-grey and brand new, and there was a broad leather band around it carrying a gleaming silver buckle. *Silver Hat !*

" Say," said Barbee, " that's a mighty fine hat you're wearing, stranger. Wonder where a man could get one like it? It's got a silver shine to it, ain't it?"

The stranger took the hat off, twirled it on a long finger, regarded it pridefully and clapped it back on his black-haired head.

" Got it over at Silver City," he said. " Bought a two-bit bag of peanuts over there, and they gave the hat away as what they call a premium."

" I'll give you four bits for it," said Red Barbee innocently, young Barbee being very good at the innocent act.

"No," said the stranger. "I'm hanging on to it. Supposed to be good luck."

"I don't know yet about that dollar," said Big Mouth. "Seems to me I win."

Over the bar was the usual bold painting of a very flauntingly voluptuous lady and, under that, a long mirror. Men, no matter how comic or tragic or downright empty their faces might be, always looked in the mirror and touched up their moustaches and all that. The Kid from Virginia, young and keenly aware of himself, at the moment like an actor in his dressing room, looked himself over. But it happened that the mirror also reflected the double-swing doors opening upon the sidewalk. The doors snapped open under the impact of a burly shoulder and a squat, florid man with his clanking spurs on came in. What Morgan noted of him was his hat: he wore a brand-new, silver-grey Stetson, wide of brim and tall of crown, decorated with a broad leather band carrying a big, light reflecting silver buckle!

"Silver Hat," he decided, and swung about to look at the man's self, not just his reflection. And, moving thus abruptly, he knocked off the bar with his elbow a brimming glass which the man standing on his left had just poured.

This man, not without some justification, swore; a man does hate to have his liquor spilled. Morgan was instantly aware of his awkwardness; despite his interest in the man with the silver hat he turned swiftly to make apologies. He confronted a young man who was obviously pure Spanish-California. Of about Morgan's age, he was of the dandy type from his enormous sombrero, his tiny moustache, his flowered vest, to his embroidered pantaloons, his dainty, high-heeled boots. He even had a delicate white cambric handkerchief in his hand.

"I'm sorry about that, sir," said the Virginia Kid. "Will you have a drink with me?"

The Spanish-Californian, who looked about to be reaching down into a tall boot for a dagger, melted instantly and bowed and gave Rob Roy a charming, white-toothed smile.

"It was all my fault, Señor," he said liquidly. "I put my glass in your way. But yes, I will be glad to accept from you. And maybe then you will allow me? My name, Señor, is Benito Fontana."

" Rob Roy Morgan," said the Virginia Kid, and they shook hands very formally.

Meantime the burly man in the high, wide and handsome Stetson clanked up to the bar and slammed down a twenty-dollar gold piece. He said to the bartender:

" I feel like an ol' man that ain't had a drink since the day he was born. If I get obstreperous, just throw me down, hog-tie me and pour two-three quarts of forty-rod down towards my gizzard."

The bartender set forth the bottle.

Young Morgan chanced to glance down along the bar. He saw Big Mouth and Red Barbee drinking together. He saw the man with them, a man in a big silver-grey hat. And then, when the swing doors opened again and a third man came in, wearing a hat wide and high and silver-grey and silver-buckle-banded, the Virginia Kid reached for his drink and poured it down and said to himself, " That makes three; wonder how many more?"

There were three more. They came in at intervals. They didn't seem to know one another or to note any similarity in hats. One was a coal-black negro, who stood almost seven feet high; one was a small, wiry Indian; one a clean-cut, dark man who looked like a gambler who knew how to deal his cards off the bottom of the deck. They had nothing in common —except their hats.

Morgan began to laugh. His new acquaintance, Don Benito Fontana, looked at him questioningly. Young Morgan lifted his shoulders and pulled his hat-brim down and rolled a cigarette.

" You laugh, Señor?" said young Fontana. He spoke his English precisely and well, but a Spanish bouquet floated about his words. " I do not see anything funny."

" There was a stage robbery to-day, Don Benito. At least two men were killed. The money box was stolen. It was said that the road agents were led by a man called Silver Hat! Right now, in here, we have six Silver Hats!"

Young Fontana looked, counted, considered and smiled.

" You are right, Señor," he said. " It is something to laugh at. And now you are going to do me the honour to drink with me?"

They drank together, experienced a casual liking for each

other, and became fairly well acquainted. And the predatory Virginia Kid learned that his new friend was a scion of the aristocratic and presumably wealthy Spanish-California family of the Fontanas of the Hacienda de la Mañana—and that the lovely valley which with a comprehensive sweep of the arm he had called " my place " belonged to the Fontanas, and that the fine, whitewashed buildings he had seen drowsing in the late afternoon sunshine constituted the Fontana home. The two had another glass together and Rob Roy Morgan was invited to visit the Fontanas—and to bring his friends.

Could a Fontana offer less? Was not hospitality as sacred as honour itself?

The young captain of adventure tucked in the corners of his mouth and accepted freely what was so freely proffered, and there was a gleam in his eyes.

At times in flights of poetic fancy, men's lives have been likened to streams, rivers " darkened by shadows of earth but reflecting an image of heaven." Small rivulets, some of them, some wild cascading torrents, some broad, placid rivers. And other makers of similes have thought of men's lives as tenuous threads, often in snarls and tangles, at times stretching straight. Varicoloured threads, black and red and white, some of coarse cotton, some of fine silk. To-night, in Twenty Mile, it would seem that the comparison of men's lives to threads was the more apt.

There were men in Twenty Mile who had never seen one another before, men who had known one another of late or years before. There were men whose life threads were jet black, men whose life threads were pale and colourless, others of bright crimson. A lot of these threads were getting entangled at Twenty Mile. Not all were the threads of men's lives; there were the lives of women and girls, and there were all colours from snow white to lovely lavender, to pink and, like the men's, black and red.

One of the men in a silver-grey Stetson, a loud-mouthed man, was talking. One would have said that already he had been drinking; perhaps he was just the blab-mouth kind. He said:

" I saw her. I saw her myself. With my own two eyes. Hell, it ain't just a wild Injun story about the Golden Tiger Lily girl! She's real, and she's prettier than that there picture over the bar mirror. She dresses with flowers in her hair and she's almost naked but she wears a bearskin or something. And she ain't no spirit neither, like the Injuns say she is. She's flesh and blood, a white girl, too.'' He poured down his drink and slapped the bar with a heavy, horny hand. '' Me, I'm going to set a bear trap and ketch her. Once a man tamed her, she'd be nice to have around.''

Men laughed. The Kid from Virginia came close to sneering; his upper lip did twitch. But the man standing with him and Smoke Keena listened gravely and with interest. At the end young Don Benito Fontana said to Rob Roy Morgan:

'' It is part of the truth, Señor. Me, I too have seen her. One night—there was a big round moon—at the edge of our Rancho, above the house where the forest comes down—She is no flesh and blood girl, but a spirit.'' He crossed himself.

CHAPTER FIVE

'' It is still early,'' remarked young Fontana. '' Me, I must step over to the post office to see if the stage has brought anything. Then I am riding home and you are to come with me; we can be in time for supper. And you will stay with us awhile; my father and mother will be honoured. And if you have some friends to ride with us, oh, we have lots of room and they are as welcome as the sun coming up in the morning.''

Certainly Rob Roy Morgan would be glad to ride with him. Curiosity, if nothing else, made him accept so spontaneous an invitation. He had his eye on the broad acres of Hacienda Fontana, had from the first view of it found it exactly what his soul demanded. And curiosity was lively with him. There was another matter which he wanted to look into: For some time he had been mildly curious about the Old Man and the Blind Man; to-day, noting how they were gathered in by McWilliams and his pretty daughter Barbara, like old friends, he wanted to know all about their relationship. He said to Fontana:

'' You go to the post office, I'll go get my horse. We'll ride together. I'll bring along just one of my friends.'' And to Smoke Keena he said, " Shake with Don Fontana. Don Fontana, my *amigo,* Nancy Keena."

Fontana touched his hat, then offered his hand. Smoke Keena said, " Howdy, Don." Then while the young Spanish-Californian visited the post office, where he was rewarded with two month-old newspapers, Morgan and Keena went to the stable for their horses. Morgan laughed softly.

" Look how things work out," he sad lightly. " I told you I was crazy about this long valley and the big houses down at the other end and all that; well, right away I'm invited to come and stay awhile! If I like the place as much as I think I do, it will be mine before long."

" Big talk," grunted Keena, " don't ring down on the bar like gold pieces."

" Big talk," grinned Morgan, " is just the boiling over of big ideas. And no man ever got to the high places without big ideas. You got a right to keep your mouth shut."

They got their horses, saddling the fresh ones they had led, Morgan riding Snow White, and found Fontana waiting for them and ready to ride, in front of the Pay Dirt.

" There's just one thing, Don Fontana," said Morgan. " There's a couple of old gents, friends of mine, visiting right now with Mr. McWilliams and his daughter Barbara. I want to pass by and tell them I'll be seeing them before long. I heard somebody say McWilliams has just bought the store here."

" Yes, yes," nodded Fontana. " I have heard about him, about his good wife and little daughter, too. They live in rooms that have been built on behind the store. I am going to show you."

They pulled up in front of the store; the door was ajar and a light was burning. Entering, they found a half-grown, lanky boy sitting on the counter, cheese and crackers in one hand, a half-eaten, withered apple in the other, his cheeks bulging like a gopher's. When they asked for Mr McWilliams the boy swallowed, started to speak, came close to choking and nodded his head and pointed his hand towards the rear of the store.

So, wearing their spurs, they clanked along to the door at the far end of the store, passed through it and through a tiny yard, all hard packed adobe, and to the first of the string of rooms, four or five in number, extending beyond. There was a curtain of sorts over a window, and a pale yellow light filtered through. At Morgan's gentle knock boot-heels sounded on a bare plank floor and McWilliams, in shirt sleeves and trailing a long streamer of smoke from his pipe, came to open the door.

The three callers, Don Benito Fontana being the first to do so, lifted their hats. It was the Kid from Virginia who spoke. "Mr. McWilliams," he said at his very politest, "me, I'm Rob Roy Morgan, and these are my friends, Don Fontana and Mr. Smoke Keena. We were riding by. Happens that two of my other friends "—he cleared his throat—" two of my other friends, Gran'pa Jonathan and Mr. Luke Christmas, dropped in on you. I'd sort of like to speak to them a minute."

"Come in, come in, come in!" said McWilliams cordially, and offered his hand that was like a blacksmith's. "They're here now and you're plumb welcome. Come on in."

The first person that Morgan saw was Red Barbee. Barbee sat stiffly on the edge of a raw hide-bottomed chair, his hair well plastered down, his fresh bandana knotted exactly round his brown throat, his old hat twirling slowly on an erect forefinger.

Besides Barbee, who turned a bright crimson on being discovered, there were in the room the Old Man and the Blind Man sitting side by side on a sway-backed red sofa, and pretty Barbara and her mother, a tall, severe and Scottish looking woman with high cheek bones and a firm-lipped mouth.

Introductions were made. Barbara flushed up and her eyes sparkled. She measured the handsome young Virginian from top to toe with a flashing yet comprehensive glance, the bright, gauging look of a girl of sixteen; she permitted her big eyes to rove on to Don Benito Fontana—and tarry with him a long moment. For Don Benito had not seen her until now, and a sort of wonder was in his eyes; he looked at her as though he could never look long enough. And she could feel his admiration, which was as emphatic as a loud voice in a quiet room. She blushed and looked down.

And Red Barbee glowered, and spun his hat faster than ever before.

Morgan said a pleasant " Howdy " to everybody, and then

made his limping explanation of his call. He said, " Like I told Mr. McWilliams, we're riding out of town now, me and Don Fontana and Mr. Keena, and I didn't want our party to get scattered without all the boys knowing where the rest of us had gone to. We're going down to Don Fontana's place for a while, then we'll be back up here. You see," he said directly to McWilliams, " I wanted Gran'pa Jonathan and Mr. Luke Christmas to know, so they mightn't stray and get lost. I'm right glad to learn, sir, that you and these two old gents are old-time friends of yours, so to speak."

" Sit down, sit down," commanded the jovial McWilliams. " Friends, Jonathan and Luke and us? I'd say so! Shucks, we've knowed one another nigh on forty year, huh, Jonathan? Huh, Luke? Huh, Mama? Huh, Barbie?"

Then, having put the question to sixteen-year-old Barbara, he guffawed.

" You haven't knowed 'em quite forty year yet, have you, Barbie?"

Barbara dimpled. She said in a small yet carrying voice, " I know Gran'pa Jonathan and Mr. Luke Christmas better than you folks do! I've known them since the day I was born, anyway, and that's more than you can say!"

The Blind Man stood up. He groped straight to Barbara and took one of her hands in both of his.

" Barbie," he said croakingly, " it's mighty nice seeing you again." He laughed, cackled rather, saying, " It's just like I could see you. Well, me and Luke has got to step along a spell. The boys took our horses and our pack mule down to the stable, I reckon, and they don't know how to take care of my Luke's pack; we got valuable things along and they'll likely get stole or throwed away if we don't take care of 'em. So we'll stagger along, and we'll come back and see you in the morning. And I'm going to buy you a little new dress like the last time, and another bonnet, too and maybe some shoes and oranges and candy and things. You sort of make me feel all young again, Barbie. And, pshaw, I don't mind any longer not being able to see any more; I've saw you, haven't I? And what's worth looking at? Come ahead, Luke."

" We'll be going too," said Morgan.

He and Fontana made their bows to Mrs. McWilliams and

Barbara, and Smoke Keena followed suit to the best of his ability.

Red Barbee sat tight and kept on spinning his hat.

" Coming along, Barbee?" asked Morgan.

" Not now," said Barbee, and was inclined to be sullen.

The three callers backed out, still bowing, their eyes raking the three of the family of McWilliams but centring at last on little Miss Barbara McWilliams, still urging them to stay awhile, went with them to the door.

They clattered out of town, the young Virginian, the young Spanish-Californian and the also young Smoke Keena, headed down valley along a lazily winding road for the Hacienda Fontana. It was a peerless night, all thought of light rains wiped clean away, little bright stars coming out, a warm breeze blowing playfully. Their horses hoofs beat out a lively rhythm that was like a song. The road for the most part followed the flirtatious small river that coquetted with the willows and aspens, that flung tender veils of spray against granite cliffs that invited again and again to splashing fords, that sang a low-throated song all the time, that tumbled into pools, and dived over waterfalls and then wandered at leisure through wide green meadows where flowers stood tall to rise above the luxuriant grass. A peerless night, a pleasant ride, and three young men, not long out of boyhood, riding like young kings, each with his hidden dream in his heart, each meaning to fill his hands overfull of the fruits of life. There is an old, eternal magic in a ride like that on a night like that. Who knew what was at the next bend in the road?

" There! You see the lights? That is my home, and we are almost there," exclaimed Benito Fontana. And he said, " That is a fine horse you ride, Señor Rob Roy."

Morgan leaned forward to pat his mare's shoulder.

" Her name is Snow White. She is my favourite of all horses I have ever ridden. I will race her with you on any horse you have, Don Fontana, and bet you my hat and spurs against a cigarette."

Fontana laughed. " That is a good bet for me and I couldn't care who won," he said. " Maybe to-morrow you will look at some of the Fontana horses. Maybe then you will just bet your hat and save your spurs!"

Around the massive whitewashed buildings, statuesque in the starlight, was a high adobe wall, also white with lime. The road led them on to a wide gate; the gate stood open as always it did; it hadn't been closed in many a year. They rode on at a gallop and to the front door of the big one-storied house, and the starlight seemed to grow warm and drip liquidly off the eaves of the red-tiled roof.

"You sure got a nice place," said Smoke Keena. "All kind of trees; I like trees. Oranges, ain't they? Olives and pears, too? Say, Virginia, look at the roses! Smell 'em! And honeysuckle, too! Man! Me, I'm getting homesick."

Out of nowhere appeared two Indian boys making what haste they could, which was inconsiderable, touching their ragged hats, taking the horses' reins. Young Fontana greeted them pleasantly after the fashion of the lord of the manor speaking down to a couple of loyal retainers, saying:

"Ah, Ernesto! And Juan too! You are good boys. Take very good care of the gentlemen's horses, won't you?"

He threw open the door with a wide gesture.

"Enter, Señores. The house is yours," he said.

There was an arched corridor with a place to hang their hats, and a mirror before which they could run their fingers through their hair. Then a high, arched door through which they entered the main *sala*, the living-room. Here were rugs, several candles burning in tall candlesticks, even a piano, and ancestral paintings on the white adobe walls; and there were colourful scarfs over walnut and mahogany tables and tall-backed chairs. And there was a garden of pretty girls, like flowers.

Also, first of all by rights, there were Señor Fontana and Señora Fontana. He was a tall man, not unlike a bantam rooster; she was a tall and majestic woman not unlike an argosy under full sail. He was almost diminutive of stature but so swollen with pride that he gave the effect of making himself larger, like a man lifting himself by the bootstraps; pride of race, pride of name and of blood, one haughtily tracing his ancestry back to Spanish kings—no matter though the strain came down from offshoots of the house of Juana la Loca. And she, deep-bosomed, richly maternal, soft-spoken, the mother of many, was that type of woman who is at once the daughter and the mother of pioneers.

The girls leaped up as gracefully as so many young panthers. The eldest, Zayda, was almost twenty and the youngest, Anita, was eight. Between them had blossomed the other lovely buds on the Fontana family tree. To start with then, were Zayda, Zorayda and Zorahayda, named for the three peerless princesses of the Alhambra. Then there were Aldegonda, Teresita and Josephina—and then little Anita. Of the Fontana boys there were Don Benito ushering in the guests, and presently there was mention of Don Mentor, the oldest, off somewhere or other to-night.

And every one of the little Señoritas, even to tiny, dusky eight-year-old Anita, wore a rose in her hair. Zayda, Zorayda and Zorahayda all wore yellow roses; Aldegonda, a rose so darkly red that it was almost black; Teresita and Josephina, white roses, Cherokee roses. And little Anita a pink rosebud.

Señor Fontana offered a hearty outstretched hand and a smile which made his black moustache curl upward; Señora Fontana inclined her head under its lacy black mantilla like a queen accepting her courtiers; the girls curtsied gracefully and their soft, dark eyes took instant and approving measure of at least one of the strangers. The Virginian struck more of a gallant and romantic note than he knew.

Both Señor and Señora Fontana made young Morgan and his friend, Smoke Keena, most welcome; they even strove to have it clear that these two, brought to them by their son Benito, were doing them a signal honour in stepping under the roof of their poor abode. An abode which, by the way, when Smoke Keena let his eyes wander, struck him in the nature of a palace; he had never in all his variegated life seen anything like it, never anything one-tenth so grand. And then the bouquet of young ladies— His breath was all taken away.

But the young Virginian, for his part, did his very excellent best at being at home. In his extreme youth, though he remembered but little of those first days, he had had a father and mother and a home that were thought very highly and respectfully of by neighbours for many an encircling mile. He was inclined to be arrogant, not knowing why; he, too, like Señor Fontana, could have boasted of his blood—if he had remembered the tales his mother had told him.

" Señor," he said to Fontana, " Your *rancho* is like a

thing that a man, hungry for everything perfect, dreamed. You know, I saw it for the first time this afternoon from the hilltops over yonder; we were riding down to Twenty Mile. I stopped on a hill and I looked down at your *rancho*; I could even see your houses here. You have four or five houses anyhow, Señor?"

Señor Fontana shrugged and lifted his hands, palms up. To be sure. There was the main *casa*; there was the stable and an extra barn; then there were little adobe houses, *casitas*, for a small army of Indian servants and *vaqueros*.

" It looked real nice to me," said the Kid from Virginia. " Right away at the first glimpse, I sort of liked it. A long, fat valley with wild oats growing as high as a man's head, with that crooked little river, with the pine and oak forests with game in the woods and trout in the stream, I bet! And bears, too, for a rug or a steak! And riding down here to-night——"

Señor Fontana, greatly pleased, beamed.

" You like my little place, no?" He rubbed his hands. " You make me happy, Señor." Then, using the old Spanish phrase to make a guest utterly at home, " My place, it is yours, Señor."

He got then a queer, stabbing look from the young man. The young Virginian's eyes hardened and narrowed. He said crudely:

" Not mine yet, Señor Fontana. But it's going to be! I know what I want when I see it, and I get what I want when I want it."

The old gentleman looked puzzled. His fine, frank eyes clouded. A queer twitch troubled the lips under his white moustache. He seemed to wince, wince the way a man might when pricked with the point of a dagger. But he smiled and said graciously:

" I am proud that my little place pleases you, Señor."

Then Mentor came home, oldest of the young Fontanas, a man full grown, a fine, full-bodied figure of a man, too, with his curly black beard and the thick mane of hair almost down to his shoulders, and large dark eyes that were warm and friendly and intelligent; and Mentor, like his brother Benito, brought a guest. It was the way of the Fontanas to bring guests or to attract them. Theirs was a big wide-spreading house; it needed to be, it had to be like their hearts, capable of taking all the wide world in. And Don Mentor Fontana's guest wore a big silver-grey hat.

He was one of the several silver-hatted men that the Virginia Kid had noted in the saloon at Twenty Mile. From his looks, he well might have been the leader of the bandit outfit that had held up the stage. He was brown, tall and lean and handsome; knifelike, in a way, or like a hawk, like an arrow, a flint-tipped arrow, swift and hard; like the Virginia Kid in more ways than one.

Mentor introduced him as his friend, " *Mi amigo,* Don Steve Question."

Steve Question! " That's the hell of a name," muttered Smoke Keena under his breath. " And I bet a man he's the jasper that pulled off that stage robbery. He's got eyes like it, cold, glassy eyes like a snake."

Steve Question and the kid from Virginia at the outset clashed like two rapiers. Perhaps they were too much alike. Neither trusted the other, each was ready to hate the other. There are in this world natural antipathies. There are forces like the forces of magnets. And especially strong are these forces among young people. Two may touch hands for the first time and a strong bond, friendship or hate, come into being.

The Fontana Señoritas, who did not often see handsome young strangers, were bright-eyed and rosy-cheeked. They opened their fans and made their eyes big over the tops of their fans, and made the young man from Virginia think of peacocks he had seen long ago under wide-branched oaks on green southern lawns.

But also he kept steadily thinking of something else. He had found what he wanted, and it was this wide-spreading rancho where a man had everything. He was doing his thinking in primitive terms. Here you had fat, virgin acres where you could grow anything you wanted, wheat or oranges, onions or potatoes, apples, pears, tomatoes, olives and quinces and corn. Here were trout and deer and quail. Here, for a young fortune hunter, was everything. Just what he wanted. He wanted everything. He meant to have it. Being very young, he could brush aside the little Señoritas and their fans and big eyes, and could steer straight ahead to the things which, in his eyes, really counted.

There is such a thing as love at first sight. Sometimes it may be with a woman, sometimes with a vision, a newly born ambition, sometimes with broad, teeming acres. Yes, a man could live here like a king. And without soiling his hands with toil. Just taking abundantly the goods the gods provided.

They dined bountifully. On a long mahogany table set forth with massive and ancient silver there were flowers in tall vases, there were heaping platters, there were bottles of red California wine, made on the *rancho*, laid down years before. Two slim lithe-bodied young Indians served them, over-watched by an older Indian servant, the household's major-domo. Thereafter there were cigarettes and music, the girls singing, guitars softly strumming in accompaniment. Certainly to the young Virginian and Smoke Keena it was a night of nights, a soft, infinitely pleasurable night after so many hard, bleak ones on the long trail.

And there was a moon, almost at the full, hanging low over the mountains. There was a flowery patio, a quadrangle enclosed on all four sides by the three-foot-thick adobe walls of the house, with a high, arched gateway opening toward the moon-flooded forest and mountains, and in the patio was an overflowing fountain, and there were roses and orange and pear trees and a mammoth grape vine spreading over a rustic arbor, and one fine olive tree. Señor Fontana strolled in the patio as was his custom after supper, and smoked, and enjoyed a vast serenity. There were benches and wicker-and-rawhide chairs. The newly risen moon was just beginning to filter through grape arbor and olive tree.

Rob Roy Morgan was drawn by the night not only into the patio but on through the arched gateway and into the level space beyond, under the big live oaks. He ground out his cigarette underfoot and drew a deep breath, his lean body straight, his head up, his eyes ravishing the moonlit fields and slopes and forestlands.

He stood with his back to one of the oak trees, in a pool of shadow, and looked toward the moon. The mountains were still black with the night since the moon had not yet overtopped them; the pine-and-oak-studded slopes, with here and there little level spaces, with broken cliffs in other places standing like rugged iron walls, with in one place a wild, leaping waterfall making threaded silver and delicate white lace down worn black rocks. He heard a night bird calling liquidly; from far off came the sharp, staccato bark of a fox.

Then he saw Silver Hat—Steve Question—the young man he remembered from the saloon in Twenty Mile, a man who, he thought, might have had something to do with the stage hold-up. A man whom he already distrusted, disliked and resented.

It struck him that there was something furtive about Steve Question's movements; he was sure that the man had slipped out of the house unnoticed. From the patio there still came the dulcet music; to the girls' singing and the guitars had been added a sentimental violin in the adroit hands of Mentor Fontana. Steve Question could easily have stepped out through the shadows without drawing an eye to his silent withdrawal.

Young Morgan thought, " These are funny folks, the Fontanas. They're soft, that's what; they're easy." For here to-night Don Benito had brought him and Smoke Keena, perfect strangers of whom he knew nothing, naming them his friends. And so had Don Mentor, a man full grown, done with Steve Question. He had said, " He is my *amigo*." And during the early moments of the evening it was made obvious that Mentor and Steve had never met or heard of each other until to-day.

And Morgan watched, wondering, " What brought Silver Hat here? He came with a reason; he's up to something right now. What?"

If Steve Question moved at first stealthily he had a stealthy shadow following him. Steve kept under the black shadows of the oaks all that he could; he moved swiftly through silvered splotches of moonlight; he headed toward the forested slope with the mountain range behind it, headed toward the thin creek among willows and buckeyes and slender shivering aspens below the lace-trimmed waterfall. And after him, dodging from oak to oak, hunting shadows, went Rob Roy Morgan.

Both saw what Steve Question was looking for, saw it at the same time.

CHAPTER SIX

THERE was a great flat rock, black by night-time and perhaps by daylight, like an ebony floor, its edge overhanging the glassy pool into which the waterfall came down, and the risen moon splashed it with soft luminance. And on the rock stood a slender, moon-bright girl poised like a deer ready to run. And on the instant Rob Roy Morgan guessed who she was.

And Silver Hat, Steve Question, knew who she was. He crept stealthily closer and closer, a silent, dark figure keeping in the shadows. So, too, did Morgan after him creep closer. He saw the girl and marvelled at her, at her slim, young beauty, at the strangeness of her attire. She wore a scanty little dress, if you could call it a dress, of soft furry skins, fox pelts for a guess. It came above her breasts and left her arms and shoulders bare; it reached almost to her knees. About her throat was a barbaric sort of necklace; it looked like gold coins strung on a string. Her hair was loose and come down below her waist. She was as shapely, as lovely, as a girl in a dream.

And Steve Question, slinking through the smaller timber and brush, drew on closer and closer to her. The girl was all unaware of his nearness; she stood peering down through the night, looking at the Fontana home. There was some sort of sash about her slim waist; an unsheathed knife dangled from it; the moonlight gave it a silvery sheen.

Then all of a sudden Steve Question's lean, wolfish form towered above her. He caught her in his long arms and held her tight, and young Morgan heard him say triumphantly:

" So I've caught you at last, have I, little Golden Tiger Lily! And I didn't need a bear trap after all!"

She started to scream, being so taken by surprise, but stifled her scream, knowing it to be so without avail, and reached for the naked blade swinging at her thigh. But Steve Question laughed at her and was as quick as a striking snake, and caught her wrist, holding it locked tight in his iron grip.

" I knew it was you, Little Tiger," he said, " who had raided my cache. Look at the necklace you're wearing! I bet a man you've got forty twenty-dollar gold pieces strung round your neck! Say, eight hundred dollars! All mine, too. Ain't they too heavy for a little kid like you to carry?''

She hadn't spoken a word. She didn't speak now. She relaxed in his overpowering grasp and Rob Roy Morgan, watching and not ten feet away, understood that she meant to employ guile against superior physical strength. Let Steve Question but loosen his grip upon her for a minor fraction of a second and she'd slip out of his embrace and be away like any little wild, frightened thing of the forests.

But Steve Question did not mean to let her go.

'' I've been looking all over for you,'' he said, '' for quite a spell. I saw your tracks once and tried to track you down. I got a glimpse of you once, but you saw me and ran, and I couldn't ever come up with you; I lost you where the trees were so thick a man couldn't see twenty feet ahead. I saw your tracks again up here where I had a gold cache, and I knew it was you who sneaked in and stole a good part of my hard-earned wealth! And now I'm going to keep you, now you're going to pay me back good and plenty! You're my girl now, understand?''

He bent her backward, his arms tightening about her lithe body, he brought his face close down to hers.

'' Kiss me, you little hell cat,'' he said. '' And if you try to bite me I'll damn near kill you.''

Then Rob Morgan, not liking the man to begin with and feeling queerly drawn to the girl, stepped out of the shadows and on to the flat, black rock.

'' Let the girl go, Question,'' he said. '' She wants no part of you. Let her go.''

Steve Question whirled on the instant, and on the instant the girl wriggled free and leaped clear across the pool and vanished in the dark timber beyond. Morgan heard her gold coins jingle like soft golden laughter.

'' Why damn you, Morgan,'' said Steve Question, seeing who it was.

His hand going down to his gun was quick but not quick enough. Morgan's fist was already doubled and came up like an iron piston, crashing into Steve Question's cruel mouth. Question went staggering back and Morgan struck again and Steve Question, off balance, plunged full length down into the pool, went all the way down, out of sight. There was left just a silver-grey hat floating on top of the troubled water.

Morgan, with his hands on his hips, stood at the edge of the black, flat rock and looked down. Bubbles came up and then flailing hands, arms and a head. Steve Question gasped, choking with the water he had gulped.

" Help ! Get me out ! I can't swim ! "

" Drown then, damn you," said young Morgan, and went away, turning back to the Fontana house. For a moment he was impelled to follow the girl, but he shrugged his shoulders instead. Anyhow there'd be no finding a wild thing like her in the night time in the woods.

All this had required but a few minutes, ten minutes or fifteen perhaps. In the patio Señor Fontana, his hands clasped behind his back, was still pacing up and down, enjoying the night and his cigarette. Guitar, violin, snatches of singing and girls' light laughter still mingled pleasantly with moonlight and the fragrance of the garden and the gentle susurrus of the night breeze through the trees. And Rob Roy Morgan, returning, thought, " This is my place. I like it the way it is."

He even thought, " If I have to, I'll marry one of these girls. I'll horn in here and stay. I don't have to grab everything in one day, but it won't be long. My place."

And with a new eye he looked the girls over, all the way from Zayda to little Anita. He didn't want a girl; they were no part of his scheme of life. But one of them might be a stepping stone.

And, so suddenly that it came almost as a shock to him, he found himself remembering the girl up there under the waterfall. . . .

Mentor asked, " My friend Steve Question, has he been outside with you?"

Rob Roy had been taught while a little boy that there were certain things which a gentleman did not do. He had forgotten or ignored most of the preachments of his very early youth, but he did not lie. He had no stomach for a liar. He himself was no coward and he considered lying sheer cowardice. He answered now in a manner which was as good as a slap in the face. He said bluntly:

" Your friend Steve Question is no friend of mine, Don Mentor. Don't ask me about him."

His rudeness was a shock to all the Fontanas; the old man's face stiffened into a mask, Mentor pulled at his moustache, his hand over his mouth, and the girls looked startled, then horrified, their eyes growing big as their singing voices were stilled or their quick little hands grew rigid upon fan or guitar strings. Even Smoke Keena quirked up his eyebrows.

Señora Fontana, rising majestically from a rocking chair in a shadowy corner of the patio, spoke softly yet none the less firmly.

" My daughters," she said, " it is time for you to retire. The gentlemen will want to talk and have their cigars and wine." She inclined her head graciously to her guests, said a quiet good-night, added a smile and another good-night to Señor Fontana and led the way into the house. The girls said their good-nights obediently, sounding reluctant, and followed in her wake so that there was a sort of procession like that of an argosy under full sail with a convoy of smaller craft bring up the rear.

In the patio there fell a silence, not only a silence but a deep hush. For a moment or two it seemed as though the little night breeze was holding its breath, as though the fountain spray remained suspended in the air. Smoke Keena spoke up, his sudden voice sounding loud and harsh.

" You've sure got a great place out here, Mr. Fontana," he said. " Seems as though you'd got pretty much all a man could hanker for, I don't know how many fat acres, but thousands, I reckon, and cattle and horses and all sorts of wild game, and even fruit trees and maybe wheat and vegetables. Only it's awful damn quiet, ain't it? I'd think you'd be glad to hear a kiote howl! Come early night time, like now, what do you do to keep from going crazy with the stillness and all?"

Señor Fontana's smile was cryptic in the brightening moonlight. He spoke serenely.

" We sit here in fine weather and are content, Señor. We look up at the moon and the stars the way we are doing now, and watch the shadows of our pear and orange and olive and oak trees. We look over the wall to the mountains where the pines whisper among themselves, where the water comes down in the waterfall, and sometimes we see the deer passing through the light into the dark. And sometimes we just shut our eyes and listen to how still it is, and then we hear little noises that come out of the trees, out of the mountains, out of the ground—out of the night."

Smoke Keena's jaw dropped. He didn't say it but he thought, " Crazy, is he?" For this sort of thing was beyond Smoke Keena's ken.

Don Benito stirred restlessly. He took up the answer and the theme where his father left off.

" And here at casa Fontana there were other things, too, of an evening, Señor Keena," he said, speaking almost urgently. " We have music, like you heard to-night. Then sometimes we have friends, and we dance and play games, charades, you know, and things like that. And even at night, in the fine weather, sometimes a barbecue. In the daytimes we sometimes get our riatas over a nice, big bear up in the hills; we bring him down and put in a special corral just for that, and a strong young bull, and they fight!" His eyes brightened; a shaft of moonlight striking them made them glitter at once both liquidly and like hot little fires. He shrugged and sat back and said, " Then, at times, we play at cards."

Here was something that Smoke Keena understood.

" Poker?" he said briskly.

" Oh, yes," said Benito. " Poker is a nice game."

Rob Roy Morgan heard little of their talk, heard that little absent-mindedly. His thoughts were elsewhere. He was thinking of Silver Hat, of the girl in the strange, savage costume, of the necklace she wore of twenty-dollar gold pieces. Stolen from Steve Question's cache, so Steve had said. And where did Steve Question's gold pieces come from? Stage robbery, other robberies, like to-day's. And the wild girl had spied on him from some dark thicket and had found his treasure trove.

Well? Whose now, the accumulated gold? Steve Question's? By rights, no, for Steve Question had stolen it, had committed murder to come at it. Whose, then?

" Mine," decided Rob Roy Morgan. " Just as soon as I can find it."

Then it was that Steve Question came stalking into the

patio. He was soaking, sopping wet; water dripped off him and made black stains under his boots; his silver-grey hat looked like a wreck and ruin. And on his face, in his eyes, was a flaring rage.

Young Morgan rested lightly on the balls of his feet, almost on tiptoes, and his hands were on his hips and his eyes were watchful. Here was just as good a place, now just as good a time as any, to finish what had so recently been started.

Don Mentor jumped up.

" *Mi amigo !* " he exclaimed in consternation. There was light enough to show him Steve Question's face, the look in his eyes, his battered mouth. Señor Question ! Tell me ! "

Steve didn't even look at him. His eyes and Morgan's clashed. There was threat in Steve's eyes, there was hot challenge in Morgan's. They looked at each other like two strange dogs taking stock of each other. Morgan waited for Steve Question to make the first move.

Steve was the older man by ten years. He had had more experience, he knew at first hand more of the fatefully dangerous spots of life; he knew that a man could be full of animal exuberance at one minute, dead and done with a handful of seconds later. Maybe he was realising that his guns, after his fall into the pool, were not altogether to be trusted. Maybe he read something in the other man's glance that made him cautious.

Then he turned to Mentor Fontana. He said, seeking to make nothing of the affair :

" I did a fool thing. I walked up to the waterfall, just looking around; I slipped and fell in and damn near drowned." He wiped his swollen lips and looked at his hand to see whether there was a trace of blood. " Hit my head on the rocks as I went in," he said.

" Come ! " said Mentor. " You must have some dry clothes. You will catch cold. Come with me."

The two went into the house, to be gone some fifteen minutes. When they returned Steve Question was decked out in Don Mentor's best, silk shirt, flowered jacket, fine pantaloons, high-heeled hand-made black boots. And Steve was smooth now after a cool, devil-may-care fashion, and sent a puff of cigarette smoke skyward. He said lightly :

" When I came in you boys were talking about poker,

huh? Is there a game coming up? I'd sort of like to be counted in."

" Why of course!" said the always eager young Benito. " If you gentlemen care to play, it is always a pleasure." He turned bethinking himself, respectfully to his father. " If these caballeros would like some cards—*No*, papa?"

Señor Fontana's mask was melting; he did not look altogether serene or happy now. He was unsure upon several points, and apprehensive. He had seen the looks stabbing back and forth between two of his stranger guests and he was not quite convinced, not being a fool, that Steve Question had merely slipped and fallen into a pool. He had taken stock of Steve's battered mouth. And he wondered what the man had been doing on the mountain flank—and where Morgan had been at the same time. Nor had he enjoyed some of Rob Roy Morgan's crude observations.

Yet it remained that these were his guests, under his roof. He made a very formal bow and said courteously:

" If these gentlemen would enjoy it, it would be a pleasure." But at the same time he looked reproachfully at his younger son.

" Fine!" said Smoke Keena. " Better than just squatting here, listening to how quiet everything is, ain't it?"

Señor Fontana gently smoothed his luxuriant black moustache. To his son he said:

" We are going into the house then, Benito. You will go ahead and have everything in readiness. Tell Ernesto we will want some very good wine; he will know."

Don Benito said, " Yes, papa," and sped into the house on feet that were almost dancing in their high-heeled boots. Señor Fontana made a gesture for the others to follow, and the five of them entered the main *sala*, softly illuminated by the mellow glow of a dozen candles.

Ernesto and Benito came in together, Ernesto carrying a roundish table—not quite round, not strictly to be named oval, a sturdy and not unlovely bit of homemade work, heavy oak from the Fontana acres, Benito with a small wooden box in his slim, agile fingers, the box, too, of oak but highly ornamented in bright colours, a smiling young girl, a leafy bough, flowers and of course, a dove with little pink feet—the work of Señorita Aldegonda Fontana, the artist of the family.

The box contained the cards, half a dozen decks. All used decks, not a fresh one among them.

Ernesto crawled away—from all that Rob Roy Morgan could see of him, the boy's top speed could only be calculated in inches, or their fractions, but presently he inched back bringing tray, bottles, and clean shiny glasses, that looked like crystal. And after a time he oozed in again bringing small tables, half a dozen of them before he was through, so small that you might have called them stools. Like the poker table, they were home-made, oaken and honest. On each, at each player's right hand, were set bottle, glass and tobacco and papers for cigarettes.

Five men sat down to play: Señor Fontana and his two sons, Steve Question and Smoke Keena. Rob Roy Morgan remained standing; he hadn't even taken his hat off. He was thinking of a girl dressed scantily in furs; of a necklace of gold pieces. He looked them over, the five players, the bottles, the used decks of cards. He said:

" Me, I'm going outside for a smoke in the moonshine. It's sort of nice outdoors to-night. Maybe later."

He turned his back and went out, but out of the corner of his eye he watched Steve Question, not trusting him in anything, feeling that Steve would rather shoot a man in the back than take an unnecessary chance of getting shot in return. He passed through the patio, made a widely curving arc under the live oaks, and then went as straight as a string to the pool under the waterfall. It was not that he had any great hope of finding her or her gold pieces.

He stood on the black, flat rock that was like a floor, jutting out over the pool that was all froth and bubbles at the upper end where the waterfall dived in, all glassy smoothness at the other end. He wondered how Steve Question had managed to claw his way out; quite a job Steve must have had of it, and scared white all the time.

He looked across the pool. It was rimmed all about with tall ferns; it was longer than it was wide, but its width was such that he asked himself whether he could jump across it. The girl had done it, done it as lightly and easily as a cat can jump up into a chair. But Rob Roy Morgan shook his head; he didn't hanker for a bath such as he had just given Steve Question.

He found a way to go round the pool, down below, then across its overflow, then up a steep to the spot where the girl had leaped. He saw where the ferns were broken.

The moonlight came to his aid, piercing down through the pines. He found other broken ferns where she had fled up the mountainside. He told himself again that it would be no good to try to follow her, but follow her he did. When there were no more ferns to be trampled underfoot there were bushes, without a trail, and the light here and there, slanting down through the black timber, sufficed to show to his keen young eyes, eyes used to following track and sign, broken twigs hanging down from the bush tips; she must have gone like a young tornado!

And then, in a pool of fortuitous moonlight, just after he had beaten his way through a thicket of ceanothus, he did find something. Something which catching the moon rays just right, flashed back up into his eyes like a jewel. It was a twenty-dollar gold piece, and it had a hole drilled through it, close to the rim.

So, in her wild flight, her necklace had broken, snared no doubt on a branch of manzanita or buck brush, left as of no consequence in her fright and headlong dash to escape. Morgan stopped and looked for further coins.

And he found them, some scattered across several yards, a small pile of them in a little hollow. All were pierced, close to the rims, with tiny holes, and he even found a buckstring thong which had held them. He gathered up thirty-seven gold pieces. He estimated cooly, thirty-seven times twenty, that's almost seven hundred and fifty dollars. He slid the coins into a small buckskin pouch which he carried, a pouch which had at times held only parched corn but which happened to have money in it before he added the gold pieces. Bright gold which did not belong to Steve Question, because he had stolen it; money which did not belong to the girl, because she had stolen it from Steve Question's cache; money which did belong to Rob Roy Morgan—because he had found it and picked it up and put it in his pocket! It was all very simple, very clear, superbly logical!

He fancied there were more gold pieces strewn around, but why trifle with them? He strove again to follow her trail.

But within a few minutes he gave up the quest, gave it up

D

at least for the night. Of a sudden the brush discontinued; then came the pines, widely spaced, dead pine needles underfoot, nothing to show where any one had passed. She might be within a few yards of him, hidden in the dark; she might be a mile away.

He wondered about her. More and more he wondered. He stood there for a long time, trying to answer the question he asked himself about her. So she was not just a legend after all, but a real flesh-and-blood girl. That was one thing, and question number one answered itself. But how explain her? Where was she now? Running free where had she gone? Where, in these harsh mountains rising more and more steeply behind the Casa Fontana, would she find shelter? Had she by now crept into a cave somewhere, curling up among such skins as she had used to make her little dress? How did she live? All alone in the wilderness? How? And why?

And the gold pieces? Out of Steve Question's cache, which must be near here. Had she taken it all, hiding it away somewhere, or had she taken only the few coins she wanted for her necklace?

He gave over looking for her to-night. His thoughts travelled from his buckskin pouch down to the Fontana home. They were deep in their poker game by this time. A sudden broad grin chased away all the serious concentration which his face had registered: might be fun to sit into the game with those gold twenties!

He returned to the house. The players had warmed up and were deep in their game. He stood looking them over, looking at the cards and stacks of coins on the table. They didn't use chips, just silver and gold with now and then a greenback. To be sure, he didn't know how much each man had put in, but the tallest stacks were where he rather expected to find them, in front of Silver Hat, Steve Question.

He saw that there was still a vacant chair, brought by Ernesto, with its little side table decorated with unopened bottle, tobacco and papers. He sat down.

" Deal me in," he said, and was pleased somehow to have Steve Question straight across the table from him. " Coach me up, Nancy," he said to Smoke Keena. " What's the game?"

" Draw," said Keena. " You know that already. Jackpots. Draw to straights and flushes. Ante, before you look at your cards, what you like. Nobody's said anything about any limit."

" Sounds like a nice little game," said Rob Roy Morgan, and reached for his buckskin bag.

He was dealt in. He fumbled in his pouch and extracted a dozen silver dollars, a couple of gold fives and tens. He put the pouch down at his right hand.

He and Steve Question appeared to ignore each other. Yet neither of them missed a single gesture, a single slight change of expression of the other.

Don Mentor, dealing, put up a dollar ante and they all came in. Steve Question, going blind, doubled the ante and again they all came in. Mentor dealt and so the game, which had paused briefly on Morgan's entrance, got going again.

Young Morgan eyed the cards narrowly, watched their backs as they were held in the several hands, as they were discarded, face down. Cards they were that had been used many a time. When Benito bet twenty dollars on his hand, Morgan stayed out. There was a slight duel between Benito and Smoke Keena, the others out of it before the end. At the showdown Benito raked in the pot, good for a hundred dollars or so, and he and Keena spread out their hands, face up.

And it was Rob Roy Morgan's deal. Gathering in the deadwood, he was very leisurely about dealing. He was still interested in the backs of the cards, Keena's and Benito's. It was so easily to mark a deck, so hard to note the markings unless you had made them yourself and knew just where to look for them. He shuffled slowly. He put up his dollar ante.

He dealt as clumsily as he could; he made the cards appear to stick together even when they didn't. He lifted his eyes to Señor Fontana.

" Haven't you got a fresh deck?" he asked.

Fontana shrugged and said, " I am sorry, Señor. When Benito was in town he tried to get new cards; there were none."

Morgan finished dealing, and he watched the back of every card. When he had done he looked again at the stacks of gold and silver at each man's right hand. Steve Question had the most money, but then again Morgan did not know how much of it was Steve's to begin with. Señor Fontana's pile was low and thin. Mentor had something like fifty or sixty dollars in sight. Smoke Keena was down to his last little heap of silver dollars, not a gold glint in the stack. Young Benito Fontana didn't appear to have done much damage to himself; next to Silver Hat, Benito had the most money in sight.

And Rob Roy kept on studying the backs of the cards.

And, furtively, he studied the faces of Steve Question and Benito Fontana. And he came to the decision that both Benito and Steve Question were watching the backs of the cards as closely as he himself was doing. So they were marked, were they? At this time of life it is natural to leap to conclusions: He made up his mind that the Fontanas were crooks, card-sharps, men who, under the gracious cloak of hospitality, fleeced their guests with cold decks. Small wonder that Mentor met a stranger and called him " *mi amigo* " and brought him home, Mentor having no doubt noted that the stranger was well heeled! And so had Benito invited Morgan and Smoke Keena—and cards had been inevitable.

So Rob Roy Morgan played a canny game, taking small chances, always watching the backs of the cards, the faces of the players. His attention was drawn again and again to Señor Fontana; the old man had but a few dollars in front of him, he looked embarrassed, you might have said that he felt ashamed. He certainly had no " poker face."

Benito won the pot, not a fat one. Smoke Keena dealt. His ante was the usual dollar. Mentor doubled it and all came in. Morgan drew three jacks; not bad. He looked at faces—also at backs of cards—in a seemingly sleepy fashion. Again he was mostly concerned with Don Benito and Steve Question.

Steve shoved in fifty dollars. Benito considered, plucking at his tiny moustache, seemingly hesitant, then shoved in his fifty and added another fifty. His father dropped out; so did all, even Morgan with his three jacks before the draw. He eased himself back, poured a glass of wine, rolled a cigarette. *And watched.*

Steve Question put up his second fifty and stood pat. Young Benito, a flush in his face, that bright eagerness in his eyes, flipped away one card, saying:

" Deal me one."

The two regarded their hands, then they regarded each other. It was Benito's bet. He lifted his shoulders.

"I pass," he said.

Steve Question's suspicious eyes gimleted at him.

"Fifty bucks," said Steve, and shoved the money into the pot.

"Fifty?" said Benito. "*Bueno*, Señor. And I put in one more hundred."

Obviously Steve Question was tempted to raise, but he kept a check rein on himself. He called for the showdown. He held a very nice pat hand, but it wasn't good enough for Don Benito's four kings. Don Benito's cheeks were warmly flushed as he raked in the goodly pot.

Smoke Keena, a fond lover of poker yet not as wise at play as he was bold, fingered his few silver dollars ruefully; he glanced sideways at Morgan.

"How about it Virginia?" he asked. "Your sack sounds heavy. Lend me?"

"Stay out one hand to change your luck," said Morgan lightly. "Then I'll stake you a couple of twenties. And I'll take 'em back away from you on anybody's deal."

Smoke Keena relaxed, rolled a cigarette, poured himself a glass of wine and watched with detached interest. He didn't look at the cards, he didn't look at the faces; he did listen to voices naming bets and he did watch the money dropped into the pot.

He did not see what Rob Roy Morgan saw, a flush as hot as that on Don Benito's cheeks now staining the swarthier cheeks of Benito's papa, Señor Fontana. The old gentleman was nervously restive. He had previously only smoothed his black moustaches; now he pulled at them. He cleared his throat, started to say something, then sat back silent. And none of all this was lost on the watchful Rob Roy Morgan. Señor Fontana's stack of silver was about like Smoke Keena's. The fever of the game was in the old man's veins, but he was short of ammunition.

And young Morgan felt a feeling of elation. He wanted the Fontana *rancho* for his own, didn't he? He meant to have it soon or late. Why not soon?

To himself Morgan said, "They re gambling fools. Crooked

as a dog's hindleg, but just the same easy to take into camp. My place!"

Not even yet could he discover how the cards were marked, but marked they were, he was downright sure. He wondered if Steve Question, who had been playing longer and who was sharp-eyed, had the secret or even suspected it; he could tell nothing from Steve's face.

Well, poker was poker, marked cards or fresh deck. Morgan dealt. His own cards he flipped back close to the table's edge, under his left elbow, pulling them in with his elbow keeping them hidden. When he picked them up he held them cupped in his hand. When he discarded, he shoved the discard under other deadwood. No one got much chance to see his hand. Even when others dealt he drew in his cards swiftly, keeping them covered, out of sight.

On his deal he again drew three jacks. This time he'd play them, having no premonition of disaster. The pot was built up slowly before the draw, only fifty dollars added, with Smoke Keena out and Señor Fontana saying with a smile and a shrug:

" I am sorry, Señores, but I have no more money."

That closed the pot, but there were still four men playing, and they could do what they pleased on the side.

Mentor tipped his head back to get his cigarette smoke out of his eyes, fingered a ten-dollar coin, shoved it forward, then slowly withdrew it and dropped his cards. Steve Question shoved in twenty dollars. Don Benito was in a hurry to put down his own twenty and another on top of it. And Rob Roy Morgan took time, perhaps ten seconds, to do a bit of thinking.

This was after the draw, and his three jacks were now four jacks and a king. He thought, " Benito doesn't know what I've got; all he knows is that he has pulled down a good hand for himself. But it isn't as good as my four jacks. Steve Question is a slick poker player; he's got a hand. I'd like to rake 'em both in, I don't want to scare 'em out. What'll be a reasonable bet? Dammit, I wish I'd watched 'em play awhile."

Steve Question said sharply, " It's up to you, Morgan. Or are you out?"

Morgan said quietly, " Thank you Mr. Question. I was just

wool-gathering, thinking about something that happened a little while ago. No, I'm still in. Twenty bucks."

" *And* twenty," said Steve, and shot his forty dollars into the new pot.

" *And* twenty," said Don Benito, and donated sixty to the good cause.

That meant forty dollars for Rob Roy Morgan to play. He did not have that much in front of him on the table. He shoved his chair back, put his hat upside down between his knees and poured into it, well protected by the table-top where none could see, the contents of his buckskin pouch. He fingered through the coins, hunting out some that were not pierced near their rims. He added his sixty dollars and then an additional hundred.

Steve Question regarded him severely, and Morgan was under the impression that Steve was trying to see the backs of his cards.

" It's up to you Question," said Morgan. " Or are you out?"

" In for a hundred," said Steve Question, and added his contribution.

Don Benito pulled at his little moustache. Slowly, with nervous, delicate fingers, he slid forward the necessary hundred dollars to play; hesitantly he toyed with what remained of his stack, then added fifty dollars.

Morgan covered the fifty, then dug around in his hat again. He'd have to play the gold twenties with holes in them now. No, he found one twenty that he had brought along with him. He drew out of his hat four pierced coins and put the unpierced one on top, covering the holes, and said," *And* fifty."

Steve Question called him. Don Benito, again hesitant, called. Morgan laid down his four jacks and raked in the pot.

An odd hand it was, Steve Question with four nines, Don Benito with four tens and Morgan with four jacks. All eyes locked tight with Rob Roy Morgan's, who had dealt.

Nothing was said. You didn't question a man, a stranger, over a hand at poker unless you were ready to go for your gun. It was queer that was all.

Señor Fontana made as if to rise; he pushed back his chair, his hands corded on its two arms. He said:

" I am sorry, *caballeros*, but you see it is this way with us:

Here at the *rancho* we do not keep much money. And only last week I have sent away a thousand head of cattle that are to be delivered to a cattle dealer who is gathering beef herds for Dodge City; and my men needed money to spend for what they needed on the way. Not until they return, bringing me the money from the sale, can I enjoy myself with you in the poker. I am ashamed, gentlemen! In my own house!"

Steve Question said, with a twitch of the shoulders, " What is money, Señor? Among friends? You have a scrap of paper and a pencil? *Bueno !* Your I O U is just like gold."

Señor Fontana was abashed. Of course his sons couldn't say anything; for a moment both Morgan and Keena were silent. Keena shifted a hurried glance toward Morgan and Morgan nodded. Steve said heartily:

" Sure, Mr. Fontana. You don't need the cash laid down to play with us boys; you got a big ranch and a fine home and plenty stock and all that; sure, go ahead and bet your boots off."

It was not very elegantly expressed, and the old man came close to shuddering, came close to shoving his chair still farther back and quitting the game. But his blood was up, and he was one of those men, and their number is legion, who never like to quit a poker game either when they are behind or ahead.

He at last glanced at Rob Roy Morgan. Morgan said briefly:

" Come ahead, Señor. Use your pencil and a cigarette paper. Let's go."

So Señor Fontana drew his chair back to the table. He filled his glass and drank it thirstily; he rolled his fine, thin cigarette; he gathered in the cards, for it was his deal, and dealt them swiftly and skilfully. And Morgan watched his face narrowly; he wanted to know whether the old man, too, was concerned with the backs of the cards. But Fontana's face was again a mask, and Morgan could not tell.

The game drifted along with its high and its low spots. Señor Fontana was apt to plunge; now, backed up by his big *rancho*, a *rancho* measured in running leagues, and by a thousand head of cattle on the trail to the Dodge City dealer, he had pretty much *carte blanche*. And it became obvious after a few hands that the old man, though given to recklessness, was a seasoned poker player, a man who, the cards being equal, was as good as any of them.

Rob Roy Morgan sized up the players thus: Steve Question was an old hand at the game, was crafty and knew values and the chances of a draw, and possibly also had found out how the cards were marked. That made him dangerous. Then Don Benito: he played wildly, he took all the chances there were, he showed much of his mind in his face—*but he did know how the cards were marked!* That made him worse than dangerous. Then there was Smoke Keena: you could brush him aside. A good-enough poker player, but just run of the mill. And now, the old man: the question remained; did he, like Benito, know how to read the cards from their backs? And Mentor?

And the game rolled on.

They played all night long. In the morning Señora Fontana with Ernesto in her wake came to them in the *sala*. They stood up to greet her, the Fontanas rising swiftly at sight of her, the others coming to their feet one by one. She gave them a stiff smile and a throaty good morning; then they sat down again and she had Ernesto open windows, let the young sunlight in, allow some of the stale air, heavy with wine and tobacco, to escape. She said, " Breakfast will be ready in fifteen minutes."

During the final hours of their all-night session, these things had happened:

Señor Fontana had lost a thousand dollars, writing out his I O Us on little slips of paper; of these promissory notes Rob Roy Morgan held seven hundred dollars and Steve Question three hundred.

Smoke Keena was out of the game and dozing; he owed Morgan two hundred dollars.

Mentor had broken about even; a few pesos to the good.

Benito was red-cheeked and hectic-eyed; he was something like a hundred dollars to the good.

And one other thing: Rob Roy Morgan had kept on capping his stacks of gold twenties with a silver dollar. Toward the end he toppled over a stack in such fashion that the coins spilled halfway across the table, in front of Steve Question. And Steve saw how they were pierced close to their rims.

His eyes seemed to start from their sockets. He stared, puzzled, then incredulous, then with angry understanding. His own money! At least he accounted it his. Money that that girl had stolen, had made into a necklace! Now in the hands of the man he hated, Rob Roy Morgan. Morgan, who had knocked him over backward into the pool, who had left him to drown; Morgan, who had gone out again, who must have found the elusive girl, who had the money from her!

He lifted his eyes with a sort of dagger thrust to Morgan's. Morgan's eyes were low-lidded, his head tipped back, and there was a taunting semi-smile on his lips.

CHAPTER SEVEN

" ME, I'M here to stay," said young Morgan, and hung his hat on a nail. " And I'm telling you boys all about it. Before long I'm going to own the Fontana *rancho*, miles and more miles of the finest earth. And I'm not only going to have a fine house to live in, but a whole string of Indian servants. And on top of all that I'm going to have my pockets stuffed with money. And you boys are invited to stick along with me and grab all that's left over when I get through. That way you'll have ten times as much as you'd ever get any other way."

They hooted at him, but their hooting wasn't altogether spontaneous or honest; they were beginning to believe in the kid and what he said.

Big Mouth Altoona Jackson let his eyes rove about the place in which they found themselves.

" Me," he said, " I've seen classier dumps than this. You talk pretty big, Virginia, but you start out pretty small-like."

" Sure," said Morgan. " Start in at the little end and come out at the big end of the horn. And there's nothing much wrong with this place, considering how I'm putting the roof over our heads, the floor and beds under you, and plenty to eat, drink and smoke. All you boys got to do is just make up your minds." He sat in the only arm chair in the big, bare, barnlike room, and looked about him with satisfaction. " A dump it is, Big Mouth," he admitted. " But it's only for the time being, and at that, it's better than you boys can go out and get for yourselves."

It was well down toward the end of the road in Twenty Mile. It had been a warehouse of sorts, as big as all outdoors and as bleak as a stable. Twenty Mile had had its ups and downs, lofty ups and dizzy downs, times of gold excitement with the little town overfilled with milling crowds, with gold dust spilled freely, times later when cattlemen foregathered and it was like a miniature Dodge City. Then a dreary while during which neither raw gold nor bawling herds enlivened the place. Then came another, short-lived boom. The owner of the warehouse moved away to other parts; Blue Nose Johnson bought the building for a song. He saw the boom coming and meant to make a hotel of the place; he had carpenters and masons in and erected thin board partitions, making rooms, and added a couple of chimneys and fireplaces, and had a big room at the rear fitted up as a kitchen. Come the boom on full tide, and Blue Nose Johnson meant to gather in the golden grain.

Then Tangle-foot Collins, on a rampage as usual, shot Blue Nose by mistake, and Blue Nose almost died. Not quite, but he came so close to cashing in his chips that of a sudden he found himself homesick for Tennessee, and away he went, selling his new venture to the first bidder, a bartender at the Last Chance, for pretty close to nothing. The next day the bartender wondered why he had bought the thing; why not have bought an elephant or a camel or a lot of mud turtles instead? He asked Rob Roy Morgan six hundred dollars for the place, lock, stock and barrel. Morgan paid him three hundred and fifty dollars, and thus became a solid citizen and householder of Twenty Mile.

He and Smoke Keena had ridden back from the Fontana home in the early morning, Smoke Keena half-asleep in the saddle after an all night of it, Morgan wide awake and of a mood to pounce on life and take it by the throat. He estimated that he had spent a worth-while evening. He had seen the Fontana *rancho* from end to end, the big house and outbuildings included; he had picked up several hundred dollars in gold that the wild girl had dropped; he had won at poker; he held Fontana's I O Us for seven hundred dollars. He said to himself as he rode across the broad, fertile acres, " Me,

I already own seven hundred dollars worth of all this!"

He knew what he meant to do; it was very clear to him this golden, sun-shot morning. California was the land of gold; men went out with picks and shovels and their bare, blistered hands and clawed the gold up out of the earth. They didn't keep the gold long, the beautiful yellow stuff for which they had laboured so enduringly. It went into other hands. After a while it was minted into gleaming, tinkling coins. It went into the hands of other men, bankers, gamblers, businessmen. It accumulated. Then now and then, rather often, too, men like Steve Question came along; men who held up stages, who robbed banks, who piled on to trains and looted the strong-boxes. These bandits hid their gold for a time, not wanting to flaunt one day what the day before they had dipped their hands in blood to come by, not hankering for swift retribution. And it seemed to Rob Roy Morgan that in the whole set-up there was a role meant for him to play. Consider those twenties with the little holes through them; he had reasoned the matter out entirely to his satisfaction, the proper ownership of them. Now of course what he had gleaned was not the whole of Steve Question's hoard. There were points to be investigated: Where was Steve's cache? Had the girl looted it, making a clean sweep, hiding what she had not required for her own personal adornment, under a rock, in a hole somewhere on the mountainside, in the timber?

It might pay to keep an eye on Steve Question. He had gone looking for the girl last night and found her; he knew something about her, about her habits, maybe. And it might pay for Rob Roy Morgan to look for the girl on his own account.

These and kindred thoughts and speculations entertained him, but he was inclined to keep them to himself. He spoke to his fellows of other things.

He had them all assembled in one of the larger rooms, one with a fireplace, with a table and benches and chairs; a room he had made his own personal headquarters since it connected with another room which he fancied best of all for his bedroom. He took the best in the house and made no bones of it; it was his, wasn't it? He'd bought and paid for it, and he was well assured that the best was none too good for the man who could get it.

So Morgan had gathered them all here, Smoke Keena and

Tony of the shattered wrist, Big Mouth Altoona and the Old Man and the Blind Man, Red Barbee and Charlie Duff and Buck Braddock, and a final trio who were much alike, being furtive and shiftless and nearly always together, Slim Pickens and Shorty Skinner and, a new man in their band, Baldy Bates.

" Like I told you boys," said Rob Roy Morgan, " I aim to stay in this neck of the woods. I like it. It's the finest country that ever was. There's lots of fine land and forests and water and grass; there's more gold flowing free than you can shake a stick at; the hunting and fishing make a man's mouth water. And I aim to have me a whale of a ranch, thousands of acres with cattle and horses, and the land will take in valley and forests with water and game and gold."

" You'll keep saying that so much you'll come to believe it yourself," chuckled Altoona.

" You sure talk mighty big, Virginia," said Smoke Keena good humouredly. He cocked a quizzical eye at their immediate surroundings, rough plank floor, warped and sagging rafters festooned with dusty, fly-laden cobwebs, crude partitions rising about as high as a man's head, no ceilings, the room giving the effect of big wooden boxes with their tops off. " This ain't exactly what you'd call a palace," Keena said, and grinned at the others.

" There ain't a hell of a lot of fat acres with cattle and horses and rivers and things around it, I notice," put in Buck Braddock. " Seems as though——"

" You're right welcome to roll your blankets and clear out of it as soon as suits you, Buck," said Morgan. He paused a moment, then went on: " I paid three hundred and fifty dollars for this place; I mean to keep it a short spell, then sell out when I get ready to move on to my real place. And if anybody here wants to take a bet it's that inside six months I sell out for anyhow seven hundred and more likely a considerable sight more; it's in the wind that boom days are headed for Twenty Mile.

"You boys are welcome to stick around; I'm putting a roof over your heads and beds under you, and most likely when you all go broke I'll feed your hungry bellies. And for that, when I want something done I'll tell you, and you'll do it. What's more, any of you boys that show you're any good will soon be drawing wages from me, and maybe, sometimes, a split on a pot.''

The trio of shifty-eyed, sly-looking, usually silent men, looked at one another, then back at Morgan. Slim Pickens, sallow, yellow-haired, with a long thin jaw and large buck teeth, spoke up in his thin, reedy voice, a voice which always seemed to have a querulous quaver in it.

'' You talk about splitting a pot,'' he said. '' How come, Morgan?''

Morgan ignored him, though meaning to get to him in a moment.

'' You boys say I talk big, and so I do. Who's got a better right in this crowd? Look here: We blew into Twenty Mile yesterday. We all spent a few bucks in the bar-rooms. Then we did whatever we felt like, this being a free country. I'm asking you, how many of you have got more money to-day than he had yesterday? Hell's bells, what man of you has got as much as he hit town with?''

'' Us two ain't spent nary a cent,'' cackled Luke Christmas, speaking for himself and blind Gran'pa Jonathan.

'' Made any money?'' asked Morgan.

'' Well, as to that, young feller, there ain't been but a mite of time, and——'' Smoke Keena was the only other to make any reply to Morgan's inquiry; he said with a rueful sort of half-grin, '' Me, I lost my shirt last night playing poker. Wasn't much of a shirt, so to speak, but all I had,'' He rolled his eyes sideways at Morgan as he added, '' And I went in debt to another feller for two hundred nice big round silver dollars.''

'' Tell them where you got the two hundred, Nancy.''

Keena shrugged. '' What's the use? They know I got it from you.''

And I still had three hundred and fifty to buy this shack that's roofing you boys right now! And take a look at this.''

He did it after his own fashion, with a flourish; he dragged out his buckskin bag and dumped its contents on the table. Men craned their necks and went goggle-eyed, all but blind Jonathan, and he clawed Luke Christmas by the arm to be told what was what. They saw a nice little heap of golden twenties with a scattering of silver dollars; they scarcely noted the scrap of paper neatly folded which Morgan had put down with the coins.

He looked his youth just then! There was the hint of a flush in his darkly tanned cheeks and a glitter in his dark, long-lashed eyes like a girl's. And though he did not lift his voice it was vibrant with triumph and with challenge.

" I don't count my winnings, I never count my money," he said. " But I'll bet a man there's better than a thousand dollars on the table—and I rode into Twenty Mile yesterday with forty bucks in my poke. And there's this scrap of paper; it's old Fontana's I O U for another seven hundred dollars. And you know who old Fontana is and whether he's good for it! He just sent off a thousand head of cattle to the market last week and he's got a lot more than that left, and he owns more land than you could ride over in a week!"

He let all this sink in while he stared down his nose at them, he standing, a tall, erect man, the rest of them seated on chairs and benches.

Old blind Jonathan was clawing at Luke's arm now and whispering excitedly, " Is it so, Luke? Is it so?" and Luke muttered, " Yes. Keep still. I'll tell you later."

" Figure it out for yourselves, boys," said Rob Roy Morgan and gathered up his coins and precious scrap of paper. " Over a thousand in cash, *and* this shack paid for in full, *and* two hundred dollars Nancy owes me from yesterday, *and* a seven-hundred-dollar interest in the Fontana *rancho*!"

" Where in bright blue blazes did you get all that gold, Morgan?" demanded Altoona after a speechless moment during which his big mouth had looked bigger, wide open, than ever before. " Robbed a bank? Held up a stage?"

" No," said Morgan. " Not in my line, Big Mouth. That's breaking the law, and a man runs too many chances."

" Must have stole it, then!" muttered Altoona. " Only I'd like to know where!"

" I'm no thief, damn you, Big Mouth! No, I didn't steal it; that's running the same sort of chances highway robbery takes you into. I came by it honest. Some I picked up at cards, some I "—he grinned tantalizing at them—" some I picked up another way."

Again the trio looked swiftly at one another, and again Slim Pickens spoke for the three of them.

" We go on your pay roll now, Morgan, me and Skinner and Bates. And we don't care a whoop in hell where you got your money or how."

And he spat on the floor for emphasis.

" Why damn you!" shouted Rob Roy Morgan. " You ever spit on my floor again and I'll kill you!"

For the second time they saw him flare up into sudden, terrible rage. Slim Pickens remembered the other time well enough, and what had happened to half-breed Tony. Pickens stood up hastily, wiped the spittle with his boot and returned to his bench alongside Skinner and Bates. He ran his tongue along his lips, he pulled at his lower lip; he blurted out the first thing that popped into his head, eager enough to change the subject. He said:

" How about them two old men? You ain't going to keep them on the pay roll, are you, Morgan? They ain't no good to us; one is blind and the other's not much better than a cripple, and when time came to split a pot——"

Morgan heard him out, suddenly quiet and patient, but his eyes were still angry, drilling into Pickens', and Pickens bogged down there.

" You mean, Slim, that there'd be a bigger share for each man, more for you, if our number was cut down. That's it, huh, Slim?"

Pickens shut his mouth tight, hunched up his lean, narrow shoulders and started making a cigarette; that way he had an excuse to lower his eyes to the work of his hands.

Morgan said, and his voice was as cold and cutting as the edge of his own bowie knife, " Yes, by thunder, I am. As long as those two old boys want to stick, they're with us and it will be share and share alike in everything. For one thing, that's because they've got more sense than the rest of you stuck together. Besides, they are old, and the going is tough for them, and they've been with us too long to turn off."

He stepped over to Tony, the half-breed, brooding in a corner. He slapped Tony familiarly, in friendly fashion, on the shoulder.

" How's the arm to-day, kid?" he asked.

Tony made a face. " She's all right, I guess, Señor Morgan. She hurt like hell!"

" Had a doctor look at it yet?"

" No."

" You crazy fool! Well we'll find a doctor right away.
Go get yourself a drink at the Pay Dirt Saloon; wait for me
there! I'll be along pretty pronto."

Then he said to the others, " Now you boys scatter; get the
hell out of here to do your thinking. All but you, Nancy,
and you, Barbee; I want to talk to you two."

The men went out; already they were taking orders without
a murmur, at least without a murmur for Rob Roy Morgan to
overhear. The shifty-eyed three went out first; through the
open door Morgan saw Slim Pickens spit in the dust. The two
old men were last out, holding hands.

Morgan sat down in the one big and fairly comfortable
chair that stood in front of the fireplace, clasped his hard,
brown hands behind his head and lifted his boots to the table-
top. Red Barbee and Smoke Keena drew up their chairs,
sensing that whatever Morgan had to say would not be shouted
to the housetops.

" Knowing our little gang pretty well," said Morgan,
" I've a notion that you two are the best men of the bunch,
and I want to count on you like my right hand and my left
hand. Suit you?"

They looked at him steadily, their thoughts in their eyes,
frank and unhidden. They had taken fresh stock of him
lately, they were doing the same thing now. He, on his part,
had been frank enough, certainly outspoken; not his words
alone, his attitude bespoke a sort of arrogance which men like
Keena and Barbee found it hard to stomach; they were used
to living their lives in their own ways, free and untrammelled,
with no one to account to, and at the jump Rob Roy Morgan
was rather at pains to make it crystal-clear that he meant to
dominate. They were to head in where he told them, and how
and when he dictated, or he had no use for them.

Hard to swallow, that, naturally. Yet somehow both felt,
albeit with vague uneasiness, that already his spirit did dominate theirs. And standing as tall and emphatic in the
memories of both of them as a lofty spire of rock towering
from a level plain, was that heap of gold on the table—and
that significant scrap of paper—and Morgan's words: already
he had a seven-hundred-dollar interest in the lordly Fontana
rancho.

E

Morgan made no attempt to hasten their answers, nor did they hasten. Smoke Keena, nursing his customary chew of tobacco, sat with his chair tilted back, staring at the fireplace. Barbee looked curiously at Keena, then at Morgan—then slowly and deliberately lifted his boots to the tabletop as Morgan had done. There may have been a quiet eloquence of meaning in the gesture: If he meant to become Morgan's man it would be understood at the outset that he wasn't going to do any cringing and boot-licking.

Keena said after a couple of silent minutes, " Suits me, Virginia."

And, with no further delay, " Suits me, Morgan," said Red Barbee.

" About the stage hold-up we saw yesterday," said Morgan. " The road agents got away with the strongbox, and men are saying around town it had anyhow forty thousand dollars in it, a lot of it gold. By now the loot is cached somewhere, and the safe way for the highwaymen to play their game is to leave it where it is for a spell before they start spending it. And last night we saw half a dozen Silver Hats in town. Folks figure that one of them was the bandit leader. They don't know which one. Maybe they figure all of them had a hand in the thing; they don't know and can't prove anything."

" It's a cinch," said Red Barbee, " that they're all in cahoots, showing up the way they did in those fool hats."

" It's no such thing," Morgan retorted. " If any one asked where they got their lids, and they felt like answering, they could give a hundred explanations. Maybe they didn't even know each other; maybe straggling into town, they came by some trading station or come up with a pedlar who was selling the hats cheap, so cheap they bought them. It would be easy to make up a yarn like that; it would even be easy for it to be true—provided the real Silver Hat had arranged it."

" Why shouldn't he?" demanded Keena.

Morgan shrugged. " So that all would be suspected, no one in particular, then no one at all. Now I want you boys to be good mixers to-day, loaf in the bars, talk a lot without saying anything, stretch your ears, keep your eyes open, and see what you can find out about this set-up. There's a name for buried gold. They call it treasure trove. That means it belongs to anybody who can get away with it. And now I'll give you something definite to go on; keep it to yourselves: the bandit leader is Steve Question."

" I had that same hunch," muttered Smoke Keena.

" It's not a hunch with me, Nancy. I know. Never mind how I know; maybe you can guess. Anyhow take it from me that I do know that the big gun in that bandit crew is Steve Question."

" Fair, enough," said Keena. " What you say goes, Virginia."

" You can talk with him like the rest. He'll be glad to have a few drinks with you. He'll want to find out all he can about me. Don't tell him anything that counts. You can tell him I'm a wind-bag, a blow-hard and a fat-head."

Again for a time, each man deeply thoughful, they sat silent; they were almost without any movement, only Smoke Keena's jaws working slowly and gently with his cud. So quiet was the room, in fact, that they heard the gnawing of a rat or mouse in the woodwork.

It was a mouse. Near the fireplace, directly in front of ruminant Smoke Keena, some ten feet from him, was the small hole which the rodent used as his doorway. In the hush of the room the little creature peered forth, its bright black eyes like polished jet. No man of them stirred as all three men watched idly.

The mouse came all the way into the room.

Even then Smoke Keena did not stir in his chair, but from his puckered lips there shot a long and accurate stream of tobacco juice; it drenched the mouse, it all but drowned him, it for the moment blinded him. He reared up on his hind legs and pawed frantically at his streaming eyes.

A shout of laughter burst from Rob Roy Morgan. Smoke Keena roared with him, and Red Barbee snorted and joined them in laughter. The mouse went running about the room, finally blundered through an open door and vanished, scattering drops of tobacco juice.

The three men stopped laughing at the same instant. All three remembered Slim Pickens. Certainly Smoke Keena had done the more thorough and certainly far more spectacular job.

" Nancy," said Rob Roy Morgan in a queerly suppressed

voice, " you go get a rag and mop that up. I'm damned if I'm going to do it, and somebody's going to."

Keena's face went red and his jaws corded. He stiffened from head to foot—then of a sudden he grinned.

" It was one damn fine shot," he contended.

Morgan and Red Barbee were waiting outside when Keena came out to join them. The three moved down the road toward the heart of the town. Morgan put his hand on Keena's shoulder and gave him a playful shake.

" Say, Virginia," said Keena, " if you got any sense a-tall, you'll keep an eye peeled on Slim Pickens. I don't know about Tony, in spite of what you did to him. But you watch Pickens, and likewise his two side-kicks, Skinner and Bates. *Sabe ?* "

" Thanks, Nancy," was all that Morgan said.

CHAPTER EIGHT

ALREADY there were thousands of gold-seekers in California, digging down for the root of all evil, as some drolly called the yellow stuff, from the long sweep of the white-beached coast to the steep slopes of the Sierra Nevada; already there were many tall-masted ships whose idle hulks rotted in San Francisco bay for the simple reason that their crews had deserted, caught in the gold rush, and none could be found to man the ships except such derelicts as might be shanghaied along the Barbary Coast. Already had the lusty shout " Gold!" raised in '49, echoed all round the world so that now Englishmen and Chinese, French and South Africans, rubbed elbows and knifed one another all up and down the Mother Lode.

Already was gold an old story, proven a true story and a compelling one. Some years had glittered by, trimmed in gold and black and crimson, since the first word of the discovery had reverberated in the most distant ports.

But before the orgy started, a sort of maelstrom into which were drawn more and more thousands of adventuresome young men who had harkened to the call of the Red Gods, there had long been pastoral California, a fruitful land of vast *ranchos,* free and generous gifts of the King of Spain to his favourites; *ranchos* like that of the Fontanas. So now you had a young California where the serene and placid Land of Mañana and the hectic Land of Golden Tumult, cheek by jowl, regarded each other as across an abyss. So close together physically and geographically, so distantly remote one from the other spiritually.

There were all sorts of birds of prey winging into this promised land, witness such as Rob Roy Morgan, as Steve Question, as Smoke Keena and Red Barbee—and the shifty-eyed trio of Pickens, Bates and Skinner. Hawks, eagles, buzzards. And already here were the doves, the old Spanish-California patriarchs, simple and trusting and guileless, most of them. And then there were those individuals halfway between—sons of the patriarchs—such as Don Benito Fontana. Young, their roots in the halcyon days, their eyes watchful of the new influx, men partaking of both elements.

Thinking of Don Benito Fontana, Rob Roy Morgan sent Keena and Barbee along to the Pay Dirt, saying he would be with them soon, and stepped into the General Store, an emporium of sorts where you could purchase nearly anything you could lay your mind to. Here was the place to come, the only place of the sort in Twenty Mile, whether you wanted hardware of any type or dry goods, suits, hats, shoes and all the rest, or groceries; the Twenty Mile Mercantile, it called itself, and in a sign over the door was the legend familiar in more than one raw western town, " Anything from a Tooth-pick to a Coffin."

Morgan asked for a deck of cards. Sure, they had cards; how many decks?

" Got plenty?" Morgan asked.

" Been selling a good many lately; got about a hundred decks left."

" Just get 'em in?"

" Hell, no. We always have anyhow a couple of dozen in stock."

" Just two decks this trip." Morgan paid for them and went out. So young Fontana couldn't find a deck in town, huh? " Thought so," thought Morgan complacently, and crossed the street to the Pay Dirt.

It was only mid-afternoon, and there were but a dozen or so

men in the big, barnlike room. Among them he saw, at the far end of the long bar, Smoke Keena and Red Barbee and Silver Hat Steve Question. Morgan paid them no attention after the one quick glance. He saw Tony of the broken wrist at the other end of the bar, a glass before him; Tony's face looked warped and twisted; he was holding his injured wrist in a tight grip. Morgan went over to him.

" Put your drink down, kid," he said. " It'll help dull the pain. Then we go dig up a doctor." The bartender stepped over to ask him his pleasure, and Morgan asked of him, " Where do we find a doc? My friend got his arm hurt."

" Doc Bones has got a shanty on Back Street; it's his office, too, and he's as apt to be there as anywheres this time of day. Go down the alley, turn right, and you'll see his sign."

Morgan and Tony went out together, followed directions and found a small board shanty with a faded, crookedly painted sign over it, " Dr. Bonner, M.D." The door was open and they went in, entering a small, bare-floored, bare-walled room furnished with a cot, a couple of rawhide-bottomed chairs and a long table cluttered with pamphlets, bottles and a confusion of litter. A sharp voice from the rear room called out, " I'll be out in a minute."

They sat down and waited. They heard the clink of coins; they heard the sharp voice saying, " I'm stepping on your neck, Johnnie Lingo!" They heard the clink of bottle and glass, then the sharp voice again, this time in a brittle, not very pleasant laugh along with the words, " Lay down to my four little bullets. Now deal me out for a hand or two, you jaybirds, while I attend briefly to my professional duties."

The door opened then and Dr. Bonner—Doc Bones to Twenty Mile—came in, a youngish man as skinny as a rail, something more than six feet of him longitudinally, wearing a dirty-white shirt, a long tailed black coat, black corduroy breeches stuffed into black, shiny boots. He was smoking a big fat black cigar. He had eyes like a bird's, round and shiny and black.

He looked his callers over shrewdly.

" Fight, huh," he grunted, picking up Tony's wrist.

Tony winced. " My gun goes off and shoots me," he said. " Ouch, Doc, that hurts!"

" I'd think it would," snorted Doc Bones.

He tore off Tony's blood-soaked bandage, got a basin of hot water, washed the wound, stared at it, felt it with quick, light finger and thumb, got a probe, probed the wound, washed it out with a pinkish solution—puffing continuously at his cigar, he dropped hot ashes on it, brushed them away, and proceeded. He poured something out of a bottle upon the raw flesh, and Tony's face screwed up and Tony's white teeth gritted.

" Hurts you more'n it does me," said Doc Bones, one of his pet jokes, and went along with what he had to do, which was to paint the wound with another solution and then bandage it with a fresh, snowy-white bit of cloth.

" You'll do, mister," he said. " Lucky you didn't get your hand blown off. Nothing bad; mostly just the meat torn off the bone, and the bone hardly more than nicked. Come back to-morrow, same time. Ten dollars."

Morgan paid the ten dollars and they went out.

" *Gracias*, Señor," said Tony.

" One more thing, Tony. The boys sort of miss your music. Go buy yourself a new guitar. Get a good one, I don't care what it costs." He gave Tony forty dollars " You can get it over at the store; I saw a dozen of 'em. Get the best, and if it's more money, let me know. Then go over to the house and lie down and take it easy." And he stepped away hurriedly leaving Tony staring incredulously at the money in his hand, then after the swiftly departing figure.

Morgan went to the livery stable to look at his horses, Snow White and Jet; he was thinking that the animals, if left boarding there indefinitely, would eat their heads off, because he knew that in a town like Twenty Mile everything was sky-high. The thing to do was build a corral back of his new place, get a load of hay and some grain, establish his crowd's small herd there.

Just as he entered the wide double-doors of the stable he encountered the Old Man and the Blind Man coming out; their arms were filled with their miscellany of possessions.

Luke Christmas said, " Hallo, Morgan. We're moving our truck over to the new diggings. Nothing like getting settled."

Morgan nodded, went on into the semi-dark, lofty building that smelled sweetly of hay and crushed barley and oats, not so sweetly of saddle and harness leather, not sweetly at all of other by-products of the business. He saw nothing to find fault with in the accommodations given his horses, slapped Jet affectionately on the lean, clean shoulder, took Snow White by the ear as she nuzzled him, and made his way back to the Pay Dirt Saloon.

Keena and Barbee and Steve Question were still fraternising at the bar. This time he joined them.

" Hi, boys," he said. " Hallo, Question."

He spun a coin on the bar. It was a gold twenty and had a tiny hole pierced through its rim. " Drinks are on me he invited.

Drinks were served; the bartender swept the coin up, started away with it to get change, turned and came back.

" What's this?" he demanded. " The damn thing's got a hole through it. How come?"

" Has it?" Morgan asked innocently. He regarded the thing gravely, shook his head and said, " Well, that hole don't hurt it any. It's worth twenty dollars of anybody's money. Or, if it will make you happy, knock off a dollar out of the change. Like the feller says, there's plenty more where that came from."

" Fair enough," said the bartender, and knocked off the dollar.

" What did you want to make holes in them twenties for, Morgan?" asked Keena.

Morgan grinned. " Nothing like marking your own cattle, Keena, so you'll know 'em anywhere you spot 'em. " Here's how, boys."

They all said, " How," even Steve Question drinking with the man who only last night had driven a hard fist into his mouth so that even yet his lips were sore and puffed, who had toppled him into the mountain pool and left him to drown or get out the best way he could. Since Morgan had given no hint of having remembered the episode, Steve Question elected to ignore it likewise. Yet when the two men's eyes clashed for a long still moment, both fully realised that a grim sequence of primitive action had been started which there was no more stopping now than there would be in checking an avalanche short of its own furious and natural end. That they chose to be in each other's presence, with no reference made to what had gone before, was simply that each judged he had his own ends to serve by learning what he could of the other, by keeping him at least in the tail of his eye.

Morgan knew well enough that Steve Question was gravely concerned, anxious to learn exactly how he had come into possession of the gold, and Steve Question could not but realise that Morgan had taken the keenest interest and would never rest until he came upon the entire cache.

They did not speak directly to each other; Morgan addressed Keena and Barbee, as did Steve Question when he had any rare remark to make. After the one drink Morgan said a general " So long " and went out.

Meantime the two old men had arrived at their quarters with their precious possessions, and behind a closed but unlocked door—there wasn't a lock in the house—were " getting settled." First of all:

" What sort of place we got here, Luke?" the Blind Man asked.

Luke, looking the room over really for the first time, strove to describe it to his sightless crony.

" Well, Johnnie," he explained meticulously, " we got a good-sized room. It's about twelve foot wide and a mite longer'n that, mebbe fifteen foot. It's got only one door; you know where that is; no lock or latch or anything on it. We got one real wall, the outside one; the other three walls is just partitions a man could crawl over, a young man could, easy." He chuckled. " So could an old man if there was a fire and he was scared good and had to! Now, let's see. There's one winder; it's in the solid wall, of course, about the middle, betwixt our two bunks. It's about four foot wide, mebbe six foot tall; if you want it open you shove it up and set a stick under it like any winder. The stick's laying on the sill right now. The winder's shet."

" Know why they call 'em winders, Luke?" said old Jonathan. " That's 'cause when you open 'em the wind can blow through."

They both chuckled. Old Jonathan went straight back to the door, ran his fine, sensitive old hands over pretty nearly every inch of it and then began exploring the walls in the same fashion. He reached up, standing on his tiptoes; he could barely reach the top of the partition.

" There's one old chair," Luke Christmas went on.

" Better be careful when you ease down into it; its legs look
they might give." He went to the chair, sat down gingerly,
shook his body in it like a hen nesting down, and got up.
" It'll be all right if you treat it gentle," he said.

" Just two bunks and a chair, huh?"

" More'n that, Johnnie; there's what goes for a table, a
box stood on end, and it's got a candle stuck in a bottle on
top of it; it's under the winder between our bunks."

Gran'pa Jonathan continued his process of circum-
navigation.

" Go 'head, Luke," he said.

" The floor is boards about a foot wide; look out for bare
feet because they're sort of splintery. The cracks between
the floor boards ain't very wide, mostly less than a half inch.
The floor's good and sound; you can walk on it anywheres.
On the walls there's three pictures; they been there quite a
spell; guess the place leaks a bit when it rains, they look that
streaked and faded. Some feller's snagged 'em out of a
magazine. One's on the wall right opposite the winder ; it's
coloured, sort of yellow-greenish mostly. It's a lake, and
there's some mountains and pines and a feller fishing off'n a
big white rock, and a boat; you can just see the tail end of
it in a patch of willows. Then there's a picture just to the
right of the door as you come in; it's coloured, too, they're
all coloured or was. It's pretty bad faded out; looks like it had
laid out in the wet and mildewed before the feller tackled it up.
It's got three scamperish females without much of anything
on, doing a kind of hoe-down out in the grass with the sun
just coming up or going down, doggone if I know which.
Anyhow it looks like them hussies had better scamper home
for a quick hot toddy and get some duds on, else they'll likely
take their death of cold. Then on the other wall there's a
picture of a big town, and it's awful late at night because it's
mostly black-dark, just the tops of the high houses showing
up against the sky and there's a few stars, and there's a few
street lights, looking sickish, and way up in front on an
empty-looking street there's an old man, old as you and me,
Johnnie, and he's got a little white, short-haired dog trotting
along with him and it feels like they didn't have no place to
go to. And that's all the art works we got, Johnnie."

" I'd sort of like to see that picture, Luke," said Jonathan wistfully. He made his way straight to it and touched it gently with his finger tips, exploring every inch of it. " I ain't been in a big town like that for quite a spell. Show me where the houses stick up in the sky, Luke, and where the stars is, and where's the old feller and his dog."

Luke Christmas took Jonathan's hand and led it from one detail to the other, explaining as the slim fingers travelled over the picture. He added, taking Jonathan's digit between his own finger and thumb, " And right here's a lamp post; you see the old man and his pup are right under the street lamp, and that's how come you can see 'em. Here's the dog, here's the old man—and right over here is one of the houses with a light in it. By golly, the door's open, too, and you can just make out in the sort of half-dark that somebody's peeking out —looks like a woman, Johnnie—mebbe she's going to ask 'em in for supper!"

" It would be pretty near breakfast-time, wouldn't it, Luke?"

" Mebbe. Mebbe three, four o'clock in the morning. Well, like I says, that's all the work of art. Now, when you go to our winder and look out—only the winder's awful dirty, Johnnie, and it's got cobwebs and a lot of dead flies in it and two dead yellow jackets—looking out the winder you see the stable where we just come from, that's when you look as far as you can over to the left-hand side, and next you don't see nothing but the road that goes straight for about a mile and then goes crooked, because there's some little hills starting there, and there's quite a few live oaks on 'em, and higher up some pines, not very big and then the road—it's a white road and dusty—dives into a sort of little canyon and you don't see it any more. And then, as far as you can see, all the way across the winder clean over to the right-hand side, there's the mountains, and they're high and look rocky and there's lots of pines in 'em low down and halfway up, a *leetle* bit more than halfway, and then there's just bare mountains with mebbe, you can't tell from here, a mite of brush, but mostly rocks and peaks and cliffs and all that sort of truck, Johnnie. See?"

Jonathan had joined him at the window.

" Yep, I got it, Luke. Now, let's stow our stuff, will we?"

They had dumped all their belongings, bags and bundles,

on the bunks, not to have them underfoot while the Blind Man did his exploratory prowling. He sat down on his bunk —well located by now, his being farthest from the door—and began fingering the various parcels. He knew each one instantly; he could have told unerringly if any one was missing.

" That Rob Roy Morgan's a sort of funny cuss, ain't he, Luke?" he asked mildly. " What do you make of him now?"

" He's sort of spreading himself the last couple of days," said Luke. " Sort of spread-eagling, you know, Johnnie." Luke's was a mellow, low-throated chuckle. " He's just a pup, Johnnie, but of course he don't know it. Give him time——"

" He thinks he's a heller and a wildcat, huh?" Old Jonathan had the knack of a humorous chuckle, too.

" Remember, old socks, when you was about twenty-one?"

Jonathan answered soberly. " One good thing about being blind, Luke—Hell, there's a lot of good things, I notice, in everything whether it's good or bad to begin with. One good thing about being blind is that you can see better!"

" You damned old fool!" snorted Luke Christmas.

" You didn't let me get through. A blind feller gets so that he can see some things awful clear that the other fellers can't. Pshaw! Remember when I was twenty-one? I can see myself!"

" Kind of swelled up and puffy and cocky, huh?"

" Yep. Like I said, Luke, there's some things you can see better with both eyes shet. Likewise you can think better. Got yourself some high-grade thinking to do, wait till it's after dark, go to bed, blow out the candle and do your thinking."

" You ought to know better than me, Johnnie. But, talk about there being some good in most things, take this Morgan kid——"

They discussed him at length. They were tolerant old boys who had been young once themselves and who—though not all old men are like them—could see the sterling qualities in the young freebooter: they recognised a crude strength and gallantry, a fine courage and high ambition—and they saw other qualities not so fine.

" He's what you call in the making," they agreed. " Something pretty soon is going to make or break him.

Reckon it's in the cards, but you can't make the cards out 'til they're turned up.''

" And there's another man I've got my eye on," said the old Blind Man. " And that's old Mac, little Barbie's papa. When he come to Twenty Mile, Luke, he come to the wrong place. The wrong place for him, I mean."

Often enough these two understood each other without any words at all. Luke nodded slowly. He said:

" I'm nodding my head, Johnnie. I know what you mean. He's done fine for himself and his fam'ly so far; he's bought and owns the Mercantile Store, and they say you can't beat it in a hundred mile. But he's bound to slip back to his old folly like the dawg in the scriptures. Matter of fact, I'm of a notion he's already started."

" Hell's bells," said old Jonathan. " Let's get our truck stowed away, Luke."

" I'm going out and get a hammer and some boards and nails," said Luke Christmas. " We'll put up some shelves for ourselves; we'll have all our things stowed away nice and neat, and in plain sight. Easy to come at."

He chuckled again and Jonathan chuckled with him.

They were busily occupied when Morgan stuck his head in. Luke Christmas, the crudest and most casual of hit-or-miss carpenters, was nailing up his last shelf; it sloped both ways. On the other shelves Gran'pa Jonathan was disposing neatly of the last of their bags and bundles and old tobacco boxes. Morgan grinned at them.

" Making it look like home, huh? That's good. Only, damn me if it don't look more like a Chinaman's store!"

" It's only fools that turn up their noses at stuff they don't understand," snorted Luke Christmas. " Just you step in here young feller, and I'll show you a thing or two." Morgan obligingly stepped in. Luke picked up a small canvas bag and opened it's mouth so that Morgan could peer inside. All that he could make of it was that it contained a waddy mass of dried weeds. He sniffed the thing; it was faintly aromatic, but he judged a part of the aroma due to mildew.

" Them there," said Luke, " are yarbs we brung clear from th'other side the Rockies; you get yourself a dose of cholera, hawg cholera or any kind, and you come running to us, and we'll make you a brew that'll cure you in two shakes." He set the bag away and took up one of his dingy tobacco boxes; something rattled inside. He poured a dozen whitish, smooth pebbles into his horny palm. "When folks use coal oil lamps," he said, "lots of time they blow up, mebbe blow a man's head off, mebbe just burn his house down. Put one of these here charm-rocks in the oil, and she just nachrally can't explode."

He set the box back in it's place and took up another small bag. The contents of this were enwrapped in an old scrap of oilskin. Morgan made a face and turned up his nose.

"Looks like dried frogs and lizards," he said.

"Shucks," grunted Luke, and restored the specimens carefully to their place. "We got treasure here, me and Johnnie," he said with dignity, "and you fellers ain't got sense enough to know it. Why, shucks, just you get a twinge of rheumatics and here's where you come. Let Johnnie have a kittle of hot water and something to grind a couple of these medicinal specimens and a piece of cheese-cloth and an old flat iron. Makes a sort of hot poultice, he does, and none can do it better than Johnnie. Put it on the stiff joint, hold the hot flat iron on it until you drop off to sleep like a babe in its mother's arms, and——"

Rob Roy Morgan laughed and escaped.

He went to his own room and filled his cartridge belt. Usually he wore but one belt gun; to-day he added the second. He put a fresh bag of cigarette tobacco and some matches in his vest pockets—seldom did he wear a coat, unless the weather grew bitter cold, and never did he go abroad without a vest. Then he went to the stable and saddled a horse; he chose Jet, being of the mind that a black horse was best for night riding, and it was dusk before he rode out of town, with a small, tight canvas roll behind his saddle.

His departure was witnessed by a few uninterested men lounging along the wooden sidewalks, also by three keenly interested men. The three were Smoke Keena, Red Barbee and Steve Question. For Morgan had said a quiet word in Keena's ear before leaving the Pay Dirt, and Keena had managed to have the others outside, on their way to the more pretentious, comparatively elaborate Tennessee's Place, a combination bar-room, dance hall and gambling hall—with mirrors and music!

" Say! There goes Morgan!" Keena exclaimed. " Headed out of town like he was going places! Where do you reckon, Barbee?"

" Where could the damn fool go?" countered Barbee. " He don't know any place here but the Fontana's place, and he's headed straight away from it." He turned to Steve Question. " Any town up there in them there hills, Steve?"

" Go far enough and you find a town most any direction," said Steve. " About a dozen miles up that way you come to Random; it ain't much of a town, though. Then, another twenty mile fu'ther——"

" Hell, who cares," snorted Keena. " Let's have a drink at Tennessee's."

Rob Roy Morgan jogged along up the white, dusty road, farther and farther from Twenty Mile, farther and farther from the Hacienda Fontana, growing into a diminishing figure which presently disappeared altogether in that notch in the hills which Luke had described to Jonathan. He still rode along, with the road winding before him, watching all the while for a likely place to leave it, as he had no concern with Random or any other town. What he did want to do, without advertising his plan to the world, was to ride into the timbered mountain slopes, keep in the shelter and turn back in the general direction of the Fontana home.

It was a pleasant ride through a lovely country, one to which he had already given some part of that wild heart of his. The starry skies grew softly radiant, and the night was warm and still. He breathed deep, he travelled with a marked leisureliness, he revelled in the solitudes and his own dreams, he expanded to the summer night. He had far more time than he needed, his only reason for starting before the full dark was that he wanted to be seen. Now it was a different matter; hence the black horse, hence his following little-travelled ways.

Having found a dim trail which led in his general direction, which skirted Fontana valley on the side farthest from Twenty Mile, he idled along through starlight, moonlight and shadow, stopping frequently to listen to any faint sound, until at last he came to a wooded slope whence, through the trees, he could see the white walls of the old home and a few lighted windows. He dismounted and unsaddled in a brushy thicket ringed about by tall timber. He tethered his horse, made himself a casual camp bed, secured his small food pack against invasion by suspending it from the branch of a tree, and then made his way silently and in a round-about way, in order to keep to the darkest places, toward the waterfall.

He found a vantage point which suited him and sat down with his back to a big pine. From here he could see the glint of moon and stars on the fern-ringed pool, and could also see a number of open spots on the slope and had a few long vistas down through the pines. He made himself comfortable for a long wait, if need be, a hunter determined to stalk his game in all patience.

And he fell to wondering which of the two whom he sought, he was going to see first. He felt in his bones, as the two old men would have put it, that he was going to find one if not both of the two he had marked down to serve his purpose.

CHAPTER NINE

Rob Roy Morgan didn't go near his bed that night. Thinking of Steve Question, he felt assured that that individual, knowing that the Tiger Lily girl had looted a part of his loot, would want to know whether she had cleaned him out on that particular cache, or had taken only what she wanted for her barbaric necklace. Without the least doubt, give him time and not a very long time, Steve Question would both seek the marauding young woman and inspect his cache. As Morgan had it all worked out, all that he had to do was to sit tight and await upon circumstance.

His reasoning was logical as events proved. He did not have to wait overlong. Within an hour of his arrival he heard a horse's hoofbeats. He stood up, cocked his ear against the oncoming sound, made out that the rider drew on, as he had done, through the timber clothing the slope, then hastily forsook his big pine and withdrew into a clump of manzanitas where he crouched down in the dark.

He saw Steve Question, still wearing that silver hat of his.

" He ought to have a black one, too," Morgan decided. " Just for night riding."

He saw Steve Question slip down out of the saddle, saw him in a blurred sort of fashion through the brush but was sure who it was. Steve, like Morgan before him, tethered his horse in a shadowy place, then came closer, moving stealthily and without the least sound. He would stop every few steps, stand stone still a few minutes, then move forward again. Morgan crouched lower in his hiding-place.

Steve Question passed within twenty steps of him; his eyes were everywhere; he peered into all the shadows, even into the thicket where Morgan was. He came on again. Then, once again like Morgan, he found a place under a big pine and squatted on his heels and sat still, listening, watching, waiting.

She won't show up again here, Morgan decided. Not after what happened last night. She would have hid somewhere and watched; she saw Steve Question go into the pool, she saw him go away, she saw him claw his way out and go back to Fontana's. By this time she's twenty miles from here. She wouldn't even have thought to look for her scattered coins from her broken necklace—or would she?

Steve Question at last stood up. Morgan saw him move down slope, along the narrow, racing stream which poured out of the pool; where it was so narrow that a man could jump across it easily, Steve made his crossing. Then he turned back up stream. He went the way the girl had fled last night, following a dim path that might have been a deer trail.

Where he went, there went Morgan also and in a stealth equal to Steve Question's; holding back as far as he could and yet keep the other man's shadowy form always in sight. The trail led straight up the mountainside for a hundred yards, then slanted off to the right, taking an easier gradient yet always climbing. It entered presently a little open glade, fairly level, fringed with timber, and there Morgan saw his quarry clearly for a moment as he hastened through a patch of moonlight. Steve sped across this clearing and, as Morgan made out just in time to escape being detected by blundering too close, stopped in the shadows on the farther side and stood still a long time. So did Morgan stand still.

At last Steve moved along again, and so did his shadow. The dim trail led close to a dark ravine down which flashed a hurrying stream, bright in moonlit spaces, lost in the utter dark at times where it dived into tunnels made by thick-

F

growing alders and aspens and willows and tall ferns. It was hard now for Morgan to keep Steve Question in sight; more than once he lost him, but always found him again, hurrying steadily on now. Morgan quickened his pace, drawing closer, and it was well that he did so, for he was just in time to see the dark, hurrying figure quit the trail and go down into the bed of the ravine and step up on a big flat, white rock in the midst of the swirling water.

Steve sprang across, headed on upstream, and Morgan lost him in the dark under the canopy of green growing things. Morgan listened; he heard the sound of steps now as Steve Question's haste grew and he gave over some part of his stealth—and of a sudden Morgan wondered, " Is the girl somewhere near, after all?" Is she snugly hidden, watching both of us?"

In his turn he crossed the creek, using the white rock as a stepping stone, and followed on. Dark it was here, as black as nigger boy in a coal cellar; not a star-gleam pierced through the verdant rooftree of interlaced leaves. Steve Question might be standing, waiting for him, not ten feet away. What a chance that would be for Steve Question! A shot fired here with no one to hear—unless it be the wild girl who, if he could credit a small part of the tales told of her, would find no human ears into which to pour the tale of it— and later on, maybe much later, the body of Rob Roy Morgan, perhaps unidentifiable, with pockets rifled, to be found inexplicably slain. His shoulders twitched as a man's shoulders twitch when he feels a cold draft.

Then he saw a light, and judged it a safe distance ahead of him; Steve Question had struck a match. It flared up, burned down, went out. Steve struck another; Morgan could not see him through the fringe of thicket along the winding stream, could only make out the match flares. Still a third match—and then Steve Question's voice.

Morgan in his time had heard many a man curse, had known many a man to fly into a rage, but such cursing as he listened to now evidencing such a blazing fury he had never before heard in his life. Steve Question's voice grew shrill, and broke, and it seemed that the man was choking. And Rob Roy Morgan tucked in the corners of his mouth and grinned all across his face.

He knew well enough what it was all about.

Steve Question had gone to his cache and found it rifled. Looted clean. Not just a miserable seven or eight hundred dollars gone, the whole of it vanished.

" What a girl! What a girl!" Rob Roy Morgan chuckled. And suddenly he found himself hoping that she *was* somewhere near, that she was enjoying this as much as he. As much? He could picture her with both hands over her mouth to keep her laughter from betraying her! The only thing was that, as he had thought before, she was probably miles away.

Morgan hastily yet as silently as possible parted the thick growth on the steep slope flanking the stream and crept on all fours some several feet from where he had stood watching the match-flares, listening to Steve Question's wrathful voice. There were no more matches struck and he thought that he heard Steve returning.

Steve Question came downstream in all haste, no longer caring how much noise he made; the man was beside himself, poisoned with the venom of his own fury. Morgan watched him stride by, going straight back the way he had come, and then once more followed him. He saw him go straight to his horse, toe up into the saddle and ride away. He saw whither he was going: Down to the old Spanish home. It was dark down there now, all lights out, but he knew that a man like Steve Question, especially dealing with the most generous and hospitable of hosts, such as the Fontanas, would not in the least mind knocking them out at midnight, demanding a roof and a bed.

A candle or lamp was lighted down at the Hacienda Fontana. A door, mellow in yellow light, opened and Steve Question was welcomed, sleepily at first perhaps, then all the more effusively! What an honour to the Fontanas to have him give such signal testimony of his friendship.

The door closed. Steve was housed for the night.

And on the mountainside, by the pool under the waterfall, a girl was laughing!

How did he know, this Rob Roy Morgan, just what the sound of her laughter would be like? But he had known!

Now, young Rob Roy Morgan, being a man with imagination, had done a good bit of thinking of the Tiger Lily girl. He had heard of her more than once. He remembered the long, windy tales Altoona Jackson had to tell of her; he had heard some of them already. For something like ten years there had been these crazy legends going up and down over the mountains. A girl like a moonbeam, a girl who came and went at will, appearing, vanishing. The Indians called her a White Goddess and were afraid of her; if they saw her small, light tracks by a spring, on a loamy bit of soil, they gathered flowers and left them there, as on an altar, and they left deer meat and corn and whatever they had that a White Goddess might accept from them, and so befriend and mother them.

These Indians, and some white men, had seen her, or so they said. They had seen her on a high peak, and it seemed that when she lifted her white arms the sun broke through the hesitant dawn, and day came. They saw her, and it was always on some high place, when earth-shaking thunderstorms burst over the land; and when she lifted her arms, lightning drove jagged spears all about her but never scorched a stress of her wind-blown hair. All these things they said, and many others.

Where is the dividing line between truth and falsehood no man knows or ever knew. It's like drawing an exact line between day and night. You can't do it. The two merge.

There were so many tales, wild tales, of this Tiger Lily girl, be she human or spirit; some held her a vampire, and this was at a time when much was said of vampires in the world; it was said that she crept from her fastnesses in the dead of night, crept into some wagon train, stole babies, sucked their blood. It was said that she danced temptingly before young men who followed her streaming hair in the night light of stars or moon, that she led them, laughing invitingly over her white shoulder, to the edge of a precipice, that there she opened her arms to them—then she was not there, and there was only the thin light on the rim of a black gorge with the dark figure of a man hurtling down. They said of her that she ran like the wind, and no man could come up with her, that she talked with all the wild creatures, little animals like chipmunks and brush rabbits, with the birds such as quail and grouse and wild pigeons, with bears and deer, and that when she swam in the mountain pools the rainbow trout gathered about her so that they clothed her as in a shimmering gown such as a mermaid might wear. They said that she was pure spirit, and good; they said that she was spawned by the devil's grandmother, and was black evil. They said everything, as everything is always said about the unknown.

But how many had heard her laugh, as Rob Roy Morgan heard her laugh now!

He didn't know quite where she was. On the other side of the pool, he did know that much. But he had no glimpse of her. He used his eyes as a man would use diamond-tipped drills to cut through the dark places. He couldn't see her.

He realised that this was their second meeting—no, you couldn't quite call it a meeting. The second time they had been aware of each other. And he realised at the same time that, though he had heard her voice twice now, he had never yet heard her speak a single word.

There can be nothing lovelier than laughter.

Her laughing embraced him, he was a part of it; she knew that he heard it. It was as good as saying, '' Good evening, young stranger. Here we are, you and I. How do you do?''

The first words he ever spoke to the Tiger Lily girl were these:

'' I won't hurt you. Step out where I can see you. If you don't, I'll track you down if it takes the rest of my life.''

Her laughter was stilled. She didn't answer. Probe as he would with his eyes through the darkest places, he could find no trace of her. He waited.

He had schooled himself to be patient, though it did go against the grain, since essentially Rob Roy Morgan was no soft-stepping man.

And so he waited. And right away he got tired of waiting; hadn't he already to-night done his quota of that sort of stuff?

'' I've told you already I wouldn't hurt you,'' he said. '' Even if I could, I wouldn't. I don't even want to. But I want to talk to you, I want to see what you look like. You know I haven't had a chance yet to get a good look at you.''

Still she didn't answer and still he didn't know where she was. Through a long silence he wondered if she had slipped away and was already far up the black mountainside.

He spoke to her again, his voice sounding friendly, saying lightly:

'' What were you laughing at? Must have been pretty funny!'' He chuckled. '' I bet a man it was because of the trick you put across on Steve Question, robbing his cache, hearing him blow up when he made sure that you had cleaned him out. I guess no man hates getting robbed more than a robber does.''

Listening with all his ears, all that he could hear was the faint sighing of the night breeze through the pines and the splash of water into the pool, the purling ripple of water running out and forming the mountain creek. He marked that the sound of the water was not unlike that of her laughter.

'' You are on your side of the pool,'' he said presently, '' and here I am on mine, and you know I can't jump across it, and that to get on your side I'd have to go down hill a way, then climb back up, and you could run out on me. So there's no good reason at all why you don't step out where I can see you, where I can talk to you a minute.''

Never did a man's eyes stab more persistently into the dark, among shadows; a dozen times he thought that he saw her but every time it was a rock, a bush, a tree trunk, just a tricky play of light and shadow. He grew very still and listened as he had done before, sure that if she stirred he would hear her, were it only dry leaves, dead pine needles, under her light tread. And again all that he heard was the hushed breathing of the pines, the gurgling laughter of the water.

He tried to think of something to say that would tempt her forth. He knew better than to threaten her; she'd be off in the instant and lost to him on the broken and timbered mountainside.

He began to feel the complete fool, talking to her as though she were within a score of feet from him, as she well could have been—and yet it was entirely possible that she had slipped away after his first few words to her. So in the end his patience ran out, utterly exhausted. He moved swiftly, as silently as he could, down along the stream that poured out of the pool, made his crossing, went back upstream, looking for her. Another foolish thing to attempt, he acknowledged, yet he would not give over without trying. He couldn't find a sign of her, not even broken twigs of the bushes where he had fancied she had hidden, and there was no such light as would reveal a track.

Then, a few minutes later, by the merest chance, he saw her at least he was pretty sure that he saw her. He had moved both up and down the steep slope, a stubborn man loath to stop short of accomplishment when once he had committed himself to any sort of campaign, and came into a bit of clearing, a grassy spot from which, through the scattered pines, he could look down into the moonlit valley. He saw the Fontana home, white under the moon, casting its black shadow—and he saw a slight figure racing across the meadow, headed straight toward the house. He couldn't be dead sure; the distance was too great. But if not the girl, then who? Certainly it was not Steve Question. And, almost certain he was that it was a girl. And what one of the little Fontanas señoritas would be running down from the mountain at this time of night? For such as the Fontanas it would be an unthinkable scandal, no less.

And now Rob Roy Morgan was considerably puzzled. The running figure sped in all haste across the moonlit open spaces and ducked into every pool of shadow that offered itself. There was the creek that flowed down valley between the range of mountains and the houses; under the cottonwoods there was a bridge; he saw the running figure dart across the bridge, to be lost again in the dark.

In his turn Morgan made his own way down the slope, swifty too, and hunting out shadowy places whenever he could. The house was dark; he heard no voices to greet her arrival— if it did happen to be the girl—and saw no lights turned on. What her errand was, he was at a loss to so much as speculate upon. She knew already that Steve Question was there; she could do no spying in the dark—Or could she? " Maybe she can see in the dark like a wild cat!" Well, he would go as far as the bridge. If she returned to the mountains, she would naturally cross the bridge again. And he would be there to square accounts with the young lady and give her the surprise of her life; right about now Rob Roy Morgan was on the crumbling verge of losing his temper. He could fancy the little devil giggling as she slipped away and left him up by the pool talking to himself, making his tones as honeyed as he knew how.

She would either stay all night with the Fontanas—or complete her errand there and go on across the valley which here was four or five miles wide, mostly clear, fertile land with only occasional groves of live oaks—or would return to the mountains. Which?

" She won't stay with the Fontanas; for one thing, she knows that Steve Question is there, and for another, she wouldn't be creeping in like that at this time of night just to visit friends; more likely she's bent on spying. And she won't cross the valley on foot, for she knows I'm up here and she'll know I've got a horse and can run her down. What she is going to do is finish whatever she is up to and come back this way." He tucked in the corners of his mouth. " Take your time, Little Miss; I'll be waiting for you!"

No lights came on. The big house, save for its white walls and red-tiled roof, was dark with the black shadows of the oaks upon it. And all remained very still. Morgan selected his position at about the middle of the thirty-foot bridge, where a towering sycamore made a glinting roof against stars and moon. He treated himself to a cigarette, careful of the lighting of it with his match cupped in his hands, careful thereafter of the glowing end. He would give her, he estimated, some fifteen or twenty minutes in which to accomplish whatever it was that she planned; then, if she did not come back this way he would get his horse and ride down into the valley, striking across it, looking for her. If she went that way, where the grass was green and tall, he would find the path she had made. And on horseback he would have no trouble running her down.

He snorted and flipped his cigarette down into the creek. It dawned on him that he was hunting this girl down as a man hunted any wild game. Well, anyhow, he wouldn't shoot her —though he might scare her stiff with a rifle shot!

Something like ten or fifteen minutes later he caught sight of her again, or at least he glimpsed a swift, furtive figure down by the house as it darted again into the blackest of the oak shadows. Then swiftly he had some reward for his long hours of patience; he saw the figure again, lost it, found it again, and he was surer than ever that it was the girl who had slipped away from the pool under the waterfall, that she was returning in all haste, that she headed straight for the bridge.

He withdrew a few feet, deeper into the black pool of dark under the big sycamore.

She ran, faster than he had ever dreamed a girl could run,

through all the patches of moonlight, and always stopped whenever she came under one of the wide-branched live oaks where, time and time again, he lost sight of her. He could picture her standing rigidly still, peering into all places where a man might be lurking, waiting for her to blunder within his reach. But always she came on again toward the bridge.

And just before she reached the bridge he saw her clearly enough, close enough, to be certain that it was the girl of last night at the waterfall. The same luxuriantly long hair which could have been of any colour but which looked black about her shoulders, the same scanty dress of furry skins—and he made out that she carried something in both hands. What it was that she was bringing back with her he had no time to make out definitely; whatever it was that she bore in her right hand could have been a round, black box, something like a small hatbox, while from her right hand trailed something which he fancied was a great Spanish shawl, anyhow something of the sort.

No time to be sure of such details, and with little enough interest in them, as she was on the bridge at last, running straight toward him. And she was within ten feet of him when he heard her smothered gasp of consternation and she came to a sudden stop, and he knew that she had seen him.

He stepped out then and toward her, blocking her way. He said swiftly, to arrest any further attempt at flight:

" Don't run. I tell you I won't hurt. But don't try to run. I'd run you down inside twenty feet! Just——"

That was all that he got time to say; at least those were his only articulate words. An exclamation that sounded rather like, " Fuff! Poof! Blaw!" burst from him. For instead of her doing the expected, spinning about and seeking safety in flight, she ran closer to him and with all her might, which was very considerable for a girl, she flung into his face the object she had carried in her right hand—and Rob Roy Morgan, not knowing in the least what the thing was, felt that it might be a great gob of mud. It splashed all over his face, filling his eyes and mouth, for an instant completely blinding him. He pawed wildly at the stuff, finding it sticky and very messy; he clawed it out of his eyes—and then heard the light, quick patter of her running feet. He threw out both arms to stop her, and his fingers brushed her but he could get no grip upon

her. The best he did was to snatch and hold the shawl or
whatever it was. He still heard her running feet, the sound of
one racing bare-footed or in light moccasins, and then for a
moment heard nothing whatever but the water running under
the bridge. Then presently there came to him one other
sound, one from somewhere up on the mountain slope. It
was the girl laughing as she had laughed a little while ago at
Steve Question's discomfiture.

" Damn the girl! " said Rob Roy Morgan.

There would be not the least sense in trying to overhaul
her now in the dark of the mountains, strange country to him
and no doubt familiar ground to her. He used a bandana
hankerchief to wipe his face clean; he discovered what it was
that she had hurled at him. It was a big cake, freshly baked,
altogether the biggest, stickiest, gooiest cake, Morgan would
have sworn, that ever was.

He examined the flimsy, silken fabric he had blindly
snatched from her. Not a shawl, as he had first thought, but
a dainty, frilly little dress such the Fontana señoritas wore.

" The little devil! " he muttered. " The little night-
prowling thief! Robs Steve Question of his gold, raids the
Fontana home for a dress and a cake! "

Then something else dawned on him: She had been to some
trouble, some risk to pilfer dress and cake, had lost both—
and could still laught like that!

" Wait until I run you down, young lady," he said. " It
won't be long."

He shook the muck of the spattered cake off his boots, and
made a neat, small bundle of the dress.

CHAPTER TEN

Now, it struck Mr. Morgan, was an excellent time to just sit
and ponder. He went back to the big pine towering above the
pool, made himself comfortable with his back to the tree
fitting his shoulder blades in nicely about a heavy strip of
bark—and then spat freely, once, twice and again. He still
tasted cake, and damn that particular cake. He wondered
what they had made it of; what made it so infernally sticky

and gummy and sickeningly sweet? There was an overdose
of vanilla in the confounded thing, he could have sworn. Then
he fancied they'd poured in a lot of honey. He knew it was
innocent of eggs and milk, for what true *rancho*, what old
Californio, had either laying hens or, though he had ten
thousand beef cattle, had a milk cow? And how make a
cake without milk and eggs? Just pour in so much extra
vanilla and honey and chocolate, he judged, and made a face.
Some of the stuff had even run down inside his shirt; he
mopped at his chest with his bandana that was already like
a well-used doormat in mud-time. He got up and went to the
pool and washed the thing out. He sat down again and did
his meditating.

Earlier in the night he had thought to himself that Steve
Question, who might have been a tough *hombre* in his day,
was getting soft; Steve had to go down to Fontana's to get a
roof over him and a bed under him. Before that, he had
thought of Red Barbee getting soft, going crazy over a girl.
As for Rob Roy Morgan, he had made it clear to himself from
the outset that no girl had any part to play in his life. Well,
what about to-night? All that he wanted to do was follow
that confounded little trick of a night-flitting girl, grab her
by the hair, make her cower down and listen to what he had
to say.

What did he have to say?

The night was largely gone; summertime brought early
dawns, impetuous, leaping bright mornings. He sniffed the
air; funny, you could smell the dawn already. There is no
smell like that of the first few minutes; little breezes start up
and shake out newly distilled, flower-cupped fragrances, and
fill the air with the resinous tang of the awakening pines. He
got up and went to his provision pack.

He set his coffee to boil, fried his bacon, made a batch of
flapjacks to turn a golden brown in the hot skillet just greased
thinly with the bacon drippings.

The lingering shadows of the night thinned swiftly, yellow
and pale apple-green tints stretched along the horizon, then
went into glowing reds and golds, and he saw a shaft of sunlight strike upon the highest peak that rose austerely above
the black pine forest across the valley. Daytime, a new day.

He washed his utensils in the creek just below the pool,

made his pack—and the little bundle of a bright blue dress he put inside it—saddled his horse, and then dedicated a few minutes to looking for any chance sign the girl might have left behind her. He expected to find nothing and so was not disappointed at the end of his fruitless fifteen minutes or so. He went down to the bridge, carrying a double handful of ferns; with them he brushed away the last signs of the stolen cake. That had become his affair, not that of either the Fontanas or of Steve Question.

He climbed the slope again and went as far as he had followed Steve Question in the dark last night. " Where the devil did he get a name like that, anyhow?'' There was ample sign where Steve had broken his hasty way through the brush; Morgan came without difficulty to the place where Steve's cache had been. There was a spot, well protected by tall ferns until Steve had trampled them underfoot last night, where in the wet bank of the ravine a hole had been scooped out. A small iron box lay where it had been tossed aside; there was a hole and just below it a newly removed rock. No one would have come merely by chance on that hiding-place; someone had watched while the loot was being stowed away. Morgan looked for tracks and, in the wet soil in the bed of the ravine, could find none but Steve's

He went back to his horse.

Before he put his toe into the stirrup he stood for a long while, the reins over his arm, his head down, his hands busied rolling and rolling and still rolling a cigarette. In the end the paper tore and he threw the thing away without bothering to roll another. He was thinking as logically as a man could with what scraps of knowledge were his. His mental steps were after this fashion : To begin with, Steve Question had hid a pretty considerable amount of loot here on the mountain. Someone, the girl, of course, had removed it. She would have hidden it at some distance and would have hidden it well, so well that there would be little likelihood of finding it unless she were tracked to its hiding place—or unless a man made a captive of her and forced her to tell. Another thing : she knew that both he and Steve were in the neighbourhood; she had had the barest escape from both of them; she had been prowling most of the night. Now what? She would be miles away, hidden in some secret place, and fast asleep. No doubt she'd sleep most of the day.

He found himself wondering what sort of a hide-out she had. Was there a lot of truth in the fantastic legends about the Golden Tiger Lily girl? Did she, just a girl like her live all alone, always hidden deep in some wilderness or, at times, creeping forth by night, bent on marauding? Rifling a robber's gold cache or, as to-night, pilfering a pretty, flimsy blue dress and an unforgettable cake?

" All high-grade hokum," snorted Rob Roy Morgan and went up into the saddle a thought viciously. " The harum-scarum, tomboy daughter of some sheep herder or wood chopper or crazy mountaineer prospecting for a claim—and ducking out at night from some snug cabin to play her fool games."

Mounted he was tempted to wait and see what Steve Question did next, whether he tarried along with the Fontanas or rode early; and if he rode, whether he went back up the mountainside looking for the girl or streaked back to town. But it did not take him long to decide: Steve Question could have no suspicion that Morgan had ridden this way to-night, that he had followed him and knew all that he had done, and there was no use giving Steve Question any information whatever. All that Morgan needed to do now was ride back swiftly the way he had travelled so slowly last night, make his wide bend safely away from Twenty Mile, ride into town in the mid-morning along the dusty, crooked road through the hills where Steve and Keena and Barbee had seen him riding in the dusk of yesterday.

He dipped forward in the saddle, touched Jet's flanks lightly with his spurs, and rode.

In Twenty Mile, at an hour when the town was as lively as the enchanted woods about the castle of the Sleeping Beauty. with never a man on the street, he rode into the livery stable. He spent a moment with Snow White, who looked as fit as a fiddle, though he decided that a good going-over with brush and curry-comb would do her sleek hide no harm, then made his way to his local headquarters. There was that corral to be built; he'd get the boys on the job to-day. He was ready to feed and lodge them and lend them money in case of need; no reason why they should turn lazy and soft and fat, doing nothing. So that day the corral, rude and crude but amply adequate to their needs, was started. Add a wagon load of hay and some grain, and you had the new Morgan establishment ready for smooth functioning.

On the back porch where there was a tub on an up-ended barrel, and a tin wash basin and running water piped down from a spring on the hillside, Morgan washed his face and hands, slicked down his hair—and discovered Tony. The swarthy young half-breed sat on the far end of the porch, his legs dangling over, and on his lap nursed the new guitar, and a young mother couldn't have fondled her baby more tenderly. Tony's dark face split in a gleaming, white-toothed smile and his good hand brushed the strings so that the sound was scarcely greater than that Morgan had heard made by the awakening breeze in the pines.

" She is the nicest guitar I ever see, I bet the best in the worl'," said Tony in a half-hushed sort of ecstasy. " When my sick hand gets well, you going to hear music sweet as honey. *Vamos a ver !* Sure! I pay sixty dollars; I use your money, Señor, and I put the rest from mine."

" Nothing doing, kid," said Morgan. He dug into his pocket and gave Tony a twenty. " Ten for your music box, ten for another trip to Doc Bones. Better go see him now."

Tony's grin broadened.

" *Amigo*," he said in that soft, liquid voice of his, " that suits me fine! The next time I am going to get a piano, too!"

Smoke Keena came in from across the road with a supply of provisions he was of a mind to lay in while he had a dollar or so; he had an ample supply of tobacco, both smoking and chewing, and a couple of bottles. These he carried to his room and placed them, as the two old men had disposed of their treasures, in plain sight. That was because there was no place to hide them. But Smoke Keena, who could both read and write after a fashion, had supplied himself with a pencil and a couple of scraps of wrapping paper. On a raggedly torn piece of paper he drew a death's head and cross bones, and did the job so well that nearly any man, after a moment of puzzled study, could make out what the design represented. Keena chewing his pencil, his head cocked to one side, regarded his artistic work with a degree of pride. Then, chewing his tongue, he printed the words:

" Privit stock of Smoke Keena, Esq., and I'll kill any man that makes free of it. Go get yore own."

Morgan stuck his head in and laughed at him, and Keena blushed like a coy young girl. Morgan came in and sat on Keena's bunk.

" Find out anything from Silver Hat yesterday, Nancy?" he asked.

Keena had a six-inch bit of wire in his pocket. He twisted it around the neck of one of his standing bottles, leaving the ends free. On these ends he impaled his warning sign, bending the wire up so as to resemble fish hooks at its extremities, thus securing the paper.

" I'll get a padlock and put on my door after a while," said Keena. He dug into his pocket, extracted a ragged cut of plug tobacco, bit off a sizable hunk, and answered Morgan's question. " It's like this, Virginia," he said. " You can tell as how Steve Question is the sort of fellar that's got into a habit of locking up his mouth as tight as a bear trap that a bear has stepped in, a man that keeps his ears as wide open as the gates to hell. Of course he did have to spill a few words to keep me and Barbee going."

" Where's Barbee now?" asked Morgan.

Keena grinned. " Most likely over at McWilliams' place. Barbee's sure gone plumb moon-calf over Barbara." He sighed like a wind broken old horse. " At that, Virginia, she's aces; pshaw, if a girl like her took a fancy to me, why, she could bring over her bonnet, and shoes and bustle, too, and stay as long——"

Morgan snorted his disgust. " Go ahead about Steve Question," he said.

" Well, like I guess you know, he's dead anxious to find out all about you he can. Like you told us, we kept our traps shut, only dribbling things that didn't count out'n the corners of our mouths, sort of. I guess he got the idea that we didn't give much of a damn for you or your ways; that we had met up with you on the trail and had pooled our luck for a spell; that we was sticking along of you mostly because we was broke and you wasn't. Well, let's see." He chewed high and wide like a placid old muley cow enjoying her cud, swallowed and observed, " I reckon you guessed him pretty slick, Virginia. Barbee, he said something careless like about all them Mexico-dove-coloured hats showing up in a flock and said he wished he had one just like 'em, and Steve, he says as how coming down yesterday from Blue Gap, which is t'other side of where you rode last night, t'other side of Random, and beyond that, past Bottle Creek; and he says as how, riding through Bottle Creek, he stopped, like any man would, to get him a drink and there was a fellow there with a covered wagon, sort of like a store, and he was selling them hats at five bucks a throw, hats worth anyhow forty dollars, and he guessed the fellar had stole 'em down fu'ther south some-wheres, and ached to get 'em off his hands—just like you said. And——''

" Anything else?''

" Nary. He got what some folks would call right talky. But I noticed he didn't say a damn thing much. He said he had a cow ranch some place you never heard of, five, six hundred miles away, and that he'd sold a string of cow brutes and had drifted this way to look things over and have him a time and maybe stick and maybe move on. He said as how he'd seen a couple of pretty nifty girl animals, here in town, meaning Barbee's girl, and Barbee got as red as a turkey gobbler, and I guess the Fontana señoritas. That kind of jabber, and hoped to meet up with us again, maybe in a little game of poker. Of course, all the time he was fishing about you. That's about all of it, Virginia.''

" Thanks, Nancy,'' said Morgan.

" Where'd you go last night, Virginia?''

" Maybe later on I'll tell you. Anything going on in town last night?''

Smoke Keena thrust out a lower lip; he could do that with a mouthful of tobacco juice and never lose a single drop.

" We-ll, n-o,'' he said, and maybe yes. There was a game of poker. Me, I just squatted and watched awhile and went off and chased down a cold bottle of beer and set awhile and then trapped another cold bottle and come back. There was Steve Question. And there was a couple of other fellers and old man McWilliams and Red Barbee. The reason I didn't stack in with them, they were shooting 'way over my head. Old McWilliams, he can't play poker for sour apples and the damn fool don't know it, and you'd think it was time that he'd found out by now, wouldn't you? Red Barbee squidged round in his chair like he was squatting atop a hornet's nest; ever' time the old boy lost a good-sized pot, Barbee sure took it to heart. I heard one time a little fly-by-night, giggling girl say, ' Love me, love my dawg,' but I'm damned if I ever heard of a girl sayin', ' Love me, love my papa!' Hell, Barbee makes me sick."

" Me, too. What happened?"

" Barbee, he plays a kind of smooth game; he didn't lose anything and I got a notion he cleaned up for about thirty, forty, fifty dollars, I dunno. But old McWilliams, the other boys sure took him downstairs, and just left him his shirt with the tails trimmed short. He must have lost about seven hundred dollars. Steve, he got most of it."

Morgan looked puzzled, as he had a right to be. " So Steve Question was in town playing poker last night, was he, Nancy? How about you, drunk or sober?"

" What are you driving at, Virginia? Sure he was here."

" Played all night?"

" Hell, no. They started in about two shakes after you left, played over in a room back of McWilliams' store. He brought out the licker, but I do give him credit for making every man pay for his own bottle; he didn't charge 'em for using his glasses." He looked round for some likely place, such as a mouse hole, swallowed and chuckled. " Steve, he give 'em warning at the jump he didn't have all night; said as how he had to see a man about buying some hound dogs to hunt mountain cats with. And he sure kept the game jumping, one eye on the clock behind the counter all the time. In about a couple of hours he stood up and stuffed his pickings in his pocket and said, ' Buenas noches, gents,' nice and polite and went where'er he was a-going."

" Mountain cats, huh? I wouldn't put it beyond him," said Morgan, more to himself than to Keena, and Keena paid him no attention.

" Red Barbee cussed all the way home," said Keena happily. " Say, he was madder'n seven old tom cats tied together by their tails!"

" What's eating him, anyhow?"

" Hell, Virginia, it's love! Don't you know what love is? Here he sees his girl's old man making a howling jackass out of hisself, getting took to town at every jump——"

G

" They ganged up on him?"

" Sure they did! Steve Question and the two other fellers. They didn't quite show one another their cards, and they didn't quite yell out loud what they had and what the other feller was to do, but it was pretty near that bad. And when Steve got up and dug out, and old man McWilliams was broke of table money and said what about a comeback, I thought Barbee was going to have a fit and bite himself."

" Game to-night?"

" Sure thing. Old McWilliams yipped like a coyote for it, and he had red hellfires in both eyes. They said him a nice yes."

Smoke Keena, having looked round again for something to shoot at, having considered no doubt that this was his own room, swallowed.

" So'd I. Who wouldn't?"

" I'd sort of like to cut you in, Nancy. I'll stake you to a hundred dollars, you to cut me in fifty-fifty on the winnings or forget the grubstake. But you got to keep sober, and you got to play the cards as they fall, and not just what you're hoping for."

" You mean like McWilliams? Gimme, Virginia."

Morgan dug down and Keena pocketed.

" Go take a walk, Nancy. There's more'n one saloon in town, but the Pay Dirt is a good place to start. Stick to beer, old-timer. I'd like to bend 'em to-night, and I'd sort of like you to kick in, and you can do a better job of bending when you don't go out on a bender! Get all that?"

" It's kind of funny, like jokes we heard them blackfaces tell down in San Antone. I get you, Virgie."

" Why, damn you! Virginia is bad enough! Be respectful, or give me back my hundred dollars—Nanny Goat!"

He knocked off Smoke Keena's hat and kicked it through the door on his way out while Keena made a wild and ineffectual grab at his legs to trip him up.

Outside, Rob Roy Morgan sang softly, so softly that his voice would have made no discord at a funeral:

> " Old man Lute was a gol'darned brute,
> And he couldn't get the cattle
> Through the gol'darned chute,

" Singing, Ki-yi-yippee,
  Ki-yi-yippee,
  Ki-yi-yippee,
  Yippee yay ! "

And Smoke Keena, unmelodiously, chimed in:

" *Oh !* It's gittin' mighty late
  And it's gittin' mighty cold,
  And the gol'darned cattle,
  They're gittin' mighty old——"

And their two voices, making discords, agreed on the words:

" Singing, Ki-yi-yippee,
  Ki-yi-yippee,
  Ki-yi-yippee,
  Yippee yay ! "

" He's a damn-fool kid, but I'm tying up with him," said Smoke Keena.

" I don't know why, but I sort of like that damn jackass," said Rob Roy Morgan, and felt satisfied with life as he saw it running.

The poker game was arranged without difficulty; almost it seemed that it arranged itself. They foregathered in the early night, just barely time to light the lamps, in that back room at the General Mercantile Store, Mr. McWilliams' new bonanza. They came straggling in, McWilliams having left his young clerk to run the store, being obviously nervously anxious to get going. One glance at the man and you would know what he had never been able to learn through the years, that he was not, never was, and never could be a poker player. He was on edge to get started and he showed every thought in his face, despite the fact that most men could have hid every shadow of expression under whiskers like his. He was one of those men who couldn't get his money down fast enough, who was restless in his chair until the deal came to him, and who still handled a deck like a man chopping wood. Small wonder that his little daughter wept herself red-eyed, that Red Barbee cursed—that the two Old Men were worried about him.

Poker games like this one are apt to run true to form. This

one was no exception. The players were McWilliams, Morgan, Keena and Steve Question and the two men whom he had introduced into last evening's short session. Red Barbee came along, said that six was just right and seven too many for poker, said that he'd sit and watch for a while if nobody cared, that he might drop back later and take a hand in case someone got frozen out.

Morgan and McWilliams shook hands. Morgan and Steve Question greeted each other casually and Steve said, " Morgan, meet up with Hap Stroud and Ben Harper." Hap Stroud and Ben Harper regarded Rob Roy Morgan in a measuring sort of way, which was befitting the occasion. For his part, Morgan gave them a swift once-over, cataloguing them tentatively. Stroud was a big, beefy-looking man, perhaps a couple of years or so older than Steve Question, which was to say crowding thirty-five; a bovine sort of man, yet one whose rather close-set eyes were keen and alert, and who moved on his feet that were encased in small, tight boots, with lightness and agility. The other, Ben Harper, was a younger man indulging himself in his first whiskers, who wore a diamond ring, whose hands were white and soft, who looked —and so, for that matter, did Hap Stroud—to have exposed himself but little to the sunlight for some considerable time. Morgan thought of toadstools, a fat one and a skinny one. He was inclined to distrust both of them. He wondered briefly if they belonged to Steve Question's bandit crew; unlikely, unless Steve carried on most of his business after nightfall.

And the game played on.

By the time each man had dealt two or three times Morgan saw quite clearly that Smoke Keena knew what he was talking about when he said, " Old man McWilliams, he can't play poker for sour apples." There was not a man at the table who couldn't outplay him. Like many another man of his breed, when McWilliams lost a sizable pot, he just figured that he was playing in bad luck.

Steve Question and Hap Stroud and Ben Harper didn't exactly cheat; Morgan saw that and realised that it wasn't necessary. But without doubt they had played many and many a game together, perhaps with some flush fall-guy like McWiliams sitting in.

Smoke Keena, as sober as a judge and mindful of the instructions given him along with his hundred-dollar stake, played close to the table, never went out on a limb once, and at the end of the game was modestly in money. Rob Roy Morgan himself played as cannily as he knew how, having no misconceptions as to what he was up against. Only once during the long-drawn-out session did he go out on a limb. Smoke Keena had dealt the hand. Before the draw Hap Stroud boosted the pot forty dollars. Morgan glanced at his hand; he had a pair of deuces. He shoved in his forty dollars and called for two cards. He let his cards lie where they were, not looking at them.

Keena dropped out; Steve Question folded up. Left in play were Morgan, Ben Harper, Steve Question and, of course, McWilliams.

Hap Stroud promptly bet a hundred. Steve Question dropped out. McWilliams couldn't hold himself back; he shoved in his hundred. And thus it came to Rob Roy Morgan with his two deuces, with a queen behind them—and he hadn't the vaguest notion what the two other cards were, still face down before him.

He kicked in his hundred and said:

" Five hundred more, boys," and put up his five hundred and then looked at his cards.

McWilliams cursed and slammed down his hand. Red Barbee saw what he held and was almost proud of Barbara's daddy that he had self-control enough to throw away three queens. Ben Harper pursed his lips, sat a moment stonily regarding Morgan's face, then said, " Count me out."

Morgan raked in the pot. With the sensation of having the devil biting his heel, having his fun, when he put down his cards he let them lie face up. He hadn't bettered his hand in the draw; at the end he held his two deuces, a queen, a seven and a four.

" I'd had a damn good hand, though," he said and sounded apologetic, " if I'd only drawed those two other deuces."

McWilliams turned white and glared at him murderously. Ben Harper never turned a hair. Smoke Keena snorted, then guffawed. Red Barbee got up and went out.

" If you don't mind my saying so, Morgan," said McWilliams, " that's the hell of a way to play poker."

" A feller has got to learn by practice, Mr. McWilliams," said Morgan meekly.

Red Barbee kept his promise to Barbara McWilliams and met her under the big oak tree shadowing the road at the back of the McWilliams' house. Though he came early, she was already anxiously waiting for him.

" Tell me! " she said hardly above an urgent whisper, and for the first time put both her small, sensitive hands on his arm, and he saw the glimmer of her uplifted eyes.

Red Barbee was close to choking before he could answer. " Same thing," he said. " It would always be the same thing. He can't ever play with those damn—excuse me, Miss Barbara! I mean those doggone wolves. They're card-sharps, and he—well, he ain't! "

She didn't withdraw her hands; she wasn't conscious where they had strayed. She even clutched him tighter.

" You mean he's losing a lot? "

" He's losing his shirt—I mean, he'll lose everything he's got before they turn him loose. What makes me mad is there ain't anything I can do about it."

" I know." Her hands dropped then to her sides like dead weights. She sounded hopeless and wearily unhappy. " He promised——" She bit her lip. " He just can't help it. I don't care about him just losing some money; money isn't everything in the world, is it, Mr. Barbee? But he'll lose his new store, and he was so proud and happy about it—and he'll lose everything—and then, oh, I know, he will hate himself and be so terribly ashamed——"

She put her face in her hands and began to cry softly. Red Barbee stirred restlessly. With all his heart he yearned to put his arms about her, to hold her tight, to swear to her that—— What? Anyhow she was so dear, so priceless, so ineffably and angelically pure that a man like himself should drop dead before he sullied her with his slightest touch.

And still the game went on, and when Red Barbee came back they were still at it. There were red spots of hot colour upon McWilliams' high cheek bones, unhidden by his luxuriant thicket of whiskers, and he had lost nearly all of the six hundred dollars he had put in play, and was nervously fingering what driblet of coins was left to him. It wouldn't be long now, thought Barbee. Nor was it. McWilliams bet his last dollar on a hand that wasn't bad, yet wasn't quite good enough. He had three jacks which went down before Steve Question's full house.

"That's all for to-night, boys," said McWilliams huskily, and got up. "You boys play all night if you want to. I'm going home. Lock up when you get through and leave the key where I can find it; I'll show you where——"

Red Barbee, who had talked about wolves, walked like a wolf himself and had a wolfish gleam in his eye when he stepped to the chair that McWilliams had vacated.

"I'd just as lieve take a hand," he said.

But Rob Roy Morgan shoved his chair back.

"Being here, Mr. McWilliams," he said "seems to me just like playing at your house. I wouldn't care to play when you'd gone."

And so, at a fairly early hour, early for poker, the game broke up.

"Let's all step across the street and have a drink," suggested Steve Question.

A suggestion of that sort was always worth a man's taking under advisement and then promptly deciding to act upon it.

"I'm going over to the stable first," said Morgan. "I want to have a look at my horses before I turn in. I'll gang up with you boys in no time."

And this was because Rob Roy Morgan, a man who always played his hunches—just as he had with his two deuces—had a brand new hunch right now. He had kept his eyes open, he had done his level best to read men's thoughts, the thoughts of Steve Question and Hap Stroud and Ben Harper. One couldn't make much of their eyes, because they guarded them. Nor of what they said, nor exactly how they said it. But just the same, with a hair here and a hair there, picked up through several hours over a card table, a man might make of them a small delicate brush that could paint a pretty true and accurate picture for him.

"Might be a good idea if I looked over my live stock," said Smoke Keena. "I haven't been nigh 'em all day."

"Hell, no," said Morgan. "I'll look 'em all over. Shove along to the Pay Dirt and I'll gang up with you fellers while your throats are still burning with the first drink."

In the stable he went straight to Snow White's stall. She

nickered softly and nosed him; he pulled her ear and gave her lean, silken shoulder a pat, and then went about his affairs. All the money he had in his pockets, saving out only two gold twenties, he put at the bottom of Snow White's manger, spreading it out, covering it with straw, then pulling down a couple of handfuls of hay on top of it. A scrap of paper, Señor Fontana's I O U for seven hundred dollars, he disposed of otherwise; Snow White, though meaning him no treachery, might eat the doggoned thing. So with a thin strand of rope no thicker than a string, he tied it under Snow White's throat, to her tie rope. Then he slid both guns up and down in their leathers, to make sure they were free and ready, and went out, making himself a cigarette, and walked slowly up the street to the Pay Dirt.

CHAPTER ELEVEN

McWilliams insisted on buying the drinks. He was still flushed, he talked loudly, he was extravagant with words, he acted like a drunken man. And drunk he was, though not on liquor but instead with the hot, wild and heady current of his own blood. He had lost a few hundred dollars, and what about it? He began to bristle. No man but himself had made any reference whatever to gains or losses, but he bore himself as though challenged. And already, as Morgan came in, he was talking about a return game. Not right away, but soon; he had a big bill of goods to take care of and was for a few days short of cash. But he was damned and doubled damned if luck could keep running out on him without ever a let-up.

As Morgan was turning in at the swing-doors he caught sight of Red Barbee hurrying along the sidewalk about to turn a corner and vanish in a dark side road. He called after him, " Hi, Barbee! Where to?"

Barbee didn't stop but called back, " I'll be with you pronto," and dived into the dark.

Morgan, having joined the others at the bar in the Pay Dirt, having accepted McWilliams' invitation with a courteous, " Thank you, sir, and here's my respects," let his eyes rove. The place was pretty well filled with rough-garbed, bewhiskered men, most of them young, many as young as himself, and they constituted a seething and rather colourful conglomerate; you could pick out a cowboy here and there, a sprinkling of miners, the usual cardsharps and loafers and assorted ne'er-do-wells. Beyond the far end of the long bar he could look into an adjoining room through double doors standing wide open, and get glimpses through the blue fog of smoke of the several games running. There was poker if you elected for the kind of poker that was played at the Pay Dirt; there were a faro lay-out, a wheel, dice games pretty much to any man's taste. And among those looking on he chanced to see that devil's trio which belonged to his own party, Slim Pickens and Baldy Bates and Shorty Skinner.

And by chance at that moment Slim Pickens looked his way, and promptly came over to join him, his two side-kicks trailing along.

" Hallo, Morgan," said Slim. And then, " Hallo, Steve."

Both Morgan and Steve said the required, " Hallo, Slim." And while Steve carelessly invited, " Have a drink, boys," Morgan did his quick bit of wondering how well Slim Pickens and Steve Question had got to know each other.

" Count me out, boys," said McWilliams. " It's getting late and I've got to open up the store early in the morning; there's a string of wagons pulling out and they want to stock up."

" One more drink, McWilliams," said Steve.

" Dammit, no!" said McWilliams, and went out, homeward bound, looking like a black cloud.

Steve laughed tolerantly. " The old boy's sorta fed up," he said. And then to Pickens, " Here, Slim, meet with a couple of fellers I just run into yesterday; they're all right." And so there was a bit of handshaking, Slim and Baldy and Shorty saying their " Howdy's " or " Glad to know you's " to Hap Stroud and Ben Harper. And drinks, on Steve, were enjoyed by all.

" Me, I'm going to have a look-see in the next room," said Smoke Keena. " I might take a look at the wheel or maybe sample that faro lay-out. How about it, Morgan?"

" Not to-night." Morgan stretched and yawned. " I'm going to roost."

Keena moved away to the gambling room. Morgan was

turning to leave the bar when Steve Question said, " What's the rush, Morgan? It's early yet. Better have another drink."

" Not to-night," said Morgan and went out.

Steve Question was at his side as he reached the sidewalk. " Look here, Morgan, I'd like to have a word with you."

" Blaze away. What's on your mind?"

" A good deal. How about going some place where we can talk?"

Rob Roy Morgan, rolling a cigarette, leaned back against the wall. It was a good comfortable feeling to have his shoulders against a solid wall.

" Suits me right here," he said.

Steve Question rolled his own cigarette. For a moment or two he didn't have anything to say. He at last lighted his cigarette; he threw the match, still blazing, out into the dust of the road.

" Some other time then," he said carelessly, and turned back into the saloon.

Morgan moved along toward home; he did as many alert men did in little towns like Twenty Mile and walked down the middle of the road instead of using either of the wooden sidewalks, and his thumbs were hooked into his belt. He walked steadily, neither fast nor slow, and under the low-drawn brim of his wide black hat his eyes were restless. He noticed little things to-night; maybe he was shying from them like a skittish pony from the dead leaves wind-blown. Nothing tangible, yet a sense of menace, the veiled looks in three men's eyes—a trifling remark: " Meet up with some fellers I just run into yesterday." No need going to the bother of all that talk——

The street was empty; it was late for newcomers to be straggling into town, too early for most of them to do more than just think of getting going, homeward bound, after another drink or so or after another few whirls at the wheel, cards or dice. Saddle horses dozed along hitching rails.

Then a couple of men lurched into the street from the mouth of a dark alley; they were ahead of Morgan and, like him, chose the middle of the road, and they appeared to be pretty nearly dead drunk. They proceeded arm-in-arm, stepping loosely, requiring a pretty large part of the thoroughfare for their onward progress. Morgan stepped aside for them, and they stumbled into him. One of them caught him by the arm and said thickly:

" Say, feller, we're jus' havin' li'l frien'ly—hic—arg'ment. Is this Thursday or is it Sat'day?"

" Gentlemen, I am very sorry," said Morgan politely, " but I don't speak English."

A quick jerk freed him, and he continued on his way, but kept watch on them out of the tail of his eye. He heard them muttering; they stood swaying where he had left them; then, still holding on to each other they turned and followed him. Still he walked neither fast nor slow, trying to have his eyes everywhere at once. A night of the sheerest trifles, the unreadable looks in men's eyes, an unnecessary and doubtless lying explanation—a flaring match thrown into the road in a bright arc—two drunks accosting him, slowing him down, asking the day of the week.

A pistol shot ripped through the silence, and Morgan knew that it came from behind him, and yet only half turned, trying to hold himself ready for anything. The figures of the two men still were clear in the middle of the road; he saw a glint of moonlight on the gun in the hand of one of them, even made out a tiny, ghostly puff of white dust rising from close to the man's foot. Of course the gun could have gone off accidentally, but here was one more trifle and——

Morgan at the moment was just about to turn the corner into the side road that would bring him within a few steps to his own place. He swung the corner and found himself almost in the arms of four men. Every man's hat was pulled low, every man's face hidden under the mask of a big bandana, and in every man's hand was a ready weapon, the four muzzles nosing into his body.

" Take it easy, Morgan," said one of the men.

Morgan took it as advised. There was really nothing else to do unless he were of a mood for suicide.

" We'll mosey along like we was all good friends," said the man who had already spoken. " Let's go."

He stepped to Morgan's right side, another man stood close to him on the left, the other two dropped in close behind. For reminder he had a good jab in the middle of the back by the nose of one of the rear guard's guns.

They crossed the street, slanting away from the heart of

the town and toward the stable, and for a few steps Morgan believed that it was the stable that they were bound for, that somehow they had guessed a part of his secret deal with Snow White. But they turned the first corner into another dark cross road, passed a dozen dark houses, turned another corner, moving toward the scattered shacks and shanties on the fringe of the village, squat, unlovely places where the road petered out and there were only crooked paths through buck brush and pines. Ahead, where there was a road of sorts again, Morgan saw a spreading oak tree and recognised it. It overshadowed the McWilliams' house.

One of the men said softly, " There's a feller and a girl standing under that big oak." The man at Morgan's right said warningly, " Keep your trap shut, Morgan; we're going past that place." Then the four not to appear furtive, lifted their voices into a natural tone, talking at random, saying nothing of any significance, and as they drew nearer and were forced to pass through the moonlight, they drew their bandanas off and stuffed them in their pockets. Their hats they kept well down over their eyes.

Morgan got only the vaguest of glimpses of the two under the tree, withdrawn into the shadows, and did not at the moment think of Red Barbee. But Barbee, watching the five who stepped along more briskly now, knew Rob Roy Morgan in an instant, knew him at first from his carriage, then from his long-legged stride. But at the time Red Barbee had no more interest in Rob Roy Morgan, what he did or where he went, than he had in a shooting star which he had glimpsed at about the same time and that he was scarcely aware of having seen. Barbee was busy, his heart in his work, comforting Barbara—trying to comfort her, rather.

He had promised to report the end of the poker game and its results to her, and late as the hour was, the summer dawn not far off, he found her waiting for him under the oak. He had hurried to the meeting until he came close enough to see her little short-sleeved, white dress standing against the black bole of the tree and then his steps began to lag. It was going to be hard, telling her.

" I—I know," she said, and her hand was at her throat and he knew that already there were tears in her eyes, because in her voice there were tears too. " I can tell by the way you walked——"

Barbee shuffled his feet and cleared his throat and began spinning his hat slowly on a horny forefinger. He wanted to swear; he wanted to go get McWilliams by the back of the neck and boot him all over town; he wanted to pull the girl into his hungry arms and comfort her without words.

" Tell me, though," said small Barbara, trying to sound brave, " did he lose very much?"

" About six hundred dollars," said Barbee, and hung his head and sounded and looked apologetic, quite as though it were all his fault and he admitted it.

" Oh, Will!" the girl gasped.

So Red Barbee's name was Will—or Bill or William—and Barbara knew it already, while not a single member of the group that Barbee travelled with ever thought of his having any given name but Red.

" Maybe you think I'm just money-crazy, Will," said Barbara. " But I'm not, truly I'm not. But in two nights daddy has lost over a thousand dollars and his new store isn't all paid for yet, and I know he has already ordered more supplies and—he'll be back at pick and shovel again, and this time I think it will just about kill mamma."

Barbee shuffled his feet again, started to spit, checked himself in time and gave his hat an extra twirl on the pivot of his finger.

" He oughtn't to play poker," was all he could think of to say. " Anyhow he oughtn't to play with strangers in a town like Twenty Mile."

" He ought never to play! He knows it, too—anyhow he knows it between spells. Will, last time he went three years without touching a drink of whisky or a gambling card. But when he starts—well, it's sort of like he'd had some sort of poison shot in his blood. He gets started and can't stop."

" Until he's cleaned? And he always loses, don't he?"

Barbara, her lips quivering, could only nod. Barbee was tongue-tied, bereft of any word to say, even of any clear thought of the least value at a time like this, since he couldn't very well obey his two top impulses, to take the girl into his arms, to go booting her father from one end of Twenty Mile to the other.

Presently Barbara spoke in a quiet voice.

" Will you saddle my horse for me, Will? While I slip in and change into some riding clothes? Daddy will be in soon, and mamma will wake up then, and she'll know what has happened and—Oh, Will, I don't want to be here then! I can't stand it! I'm going for a good long ride; it's almost day."

" It ain't day yet for a while," said Barbee. " Sure I'll saddle for you, Miss Barbara. Then I'll go get my horse——"

" No, Will. Please. Oh, thank you, but I want to be alone. You understand don't you?"

" I guess so," said Barbee disconsolately. And it was almost daylight.

Meantime Rob Roy Morgan had been escorted a couple of hundred yards farther along, steered into a winding trail through the scrub timber, and was brought to a stop before a rambling, black blot of an old building that looked like a disused, sway-backed barn. Something of the kind it obviously had been and in part still was. There was a big windowless front room in which were a few bunks along the walls, a half-dozen dilapidated stools and chairs, a rough table with a coal-oil lamp on it; beside the door through which they entered there was a second door in the opposite wall giving upon that portion of the building which still served as a barn. Morgan heard the stamping and stirring of horses and whiffed stable smells.

" Might as well lift his guns off'n him," said one of the men. " He won't be needin' 'em for a while."

Morgan's guns were lifted out of their holsters and dropped to the table well out of his reach. There was nothing he could do about it; he had still the guns of his four captors trained upon him and now, before the door closed, he saw two other men come in; he recognised them for the two drunks encountered in the middle of the street.

All this time Morgan hadn't spoken a word; he did not speak now. He made himself a cigarette, to be doing something rather than from want of it, and he was one of those men to whom the leisurely, even meticulous, rolling of a cigarette is an aid to thought. He had stepped into more than he had counted on to-night, six men instead of three—and Steve

Question out of it. These men he did not know even by sight, not a man of them. Perhaps he had seen them mingling with others who were all strangers to him, but no individual stood out.

He devoted an arrant thought to Barbee: after recognising McWilliams' oak tree, he had guessed at Barbee and Barbara. Had Barbee, so busy with the girl, so much as known it was Morgan with the other men? Probably not, and even if Barbee had realised that there went Morgan with a flock of strangers, walking in their midst, would he have noted or thought to know where they went?

" Well, Morgan, you're one of them close-mouthed *hombres*, huh?" said the spokesman of the outfit.

Morgan regarded him gravely; he'd know this man whenever he saw him again; lean and hard-faced, hard-eyed, thin-lipped, with an unsightly, bluish scar that cut from the side of his nose down slantingly across his mouth all the way to the middle of his long, bony chin, a wolfish-looking man with the trigger finger gone from one hand, a man who, from the look of him, would have fitted without discord into the sweet harmony of the Pickens-Skinner-Bates trio.

" All right, Morgan, keep your trap shut until I make you open it. Right now spill out your pockets."

And so, thought Morgan, Steve Question did have a hand in this affair after all. He was just holding back, that was all, handing the job over to men who did as he told them.

" What do you want out of my pockets?" he asked.

The other man laughed, and his scarred mouth twisted crookedly.

" You know all right," he said. " Some of us men here in Twenty Mile has had our eyes on you ever since you and your gang blowed into town. And we ain't forgot the stagey robbery, neither; neither we ain't forgot how Bandy Weaver got killed and how Tom Stukey was brought in all shot to hell! Happens both Bandy and Tom's friends of mine, of all us fellers. And we've saw how you're spendin' money like you had a lot of easy money to spend. But like the feller sez, easy come, easy go. Pungle up and do it pronto."

Morgan fished in his pockets; at the end he brought out all he had, the two twenties he had reserved when he left Snow

White, and two or three dollars in silver. He dropped the coins to one of the bunks near which he was standing.

"Want to make us laugh? Shell out! Pronto, like I said."

Morgan lifted his shoulders. "That's all," he said.

"Why, you damn liar! Do you wanta get gun-whipped? Do you want as I should break your nose and knock your ears down?"

The front door opened and Steve Question stepped in, with Hap Stroud and Ben Harper close at his heels.

"What's going on here?" Steve demanded. He looked at Morgan, looked the other men over, then asked again, speaking directly to the man with the scarred mouth, "What's going on, Spike?"

Spike—the full name as far as Twenty Mile and its environs knew, was Spike Voych—seemed actually to dwindle in stature with Steve's eyes upon him, and instantly Rob Roy Morgan leaped to the perfect correct conclusion that Spike Voych was Steve's dog to whom there had chanced to be delegated a scrap of authority to-night. Still Spike spoke up well enough, saying the words which doubtless Steve Question had put in his mouth for him.

"Glad you come, Steve," said Spike. "I told one of the boys to look you up and tell you; guess he found you, huh?"

"What are you boys doing with Morgan?" His eyes went to the table. "I see you've got his hardware." He glanced at the bunk. "His money too?"

"It's like this, Steve: us fellers have been nosing around trying to get the deadwood on that gang that stuck up the stage and killed Bandy Weaver and shot Tom Stukey up. It's the gang that rode into town along with this feller Morgan; Morgan's the ring-leader. Of course, he wouldn't have all the swag on him, not being a pack-horse, but we aim to shake him down for all he's got and see it gets took back to them it belongs to. We wanted as you should be in on it, you and some of the other main citizens of Twenty Mile."

Morgan permitted himself the luxury of a broad grin. "Quite a speech, Spike," he said. "Take you long to learn it?"

Young Rob Roy Morgan had kept himself as cool as a cucumber. Rather, he had thought that he had. What to do at any step along the line, first with four men shoving their guns into him, then with two more men stepping in, then with Steve Question and another two. Count 'em. He had nine against him—and they had his guns. So it was best to keep cool, wasn't it?

Yes. No question. But—and there is always a *but*—cool outside as he seemed to be, inside he felt his blood running the wrong way, and he felt that it was setting him on fire. He set his teeth hard; he tried to keep a grip on himself; he said to himself, " If I make a move I'll have nine bullets through me before I can bat an eye."

Nine bullets, huh? Could nine bullets or nineteen or ninety kill a man any deader than just one, placed right?

And the fury within his blood rose to his head.

Steve Question was talking. What he was saying seemed to come to Morgan's ears from afar off; he had missed the first part.

" . . . and anyhow, you got to be sure, Spike. Sure his crowd stuck up the stage?"

" Surer'n hell," said Spike Voych, the trained parrot.

Steve Question looked at Morgan. He said, " I guess they've got you dead to rights, kid. Better shell out."

Morgan licked his lips; they were burning hot. He said, " I shelled. There on the bunk."

" You got a hell of a lot more than that," said Steve. " Didn't I just set in a game with you?"

" Maybe I got stuck up before you stick-up gents got me," said Morgan. " Go through my pockets, damn you, if you feel like it." He even lifted his hands, making the way clear.

And his blood kept hammering through him, and his fury burned hotter and hotter within him. And, a queer sort of thing with Rob Roy Morgan, the madder he got, the more insistently a quiet little voice spoke within him, " Watch your chance, kid! They're nine to one—they *know* you haven't got a chance—— *That's why you have.*"

Spike Voych, so dead sure of dragging out handfuls of the only thing he loved, just money whether it be in gold or silver or greenbacks, plunged both hands into Rob Roy Morgan, and Rob Roy Morgan seething with his newly unleashed rage, as quick as any venomous reptile that ever sank its fangs into the thing it hated, dragged both of Spike's guns

H

up out of their leather, and before a man could blink an eye he brought one gun-barrel down on top of Spike's head so that that individual dropped like a slaughtered beef. And then both guns were jabbed hard into Steve Question's belly, and there was the ready click of the hammers pulled back.

" Tell 'em what to do, Steve! Dammit, you're high dog here! Tell 'em what to do! With a dozen bullets through me I squeeze both triggers!"

" Hold it, everybody!" shouted Steve Question, staring death in the face. " Hold it, I say!"

Morgan shoved both guns deeper into Steve Question's lean, flat stomach.

" Even if I didn't want to," he said, " you know what would happen if they blasted me. Just naturally I'd squinch all over—my fingers would jerk—and both guns are cocked, Steve! They'd kill me deader'n a mackerel, Steve. Sure. But look at the lead they'd be wasting! I'd get what I want with just two shots—and I didn't even buy 'em; they're Spike's."

He drove the gun-barrels so much deeper into Steve Question's flesh that Steve winced in pain. Morgan said, " Move back to the door. Open it and let me go. Do it damn quick too. I'm kind of scared and so my fingers are sweaty; they might slip on both triggers any minute."

If Rob Roy Morgan had been swung high on a volcano of fury, Steve Question's fury was no less. Yet, like many a man, he clung desperately to his life. He opened the door.

" I'm not through yet," said Morgan, in a thin voice that was like a summer whisper of wind through dead grass, dry and brittle. " Tell all these boys to take off their guns and pile 'em on the table. Better do it, Steve."

He had his back to the open door; he was as good as free, free from these nine men but not yet free from himself. Not yet free from the sort of rage that had broken Tony's wrist, that had come close to being the death of Slim Pickens for spitting on his floor.

" Do me a favour, Steve?" said Morgan.

" Sure," said Steve Question. " Sure."

" Spike's asleep right now, so tell one of the other boys to collect all the hardware and spill it on the table, will you?"

" Morgan, as sure as——"

" Will you, Steve? Just as a favour?" And he found that he could drive his two gun-barrels a half-inch deeper into Steve Questions midriff.

" Kilgore," said Steve, " do what the gent says. Pile the guns on the table."

Instantly Morgan made out which one was Kilgore, and he had sensed enough to know that Steve Question would have selected a man to depend on.

A long, thin man with a long thin neck, with an amazing Adam's apple which Kilgore seemed always to be trying to swallow, but which seemed to stick in his throat—maybe sometime in his sleep it would choke him to death—and from his wiry and puckered look the thing might have been a crab apple—stepped to the table and put his two guns down. He swallowed, anyhow tried to swallow, and went about his appointed task. Under Steve Question's eye the other men, though they bristled, allowed their side arms to be removed.

" Now," said Morgan, " tell Kilgore to take down one of them buckskin strings that's hanging on a nail on the wall right behind him and run it through all the trigger guards— and hand 'em to me like a string of fish."

" I'll be seeing you soon, Morgan," said Steve Question.

Morgan backed out. He had the string of guns, his own included, festooned over his left arm; he still had both Spike Voych's guns in his hands, always at least one muzzle burning hot against Steve's belly.

" Remember I paid for the guns," he said. " You've got over forty bucks of mine on the bunk. Now shut the door!"

Steve Question slammed the door shut.

CHAPTER TWELVE

It was almost day. The sun wasn't up, but its promise was in the eastern sky. Morgan went as straight as a string to the Pay Dirt Saloon. He hooked his heel over the bar rail and strung out his assortment of guns on the bar. The bartender's eyes stuck out.

" I want a drink," said Morgan. " A quick one. And I want a hammer and some nails and a piece of paper and a pencil. And I haven't got any money on me. I'll pay you to-morrow."

The bartender, being an old-timer, and having cast a roving glance over the hardware, and having taken stock on the look in the newcomer's eye, said, " Sure. Why not?" and put himself out to please.

And just then both Smoke Keena and Red Barbee ranged up alongside Roy Morgan. And Barbee said:

" Say, Morgan! Was it you I saw———"

" One of you boys give me a few dollars," said Morgan. " I'm short."

Keena dug down swiftly and piled up a good share of his night's winnings, in gold and silver. Morgan dragged out a twenty.

" Where'n hell, Virginia, did you get all them guns?" Keena wanted to know.

" I know." said Barbee. " I saw him straggling along with some friends of his. They got into a game. He took 'em. Right, Morgan?"

" Right, Red," said Morgan.

The bartender came back with drinks, hammer and nails, and hadn't even forgotten paper and pencil. Morgan spread the guns out on the bar. He looked them all over, then decided to keep his own. He lifted Spike Voych's out of his holsters and replaced them with weapons he knew as a man comes to know anything he has lived with, day and night, for years.

He wrote on the piece of paper, " These guns belong to Steve Question and his bunch, Kilgore and Voych and Stroud and Harper, and the rest of the boys. All they got to do is ask for them and they can have them back with my compliments." And he signed it, " R. R. Morgan, Twenty Mile, California, U. S. America, any time."

" Now," he said to the bartender, " let's do this: Right under that nice big mirror of yours, we'll drive two nails one at each end, and we'll string these guns along between them along with this open letter of mine. And Steve, my old pal Steve, and his friends, can come pick 'em up any time."

" Virginia! What the hell's been going on?" gasped Smoke Keena.

Morgan's grin was as boyish as, far from his own realisation, Morgan was himself.

"There was nine of 'em," said Morgan. "They had me shut up in a room. They had my guns. Most of 'em had a gun in his hand pointed my way. I just took their guns and got back my own and walked down town."

"Quit your damn lying, Virginia. Let's have it."

Rob Roy Morgan's grin broadened and he clapped Smoke Keena so heartily on the shoulder that Keena sagged at the knees.

"There they are, there are the guns, there's my polite little letter to them." He began to laugh. "It's near morning, boys, but I'm betting you Snow White against a wheelbarrow that before it's full day all Twenty Mile will be laughing its head off! It might be worth it, just sticking around watching for Steve Question and his gang slinking in and claiming their hardware! Come ahead, let's get out of this."

"You ain't lying, are you, Morgan?" said Red Barbee soberly.

Morgan's face froze; his eyes too seemed to freeze as he turned them on Barbee.

"I sort of take a good many things off'n Nancy," he said, "and I don't know why, but not off'n anybody else, Barbee. I don't lie because I don't have to lie. I do what I damn well please. I do it my way, and that's all there is to it. Now let's get out of here."

Late as was the hour—or early, rather—there were something like a dozen men still hanging around in the Pay Dirt, and not a man of them, except for one fellow who was fast asleep, sprawled across the bar, but had not taken this all in. More than one mouth was open, jaw dropped, as the three went out. And then as the swing-doors snapped open and then swung as Morgan and Keena and Barbee went out, they heard a great thunder of laughter.

And laughter was to prevail in Twenty Mile for many an hour. The story ran as fluidly as hot lava. Men who heard, at first laughed it off, but when invited to go see for themselves, they did go, some even that night, more and more in the early hours and all day long, to look at the string of guns festooned under the bar mirror. As tough a crowd as even tough little Twenty Mile knew were Steve Question and Kilgore and some of the rest—yet their guns hung on display, theirs for just claiming them—which was as good as to admit that a young chap named Morgan, a Johnny-Come-Lately, had taken the nine of them into camp single-handed, had made monkeys out of them, had combed their hair, as they used to say in Twenty Mile, and then given them back their toys.

None of Steve Question's crowd dropped back to the Pay Dirt that night, for after all the night was spent. And as it chanced none of them dropped in till the afternoon of the next day. All that time the guns on display were drawing crowds.

Kilgore came in alone in the early afternoon. A man next to him jogged him with a facetious elbow, pointed at the display under the mirror—and Kilgore saw, stared, read—and came close to choking to death on his apple.

Instinctively he clapped his hands to his hips. Empty holsters!

He gulped his drink and hurried out.

As for Rob Roy Morgan, with Red Barbee and Keena keeping in step as they headed for bed, Morgan said: " Oh, by the way let's drop in at the stable. I sort of want to say good night to Snow White."

" You're as crazy as a bed bug," Keena growled at him. " What for, this time of night?"

Morgan in a gayer mood than either Keena or Barbee had guessed ever came his way, said, " Just you wait and see! Snow White's the only one I let in on all my secrets. Maybe she'll give you boys an inkling."

Arrived at Snow White's stall, greeted by her soft whicker, Morgan ran a light hand over her, she nuzzled him, he put his arm round her neck.

" Good girl," he said. " I'll hunt all over town for an apple for you to-morrow, and if I can't get one, I'll bring you an apple pie, by glory! Now, Nancy," he said, " you just scratch down in Snow White's manger, over at the left-hand corner under the hay, and see what you can find. You, Barbee, feel under her chin and see if anybody left a note tied there for me."

They thought that maybe he was just plain drunk, though in a new way to them. Just the same they did as he directed.

Smoke Keena whistled softly; Barbee groped, found a bit of paper and handed it over. Then the three steered again for bed and Morgan made a sketchy explanation.

" Steve Question's going to murder you for this, Virginia," said Smoke Keena, and sounded troubled. " Him or any other of them fellers. They'll shoot you in the back in the dark. But—dammit, Morgan, how come? Nine of 'em! Hells bells, if there'd been only two or three of 'em——"

" If there'd been only three of 'em—or two—or one!" said Morgan, " I couldn't have got away with it. They'd have been watching me too close. But nine, man! All heeled, and me as good as naked! So they went to sleep, as the feller sez. And I bet a man they're going to turn so turkey-red to-morrow that they'll get sunburn!" He drew a breath as big as he had ever drawn in his life; he looked up at the starry sky; he said, " It's a pretty good world, ain't it?"

" If you've got any sense you know they're going to get you for this job you worked to-night."

" I can shoot as straight as they can, Nancy!"

" But, you jackass, there are nine of them!"

Morgan stopped dead in his tracks.

" How many of my side?" he demanded sharply.

Keena, who had gone ahead a couple of steps, swung on his heel and came back.

" That's right, Virginia. Me, I'm with you until hell freezes solid. So's Red Barbee. Am I right, Barbee?"

" Dammit, with bells on," said Barbee.

" And," said Keena, " there's some of the other boys— there's a few I wouldn't count on much, Morgan—but there's Big Mouth and Buck Braddock and——"

" There's Tony," said Morgan. " His gun arm will be pretty well quick. You'd better round 'em up, Nancy. Likely we'll need 'em."

" And damn you, Virginia, don't you go poking around alone——"

" I walk on my heels," said Rob Roy Morgan, " and I walk where I damn please and whenever I feel like it."

" Oh, hell, you make me sick," said Smoke Keena, and they went along to their quarters.

With his hand stretched out to open the door, Morgan said, " Get a line on Slim Pickens to-morrow, will you, Nancy?

You too, Barbee. I've got a notion he's a rat and smells cheese in Steve Question's lunch bucket. If he is, we'll tell him and all like him to roll their blankets and move along."

Then he entered the big, barnlike place; it was dark and still. Each man struck a match, headed for bed. Morgan, hardly had they separated, dropped his own match and trod out the spark; he had seen a thin line of light under his door. And he knew he hadn't left any light burning.

He went to the door without making a sound. He stopped and stood several minutes, listening. All that he heard was no more than the audible hush in a seashell. He threw the door open and stood on the threshold, both guns in his hands. Steve Question, on murder bent, could have been before him.

He saw a man lying on his bed, sound asleep. Who the man was, at first he did not know, because, though he lay on his back, he had pulled his hat down over his face. It wasn't Steve Question; he knew that. And there was only one man, and that man sound asleep.

He closed his door silently, stepped to the bed and lifted the man's hat from his face. The man sat up, startled, and there was a wild look in his eyes. It was young Don Benito Fontana.

" Señor!" exclaimed the boy, and blinked and rubbed his eyes.

" Make yourself at home, Don Benito," said Morgan dryly.

Young Fontana jumped up, smoothed his hair and started pacing up and down.

" I asked where you lived; I came here maybe one—two hours ago. I don't know what time it is. One of your friends told me this was your room. I waited for you here."

" Fine," said Morgan. " My house isn't quite the grand place yours is, but give me time!" He made a bit of mockery of Benito's father's welcome, and said with a flourish, " My house, it is yours, Señor!"

Ernesto took him seriously and was visibly relieved, pleased, too.

" You are a friend, Señor Morgan!"

" What did you want with me?" said Morgan bluntly.

Don Benito, about to become expansive, became confused. His dark skin reddened and he couldn't keep his hands still until he locked them together, making each prisoner and jailer of the other.

" I am in hell, Señor! Do you know what that can be to a man like me? I tell you I am in terrible hell. And I came to you! Where could I go? Do you want to be a friend to me? Anyhow, I come to you for help."

Rob Roy Morgan looked at him with coldly calculating eyes. The young Spanish-Californian was as tense as a violin string about to snap. He had been asleep, of course, yet sometimes a man asleep does not greatly rest, having carried along with him into those mysterious realms of sleep those cares of the days which grow into nightmares.

Morgan chose a light vein.

" So you're in hell and want help! Easy! You knock the last ' l ' out of hell and put a ' p ' in its place, and there you are! Even I might do a little thing like that for an *amigo*. What's got you down, Fontana?"

" I'm a liar, I'm a cheat, I'm a thief!" cried Don Benito. " I ought to be dead. I ought to go out and shoot myself and cut my throat." His hands escaped each other and were clenched into fists knuckling at his temples. " I ought to go away from everybody I love and that loves me. I ought to go out and get drunk!"

" That might help," snorted Morgan. " First, suppose you tell me what's gone sour."

Don Benito, pacing up and down, rumpling his hair, now and then dabbing at his eyes where the tears stood ready, would have been an hour getting to the heart of things but that Morgan cut him short in his ramblings, drove short, sharp questions at him and so in a few minutes had the tale.

Señor Fontana, Benito's father, had to-day received some of the money he was expecting from cattle sales; he had entrusted his son with four hundred dollars, a sum which Fontana owed for supplies purchased last month from the general store in Twenty Mile, payable now to McWilliams, who had taken the place over lock, stock and barrel, which meant along with everything else all assets and liabilities. And Benito, meaning well as God judged him, on his way late that afternoon to the store with the money in his pocket had stopped a moment at the Pay Dirt Saloon. He was thirsty, that was all there was to it——

"And you shot the wad!" snapped Morgan. "You got into a game and lost the four hundred!"

Don Benito choked on a sob and nodded miserably. The devil had been in it. He had been sure of his luck—he was going to double the money and quit—he had already gotten into debt—he couldn't ask his papa for more, he didn't want his papa to know and scold him——

"And you got into your head that you could come to me, and that I would be fool enough to stake you to four hundred dollars! Now keep your shirt on! What are your other debts? How much?"

"Not much, Señor. Just about two hundred dollars, maybe a *leetle* more. I owe to a man named Señor Kilgore; he's a nice man and honest, and he has been good to me too, waiting for the money, but now he has got to have it——"

"Poker, Benito?"

"*Si, Si,* Señor."

"Six hundred in all. Well, I don't like to be a fool, but maybe I can kick in with you and still not be so much fool after all. Squat, Don Benito; take a chair or sit on the bed and keep still. I want to think."

Don Benito folded up and his eyes were enormous, fixed on Morgan's face, and again he had his hands clasped tight together. Morgan ignored him, sat down and rolled one of his slow cigarettes. He already held Señor Fontana's signed promise to pay seven hundred dollars. Another six hundred to Don Benito now? It would be as good as gold! for he knew that if the boy defaulted, the old man would pay; there was that high Spanish pride of his! The man would pay though it ruined him—as perhaps in due course it would. Morgan felt that, handing over the money to Benito, he was by way of acquiring a thirteen-hundred interest in the Fontana *rancho*.

And Don Benito had a horse, perhaps several horses, and was inclined to brag even after having looked with a true horseman's eye at Snow White. And Morgan loved fine horses.

Morgan lighted his cigarette.

"Go to bed, Benito," he said. "We can bunk up together to-night. In the morning I'll go with you to the store and you can pay your father's four hundred. You will give me your I O U. Then you will find your friend Kilgore;

you'll tell him to meet you at the Pay Dirt and that you'll pay him there; tell him a man owes you a couple of hundred dollars and is to meet you. Just don't say who it is. Understand? Don't mention my name!"

" Oh, Señor!" Benito leaped to his feet, his face radiant, his arms extended as though he would embrace this tried and true friend of his. " There is nothing in the world, nothing, that——"

" You've made a damn fool of yourself, kid," said Morgan curtly. " Now go to sleep. Me too, I'm sleepy."

Don Benito flushed as though he had been slapped, but if even Morgan's hard hand had slapped his face just then it is likely that he would have bitten his lip and held his peace. He began removing his jacket and boots.

Morgan, as best he could, barricaded his two doors, that leading into the room that he called his office, where he dragged the long table across the threshold and stood a precariously balanced chair on top of it; the other door with a tilted chair hooked under the knob. If he should have callers, he'd wake. He emulated Don Benito in preparation for bed, blew out the lamp and turned in, a gun down by his hip, his hand on it.

It was mid-morning when the two awoke. Morgan led the way to the back porch where they washed and combed their hair and adjusted their neck scarves, Morgan's a big red bandana, Don Benito's almost a tiny shawl. They turned a corner together and went across the road to a lunch counter where Smoke Keena and Red Barbee were already wolfing down their coffee and flapjacks and allied delicacies.

" We tried your door," said Keena, " found it was fastened inside, reckoned that you was scared and might start shooting at the drop of a hat, and so came along over here. Hallo, Don Fontana."

The four repaired together to the store where Red Barbee, for one, was treated to a most pleasant surprise with a thrill in it. Behind the counter was Miss Barbara, as pretty as a picture while trying to look businesslike with a pencil behind one ear and almost lost in her clustering curls. Barbara's jaw wasn't square and never could be square, but that was what she was trying to make it this morning. The clerk was gone and Barbara, already flushed with trying to remember how much a sack of sugar was worth and whether to sell a side of bacon by the yard, had taken over. Barbee instantly remembered several small items he was in urgent need of, chewing tobacco and, yes, a big needle and some strong thread and a couple of more bandanas and a jack knife and so on.

McWilliams, looking harassed, was at the far end of the counter, pawing through some papers impaled on a tenpenny nail that had been driven through a bit of board and was left with the point up, a convenient file for letters and other documentary odds and ends. Morgan and Don Benito bore down upon him; Don Benito paid the four hundred dollars and Morgan was quick to see the fires light up in McWilliams' jaded eyes.

Barbee, too, had marked the transaction. He whispered to Barbara; in another instant her flying feet carried her to her father's side.

" Oh, this is Señor Fontana's account that you told me about, is it, Daddy? Here, I'll make out the receipt. Four hundred dollars? In full?"

She counted the money and put it into the drawer. She pencilled the receipt with quick, not too steady fingers. " You'd better sign it, Daddy," she said, and honey was never sweeter than her voice.

Morgan and Young Fontana went out. Smoke Keena, having glanced Barbee's way, shrugged and followed them. Barbee, with Barbara again attending him, was making sure that he hadn't forgotten anything. Well, if he had, he'd be back——

" Do what I said, Fontana," said Morgan. " Let's get this business cleaned up. Go and find Kilgore, make your date with him, then come get me. I'll go back to my place and wait for you there."

Young Fontana hurried away. Morgan said to Smoke Keena, " Come ahead with me, Nancy. Maybe we're going to stir up a piece of hell this morning. I don't know. I'd just as leave have you along this time, you and Barbee, too."

" Barbee! Shucks, he's liable to be hanging around the store all day."

" Not with old man McWilliams' eye on him! Anyhow he'll soon be running out of things he can think of that he's got to buy in a hurry."

Barbee came out with his bundle, stepping high and

looking like a man who had just drawn a royal flush. The three returned together to their quarters to await Benito Fontana. Morgan slipped his two new decks of cards into his pocket.

CHAPTER THIRTEEN

YOUNG FONTANA came rushing in. He had found Kilgore, but Kilgore did not want to meet him at the Pay Dirt. Don Benito had shrugged; he had said, remembering what Morgan had told him, that a man who owed him was to meet him there. If Señor Kilgore could not come, *bueno*. Some other time, then.

But it would appear that Kilgore wanted his money, and now. So, reluctantly, he had said all right. He was to meet Benito at the Pay Dirt in ten minutes.

Morgan had a piece of paper and a pencil handy. He slid them across the table to young Fontana. " Your I O U for six hundred, *amigo mio*."

Benito swept upon paper and pencil like a whirlwind. " *Amigo !* I am never going to forget this if I live a hundred years more!"

Morgan pocketed the paper but did not give him the money. He and Smoke Keena and Red Barbee and Benito Fontana walked over to the Pay Dirt. It still lacked an hour until noon.

The four lined up along the bar in front of the festoon of guns. Not a gun so far had been reclaimed; perhaps Kilgore hadn't yet had time to carry word to Steve Question and the others. A moment later Kilgore came in, saw young Fontana without at first noting who his companions were, and tapped Fontana on the shoulder. Then all four turned and he saw Rob Roy Morgan, and gave every appearance of nearly choking to death on that Adam's apple of his.

" Good-morning, Kilgore," said Morgan pleasantly. " Have a drink?"

At the far end of the bar some men guffawed; another man snorted and blew the foam off his beer over his section of the bar. Kilgore hastily took up the money which Fontana had ready for him and went out.

"If he don't kill you, Virginia," said Smoke Keena, "it won't be because he won't try."

All this was first over Don Benito's head. So concerned was he with his own predicament that he had had no thought for anything lying outside it, even the guns strung along under the mirror not in the least interesting him. Now, however, he chanced to see Morgan's note, still in place—he saw Kilgore's name there—he heard Keena's remark and recalled the impolite haste of Kilgore's departure—and at least a fraction of the whole thing dawned on him. He stared at his *amigo*.

"Señor!" he gasped, but already Morgan was on his way out. The four left the Pay Dirt and stopped to roll their cigarettes on the wooden sidewalk.

"And now I must hurry back to the *rancho*," said Fontana. "They will wonder already why I did not come home last night. Maybe they will worry about me. I will have to tell them——" He clutched Morgan's arm. "Come with me, Señor! We will tell them how I met you, how you asked me to be your guest!" He remembered his manners and made his little bow to Keena and Barbee. "You too, Señores. It will be a nice ride. I will show you our horses. We can ride over part of the ranch, too. It will make my mamma and papa happy."

"Suits me," said Keena quickly. Anything, he thought, to get Morgan out of town for a while. And besides that consideration, it remained that Keena had enjoyed his other visit at the hacienda; he had never been in so fine a place before; he liked the girls' singing, and their pretty dresses.

Morgan thought instantly of the main issue: He was here to feather his nest. The Fontanas were as soft as putty, and he coveted what they had. There was that I O U of the old man's; no doubt it could be put upon a poker table after the womenfolk had gone to bed. And, as practical in another field as Keena, he thought of a nest of hornets he had stirred up, nine of 'em who'd most likely be swarming out on the warpath before the third drink this afternoon.

"I'd like to see those horses of yours, Benito," he said. "Remember, you said you thought you had one as good as my Snow White?"

" Then you will come! And you Señor Barbee? You too!"

Keena relieved the pressure of a mouth filled with tobacco juice and then laughed.

" Barbee? Just look at him! Look at the fishy look in his eye! Man, Barbee's got a lady friend, and if you think he'd ride that far out of town——"

" Shut your mouth, Smoke," said Barbee.

" Oh!" exclaimed Don Benito. " Oho! The lovely young lady who is the daughter of Señor McWilliams? She is like a little flower, she is lovely! And Señor Barbee, she has only just come here, and will have no friends. Bring her, too, and let my sisters know her. Oh, they will be glad. You see, they too have not many friends outside our own home."

A glowering Barbee changed into a mooning Barbee: He thought of the long ride down the valley, he and Barbara alone together, letting the others go on ahead. If she only would come—if that damned old hard-head, her father, would let her——

" And," said Benito, " you will tell her that my mother will want her to stay all night and, oh, of course, as long as she will be happy with us. It would make us all happy and proud, Señor Barbee."

Barbee thought, " He's a kind of nice kid at that." He gave a hitch to his belt and cleared his throat and looked off into vague distances. " I'll go ask her," he said.

And both he and an excited Barbara were amazed when McWilliams said without a moment of delay:

" Yes, yes, Barbee. Go by all means. The Fontanas are fine people; I've already heard a lot about them. You can go now if you want to."

Barbara fled with Barbee, going home to tell her mother—and so intrigued was she that she forgot all about the four hundred dollars that those fine people had just paid in to her daddy!

So they rode down to the Fontana hacienda. Barbee explained that Miss McWilliams would be able to come later on, that they needn't wait. Besides, he had a couple of things to do before he could leave. He was thinking about shaving, about managing somehow to scrub himself; he wanted to spruce up all he could. He'd anyhow get a new pair of boots.

They rode, loose in the saddle, idling along. Morgan's eyes, roving the fat lands of the Fontana *rancho*, were not merely predatory, they grew possessive. He wanted that ranch.

Their horses were at a swinging walk. He hooked a knee over the saddle-horn. He said dreamily:

" I like your ranch, Fontana. I've got to have one just like it. Maybe this one, huh?"

Don Benito laughed gaily as at something very funny, a joke of his friend's. Then he noted the steely glint in Morgan's eyes, and his laughter stopped and a look almost of horror, such horror as sacrilege might engender, swept across his face. He said in a suppressed voice:

" Señor, our *rancho* can never be for sale. Our hearts, all the hearts of all the Fontanas, are in it. To leave this *rancho* would be to tear our hearts out by the roots."

They jogged along, mostly in silence, for half an hour. Morgan said abruptly:

" Say, Fontana, we were talking the other night about the wild girl of the mountains, that girl I've heard talk about over five hundred miles. Some say she's a vampire and some say she's the spirit of an old Indian Princess—and some say she's all in your eye, just nothing that ever was. But you said that you saw her one time. Down by your place."

" It's funny, Señor," said Fontana. " For five or six years now, I listen to what men say about that girl. Oh, she is a real something, all right. More men than one know something about her—but not very much, not any one of them." He shrugged lazily. " Yes, I saw her. If it was not her, who, then? It was moonlight. I was walking outside, looking at the moon and the mountains and watching our waterfall with little rainbows in it and with lace, like a lady's, making it a dress for the dance. And I saw her. She was— oh, she was beautiful, Señor! That is all I know. She was there one bright second, then she was not there any longer. Maybe she climbed up through the lace and the rainbows of the waterfall and up the moonbeams, and went back to heaven. That is all."

" Whew!" said Smoke Keena. " That's-a-plenty."

" How long ago?" asked Morgan.

" Maybe six months."

" And you haven't seen her since?"

" No, Señor. And maybe I dreamed it all."

" Let's look at your horses when we get there," said Morgan. He was to-day riding Snow White. He patted her silky shoulder. " You said you might have something that you thought could stack up alongside this pony of mine."

" She is as pretty as a pretty girl," said young Fontana. " And she has blue blood in her veins, oh, sure. Yes, I am going to show you our horses."

They looked over the horses first of all. There was a long barn with a hay loft above, with some twenty stalls below. A couple of Indian boys were idly doing nothing while presumably attending the dozen horses in the stalls. Behind the barn was a field of ten acres or so where a score of clean-limbed saddle horses took their ease in shade or sun.

Morgan went unerringly to Don Benito Fontana's favourite. She was a young mare as black as coal, her eyes big and clear and dark and intelligent, a superb bit of horseflesh. Morgan stepped along to her where she grew restless in her stall; she ignored him prettily and whinnied to Don Benito. And young Fontana, petting her, laughed softly.

" She knows she is *mi novia,* my sweetheart," he said. " Sometime, Señor, I am going to race you, you on your Snow White, for one mile or twenty miles! And the man to lose will give a big red apple, if he has to go to San Francisco for it, to the other man's horse!"

" Sell her?" said Morgan.

" Sell? Sell, sell, sell! There are things a man cannot sell, Señor, and you know that. As a gift, that might be possible; I don't know. But to let La Golondrina go for just money— ah, no, Señor! Never in all this life."

" We'll race sometime," said Morgan. " For a big red apple."

" We are going to look at the horses out in the field. There are not any finer horses in California, Señor. *Vamos a ver !* "

So for a couple of hours they looked at horses and talked horses, and Rob Roy Morgan thought, " This is the life of kings! And I don't believe they even know it! And I've got one thousand three hundred dollars of it in my tail pocket!"

" Look what's coming!" said Smoke Keena. " Oh, my eye Charlie! A top buggy and a red ribbon tied around the whip! And blue ribbons on the girl's bonnet!"

I

Barbara was as pretty as a pink, with cheeks flushed up and eyes dancing.

Don Benito Fontana made her the sort of bow he served for very special occasions.

" Señorita! You are going to make us all so happy and proud that we are going to think that heaven cannot be so nice a place as the Hacienda Fontana! Come! My mother and father, and my sisters, too, and my brother Mentor, they will all want to keep you so long that you can never go away!"

He embarrassed her; she didn't know how to take him. But she didn't have to take him at all, since he took her. He caught her by the hand and drew her in through the door set deep into the three-feet thick adobe wall.

" Papa!" he called. " Mamma! All of you! It is Benito, that bad boy, come home and he has brought you something nice!"

Barbara was swept away by the Fontana señoritas.

" Barbee looks sort of like a Christmas tree," observed Smoke Keena innocently.

Morgan said to Barbee, with no one else to hear, " Barbee, you're a long-eared jackass." And when Barbee's eyes, belligerent, asked him for the rest of it, Barbee got it. " You asked the old man if you could bring his daughter down here, didn't you? And he said, ' Hell, yes!' Didn't he? And you almost fell backwards getting out, didn't you, before he could change his mind? And you plumb forgot that four hundred dollars Kid Fontana just slipped him! Steve Question's before morning!"

Barbee's jaw dropped. " If the old devil does that——"

" If he don't, you go get me a wagonload of hay and I'll eat it." And for a while Barbee didn't look so much like a Christmas tree. He chewed his fingernails and glowered— until Barbara and the Fontana girls tossed themselves into the *sala* like an armful of flowers.

It was very peaceful there at the old Fontana home. Life could, at times and places, run as smooth and clear as any slow, meandering summer river.

" Oh, Will!" exclaimed Barbara when she had a chance in the corner of the patio to clutch Red Barbee's arm. " It's so lovely! And they are such lovely people! Oh, Will, I'm in heaven! And they're just the prettiest girls you ever saw!. Don't you think so?"

" No!" said Will Barbee. " You——" He couldn't get any further.

Mentor came in, he had been at the far end of the *rancho* with a couple of the *vaqueros*; shortly they would be moving a herd of cattle up to Las Manzanitas, another ranch they had some twenty miles away, higher in the mountains, where they would graze stock, a quarter or a third of their vast herd of bellowing cattle, until the end of the summer. Mentor, sun-flushed, beamed, like the rising sun at the sight of their guests.

And they had coffee, and thin, sweet cakes—a man like Smoke Keena with his jowls developed through long years as a tobacconist, could have crumpled a dozen of them into his mouth at one time—and wild honey. And the girls laughed and were forever jumping up and never sitting down.

And Red Barbee's eyes were glazed with happiness. Smoke Keena said, " I guess that's the way a guy looks in the morgue."

It was a day like a gay-coloured page out of a picture book. They rode over the most picturesque part of the ranch, the southern end. Señor Fontana, like a young colt feeling its oats, effervesced. He had the carriage brought to the door, drawn by a high-headed pair of golden bays, a carriage of which he was fond and proud, there being but one other, one down in Santa Barbara, like it in California, and both had made the long journey around the horn from Spain. He drove himself, Señora Fontana at his side, some of his daughters, Barbara with them in the back, and bright ribbons streamed behind them. There were saddle horses for the rest, and they picnicked in a lovely spot where the valley pinched in, where there were enormous oak trees and, down by the stream, big white-boled sycamores. And the girls chattered like magpies, and never, never had little Barbara McWilliams had a happier day. The menfolk sat cross-legged or squatted on their heels, and flipped stones into the water and listened to the girls and watched them make wreaths of wild flowers. And Indian servants barbecued meat and made coffee and served them on a white tablecloth that got stained with crushed grass and grape jelly.

In the sunset they returned to the old home singing, and Don Mentor on horseback alongside the carriage played his guitar, and his brother Benito sang and was as tuneful and carefree as a lark. The girls ran off to their part of the house to make themselves fresh and tidy; the men wandered away to the stable and corrals.

Don Benito had had a moment alone with his father, had given him the receipt from McWilliams for the four hundred dollars; had no more cares upon his shoulders than an accumulation of water on a duck's back. That he had signed his own I O U to Morgan for six hundred dollars did not in the least disturb him; that was some time in the vague, unspecified future, and the man who lives wisely and well—ask any of your Fontanas!—lives in the present. His father patted him on the back and said, " Good boy, Benito." And Don Benito felt like a very good boy indeed.

And Barbara did not think once all day long, or all night long, of the four hundred dollars she had been so business-like to begin with, then had forgotten. So her glorious holiday went unspoiled.

The first stars were out as the men strolled back across the meadow to the house. Señor Fontana had a moment alone with Rob Roy Morgan.

" Señor Morgan," he said, " I am glad to tell you that some of the moneys I have been expecting from my sales of cattle has come to me. I do not forget that you have my note of hand for seven hundred dollars. When we get back to the house we are going to fix up that affair."

Morgan had something in mind—nothing other than a pilfered blue dress and sticky cake. He saw an opening to come at a scrap of information perhaps. He said lightly:

" There was that stage robbery just the other day. Is it safe, Señor, for you to have considerable sums of money in the house? With, of course, many men knowing about the herds you have sent away to be sold and of your expecting the payment in cash."

Fontana laughed softly. " My father, Señor," he said, " came from Spain to California in 1769, that was with the first expeditions which came by way of Mexico City, the great Padre Junípero Serra and the others. I was born in

California. We have lived here all our lives. Never once has there been any thought, any danger, of robbery."

Morgan drew closer his objective. He said:

"You mean that not once in all this time have you had any sort of burglary? That no one has ever broken into your house and stolen so much as—as the worth of *cinco centavos*?"

"Never! Not once! You see, Señor——" He came to a full stop; a man of high honour, he must be careful always of every word escaping his mouth. He laughed. "Now, that is a funny thing! My daughters told me—I made them run away and be still. They told me that a robber——" He had to laugh again. "A terrible bandit entered our house and plundered it! He stole, what do you suppose, Señor? My little Aldegonda's pretty blue dress! And a truly enormous cake! Think of it, Señor! What a bloodthirsty villain!"

"That's an odd thing—a cake, Señor! Oh, my eye!" and Morgan rubbed his eye reminiscently.

"Pouf! It is not anything. Some *pobrecita* little Indian girl; I myself saw little marks in a bed of flowers under a window. And I told my daughters that soon they must send to town for some pretty things to make into dresses, and must have some big cakes cooked, and send them down to our good and faithful Indios. They have been with us all their lives, Señor. They are true, like gold—but," and his eyes twinkled, "the young ones sometimes want blue dresses and cakes, *no*?"

While strolling toward the patio where the lamplight through unshuttered windows showed big, white winged moths fluttering, Señor Fontana and his son Mentor had a few words to say about some ranch business. Smoke Keena snagged Morgan by the elbow.

"Chance of a game to-night, you think?"

"You still owe me money, young feller," said Morgan.

"Better get square before you lose all you've got."

"Want me to laugh, Virginia? Lose here? Pshaw. Of all the easy pickings I ever saw, it's at the Casa Grande de los Fantanas! What do *you* think?"

"Why do you suppose I'm here?" said Morgan.

And later they played poker. Concerning the game itself there is no need to go into details; again it was just a game of poker. And the important thing was what happened so briskly at the end of the game.

The ladies in the wake of the majestic Señora Fontana swept away in a bright and colourful flotilla, leaving the gentlemen to their wine and their cards and whatever other wickednesses the gentlemen indulged in, once freed of the tenderer and more refining influences of their ladies fair. Señor Fontana brought in his money box; it was a flimsy, japanned tin affair that he kept in a table drawer without any key. First of all he counted out the seven hundred dollars he owed Rob Roy Morgan, and the I O U was crumpled and thrown into the fireplace.

Benito, like a little boy, pouted with his full lower lip thrust out. He said, " Papa, I have no money. I would like to play with our friends, too." And for a moment Señor Fontana looked at his young son thoughtfully; perhaps he was wondering how it happened that Benito was not in funds. When was it—only last week?—that the boy had come to him for money.

Before he could make answer—and without doubt, after a minute of trying to be stern, he would relent and give Benito what he required—Rob Roy Morgan chose the opportunity and spoke up carelessly.

" Don Benito," he said, " look at all the money your father has paid me! Let me be your banker! Any part of it—and your I O U in return—with La Golondrina to forfeit if you lose and can't pay!"

" Gracias, Señor! That is fine!" cried Benito. " Then let me have two or three hundred dollars!"

" Benito!" said his father.

Benito laughed. " We are old amigos, Señor Morgan and me," he said. " We understand each other! And I will have to be in the best of luck—because the blessed saints would never let me lose La Golondrina!"

The paper was signed for three hundred dollars, then moved and shoved across the table, and Benito reached eagerly for the old deck of cards.

" Oh, by the way," said Morgan, and addressed Señor Fontana. " I heard you say that you had trouble getting fresh decks. I was lucky enough to find two that were left over in Twenty Mile." He unpocketed them, dropped them to the table—and while appearing to be looking at the coins he was stacking before him in readiness for the game, watched young Fontana out of the corner of his eye. And he saw how the boy's hand, as though frozen in mid-air, lingered over the worn decks.

They used the new decks, their seals unbroken; there was nothing else that any one wanted, unless it might be Don Benito, and there was nothing he could do about it. Morgan said, and appeared to be only joking, " Now kiss your little horse good-bye, *amigo* Benito."

They played a swift heady game. Benito from the outset was obviously nervous. Alternately, flustered, he played close to the table and played wild. Even his brother Mentor cocked up his handsome eyebrows at him. " You are too young to play a man's game, little Benito," he said once; the thought was in his eyes many times.

There were three Fontanas playing, and Morgan and Keena and Barbee.

Of the Fontanas, Mentor was the shrewdest poker player. His father was by far the boldest, and so the most reckless. But the old man knew what he was doing; when he bluffed his head off and when he played his four aces, he played the same game, with the same face. But it did seem that the cards ran against him. As for Don Benito, he was born to play a guitar under a lady's window, not poker.

Smoke Keena was a blundersome poker player; he was like a bumblebee in a garden. Sometimes he hit, sometimes he missed; no one would ever take Smoke Keena too seriously as an adversary over the pasteboards. Red Barbee? Cool and calculating and canny—bold when he judged it the time, ready to fold up when he saw that he was crawling out on the end of a limb. But to-night? He was thinking altogether too much of pretty Barbara, and you can't mix girls and poker. Then, as for Rob Roy Morgan, he was born to a deck of cards as Don Benito to guitars and moonlight. And he knew what he wanted, what he meant to have—and he thought to see the broad avenue leading to his house of dreams.

When they started playing they agreed to knock off at midnight: Barbee had to return Barbara to Twenty Mile early next morning, Morgan had his plans, the Fontanas also had ranch affairs, and none of them wanted to keep the ladies waiting at breakfast time or to be stale at that time.

When the old clock over the mantlepiece struck twelve, Don Benito was flat, and Morgan still held his note, with La Golondrina as silky-skinned security, and Morgan had won more than he had lost, a good deal more, not counted yet but making a substantial stack in front of him. Mentor again had done a little bit better than break even, was perhaps between fifty and a hundred dollars ahead; Señor Fontana had lost four or five hundred dollars. Smoke Keena had lost, but not more than twenty or thirty dollars. Red Barbee, who had come in on a shoestring, had borrowed once from Keena, had lost all he had.

An Indian boy brought coffee; they had cigars and cigarettes. Morgan got up and went out into the patio; he kept thinking of the waterfall and the pool below it, of the bridge across the creek—and of a girl who had raided Steve Question's cache, who had stolen a blue dress and a freshly baked cake—who had thrown the cake in his face and laughed.

Don Benito had seen her some six months ago. Morgan had seen her twice. Then she had a hide-out somewhere near; she certainly had given every indication of knowing her way about. Even now she might be watching the house—watching him. He tucked in the corners of his mouth: when lights were out, she might come down for another cake and a change of raiment! He moved along with all possible stealth, keeping in the shadows of the oaks as much as he could, to the bridge across the creek.

"Dammit," said Rob Roy Morgan to the quiet night, "why didn't I bring a rope along with me? If ever I nab that girl, I bet a man I'll have to rope her on the run!"

It wasn't that he expected to find her to-night, just that his thoughts kept straying back to her. He wanted to see her face clearly, her eyes, her mouth. He wanted to hear her speak. No girl had ever stimulated him the way this elusive creature did. He wondered, does she hole up somewhere by day, and just prowl by night?

Under the canopy of the big sycamore overhanging the bridge he glanced out across the field to the house. Lights were still on in the *sala*, which had been devoted to cards;

the rest of the house was dark save for the summer light of moon and stars; the patio was a place of mystery, of black shadows and straggling beams of light. The night was steeped in peace . . .

Morgan stiffened all of a sudden from head to foot. He saw a dark figure move swiftly across the patio, merely glimpsed, then lost. That girl! That was his first thought, natural because he had been brooding upon her. But then he saw another figure, a third, a fourth. A fifth, a man doubled over as he ran, was making his way to join the others, and Morgan saw the horses tethered under an oak. Five men at least, maybe more of them.

In the house were the three Fontana men and not a man of them armed; there were Smoke Keena and Red Barbee. Outside were not less than five men, probably six or seven. That they were bent on plunder, if not on murder bent, was as clear as the moonlight; every move they made bespoke their intention.

In the house was that little japanned box of Señor Fontana's—and how much money in it? Some thousands of dollars, receipts of his heavy cattle sale? And how did men know that there was all this money at the Hacienda Fontana?

Simple. Only to-day Don Benito had paid McWilliams four hundred in cash. He had paid Kilgore two hundred——

" It's Steve Question's crowd," said Morgan and spun the cylinders of his two guns. They turned like ball bearings in oil.

CHAPTER FOURTEEN

In the main room of the Hacienda Fontana they were getting ready to say their good-nights. Don Benito, drawn apart, was of a sudden sunk into deep moodiness; it had just dawned on him that, though he had escaped the worries of last night and this morning, he was in debt to his *amigo* Morgan for almost a thousand dollars! Was there that much money left in all the wide world? Mentor was merely thoughtful. Señor Fontana had his little box under his arm and was his customary courteous self; he didn't want to hurry his guests off to bed, but he came dangerously close to a yawn. He shuddered; that would have been something never to forget!

And Barbee and Smoke Keena had drawn together, and Keena said, " Where the devil did Virginia go?"

There were two windows opening upon the patio. They had been closed a couple of hours ago, when the night grew cooler. Now both windows were open, lifted up from the bottom, as Red Barbee, who chanced to be facing that way, saw without any particular concern. Morgan was out there somewhere——

Mentor, too, saw and stared, puzzled. Then a moment later all saw and were galvanised: two men, their faces hidden by their hat brims drawn low, with bandana handkerchiefs masking them, with the noses of their guns thrust into the lamplight, commanded attention.

One of the two men said in a voice so low as to be almost toneless, scarcely above a whisper, not a voice to be recognised even though you might happen to know the speaker, " Take it easy, everybody. You don't have to get hurt unless you start something. The first man to make a wrong move is buying himself a lot on Boot Hill."

None of the men in the room moved a muscle. The front door opened and four men entered. Like their fellows at the windows, they wore their hats low, and had their faces masked with blue and red bandanas.

One of these four, a step or two ahead of the others, spoke quickly, and his voice like that of the man who had spoken through the window, was hushed, made rough in his throat, hardly above a whisper, obviously because the speaker, with his face hidden, did not want his voice to betray him. Someone, then, whom they knew?

He said, " Do the way you're told. Stay the way you are."

His head turned like an owl's pivoting on its body; he took in everyone in the room, the two at the windows, the closed doors.

" Where's Morgan?" he demanded. " He was with you."

Out of a brief silence Mentor answered him.

" Morgan?" he said. He lifted his shoulders elaborately. " If you look well, Señor, you might find him under one of your bandana masks! Just possibly—under your own!"

And Morgan heard this, every word of it, because, stepping

as softly as a cat, a gun in each hand, he had made his way into the patio and sat close behind the two men at the windows. And he said to himself, " Sure, that's Steve Question. And Steve in another minute is going to find out that Morgan is outside somewhere—and may show up all of a sudden."

The masked bandit in the room who was giving orders had been more or less leisurely at the outset, but now gave signs of an almost nervous eagerness to have a swift end made to this small affair. He ordered in that half-whisper of his that was as keen as a scythe cutting through ripe grass:

" Put down that box, Fontana! Hurry, man! You other boys empty your pockets; turn 'em out on the table. Don't make a false move, don't go for a gun——"

A gun barrel, through crashing down on a man's head with a fearful impact, makes no great noise, especially if the man has his hat on. One of the masked men at the window melted and slumped down into the shadows, and no one heard a sound except that man's companion at the next window— and he didn't hear it in time for it to do him any good. The same gun barrel came down the second time, and there were two sleeping forms in the patio, two in so deep a sleep that it promised to last a long time. And Rob Roy Morgan whipped out his own bandana and tied it over his face and pulled his hat down—and stood looking in at the window, his two guns on the sill, and spoke. He, too, kept his voice throttled down, low in his throat masking it as his face was masked. He said:

" Steve! Look out! Watch your step!"

The man who was directing things whirled toward the window, and Morgan was sure of him then.

" Shut up, you fool!" he said angrily. " Haven't you got any——"

" Better hurry, Steve! *And look out for Nancy !* "

Now, nobody except Rob Roy Morgan had ever called Smoke Keena by the absurd name of Nancy. And instantly Keena, not being anybody's fool in particular, knew that the masked figure leaning in at the window was Morgan. Keena was bewildered, yet he knew that one thing—and he gave Red Barbee a dig in the ribs with his elbow, and hoped that Barbee, hearing the name " Nancy," was as ready as he was.

Señor Fontana, his face a dead ivory-white, his lips

thinned, his eyes burning fires, stepped to the table and put down his box. In it were many fat herds of cattle. The others began turning out their pockets.

Steve Question stepped toward the table.

After that it didn't take long.

"Get 'em, Nancy! Get 'em, Barbee!" Morgan yelled and pulled both guns down on Steve Question. "Stick 'em up, Steve, or I'll drop you!"

Both Keena and Barbee went for their guns like streaked lightning. One of the masked men, the one nearest the door, took a snap shot at Red Barbee not six feet away from him and, such was his hurry, merely burned Barbee's side and enraged him, and Barbee shot the man through the throat. A shot fired point-blank at Smoke Keena was a split second late; Smoke, firing also in haste, didn't do what he had intended to do, but the results were satisfactory: he shot the man through the gun arm, close up to the shoulder. Steve Question jerked about toward Morgan at the window, but his hand was already on Fontana's box, and he was too slow.

"Get 'em up, Steve!"

Slowly Steve Question dropped the box, slowly he lifted his hands.

The fourth of the invading party made a dive for the door. Benito and Mentor, both unarmed, were on him like two mountain cats; they dragged him down, beating at him with their fists, holding his hands, grabbing at his gun. Mentor got the gun and hammered his captive over the head with it, and so the third of the marauders went to sleep.

Morgan pulled off his mask and stepped in through the window.

"Nancy," he said, "pick Steve's guns off and give 'em to Fontana and Benito." He himself yanked the bandana down from Steve's face, and so at last was sure and was gratified to be sure that it was Steve Question. He said hurriedly, "There are two of them out in the patio, and they may come alive when we don't want 'em—Benito! You go out there and keep an eye on those two; get their guns and they'll be good."

Don Benito went out on a run.

"There may be more of them," said Morgan. "They have their horses not far off, and may have left a man or two there." He closed the front door. " Let's keep our eyes open."

" Señor!" cried Señor Fontana. " If you could look down into my heart——"

" Look out a bullet don't get down there yet before we're through, Fontana," said Morgan. " Let's watch our step——"

" Like you told Steve to do!" said Keena and laughed.

There was such fury stamped on Steve Question's face, such fury burning in his eyes, as to make the man look like a mad man, like an infuriated beast in whom no urge was left but that to kill and kill and go on killing. Yet with more than one gun barrel trained on him, Steve Question, his face drained white, stood as cold and rigid as a man carved out of ice. You thought of ice with a fire somewhere inside it, consuming it.

" Better kill me now, Morgan, while you've got a chance," he said.

Few as were the shots that had been fired, they had boomed through the sleeping old home like thunderbolts, and here of a sudden came all the rest of the Fontana household, heavy-eyed, yet wild-eyed, half-awake yet terrified, in their night raiment, some with great Spanish shawls about them, all bare-footed—even to the Señora who, for once, trailed the younger ones like a belated argosy.

They saw a dead man on the floor, the man Barbee had shot through the throat, and there was a pool of blood, bright and gay in the lamplight. They saw another man lying near him, and they thought he was dead, too, the man Mentor had hammered over the head with a pistol. At first they could not even scream. They saw Steve Question and saw the look on his face, in his eyes—the Señor Question whom Mentor had brought home as a guest, and who now came as a robber!

Señora Fontana looked at Señor Fontana, standing there so grim, with a pistol in his hand, and said quietly:

" And so you have killed them, Señor?" and then fainted dead away—luckily into a chair with two or three of her daughters rushing to her.

Mentor said swiftly, speaking in Spanish, " You girls have no business here, you had better go quick. There has been an

accident——'' His eyes roved and he moistened his lips.
'' There have been some accidents, and——''

A ten-horse team couldn't have dragged them away.
Every girl had her hand to her mouth, every girl's eyes were
wide open for every horrible detail.

'' What are we going to do with these men, Señor?'' asked
Fontana, and sounded at a loss, looking to Morgan for help.

'' First,'' said Morgan, '' I'm going to do this: keep your
hands high up, Steve; no funny business. Nancy, plug him
if he starts anything, will you?''

'' Glad to,'' said Smoke Keena, and meant it.

Morgan dipped into Steve Question's pockets. He found
some loose coins, both gold and silver, and put them into a
small heap on the table. He sought further and found a small
buckskin bag; it was heavy and jungled with soft, mellow
music, and he put it on the table.

He stepped over to the dead man and rifled his pockets;
he paid like attention to the man Mentor had half-killed; all
the gleanings went to the tabletop.

'' Have you got a good little rat-proof jail in Twenty Mile?''
asked Keena.

Mentor said, '' No, Señor. No calaboosa before you get to
Glory Hole, and that's forty miles. And——''

'' Put 'em in jail,'' snorted Red Barbee, '' and they'd be
out in half a day. Better shoot 'em. Or, there's some fine old
oak trees. . . .''

'' But, Señor!'' cried Fontana aghast. '' We are not ourselves robbers and thieves! You are not going to take their
money!''

To have shot the bandits, to have hanged them, that was
one thing. But to rifle their pockets! *No, no, no, Señor!*

'' I like to play their game their way,'' said Morgan.

'' Hang 'em, Virginia?'' said Keena.

'' No. They haven't killed anybody. And anyhow, it
would upset the Fontana girls. You and Barbee go out and
find their horses; count 'em, Nancy. Come let me know.
We'll take care of things here for a few minutes.''

He stepped to the patio window and looked out; two still
forms lay where his gun barrel had put them down. Benito,
very alert, and tragic-looking, stood over them.

'' Six horses,'' Keena and Barbee reported. '' Tied out in

the clump of oaks just before you get here. We got 'em all, Virginia. There wasn't anybody with 'em."

" That's nice," said Morgan. " Let's move the deadwood outdoors, huh?"

They dragged out the dead man, with the girls shuddering and clutching one another and turning away—and peeking through their fingers. Keena whipped the dead man's bandana off while they were still in the lamplight.

" Look what you caught, Barbee," he said. " Now, I'm damned."

Barbee looked and scratched his chin and said, " Me, too, Smoke."

The dead man was Slim Pickens.

Mentor and Benito tied Steve Question's hands, and tied them skilfully and tight, at his back. " And I brought you here as a friend!" said Mentor, and showed his teeth and wasn't at all the easy-going Mentor that Steve Question had known.

Outside, Smoke Keena said, " Virginia, if he lives, Steve Question is going to kill you if it's the last thing he does."

" Me, I've been thinking," said Morgan. " It wouldn't be any fun hanging 'em, and it would be wasted time carting 'em off to somebody's jail house." He began to laugh. " Benito, bring a bucket of hot water, will you, with plenty soap in it, and a couple of razors!"

" My God!" cried Benito. " You are going to cut their throats!"

But he brought the sudsy water and a couple of razors.

Aside, Morgan spoke swiftly to Keena and Barbee. The two stared at him for a moment then slapped their thighs and laughed and said, almost in the same words, that Rob Roy Morgan had the one glittering hunch of all the hunches.

Morgan grinned. " Sure," he said. " We'll let 'em go. Where can they go? As far as I know, the nearest place is Twenty Mile. We won't start 'em until daybreak, either! Can you see 'em riding into Twenty Mile, or any other place?" And both Keena and Barbee in high delight, beat him on the back until his shoulders sagged.

And this is what they did. With Señor Fontana and his two sons looking on and beginning to smile, with the women-folk commanded to remain within doors and out of sight—

and more or less obeying—they stripped every rag of clothes off their five living bandits. The two in the patio had been dragged along and unmasked, and had finally regained a headachey consciousness; one of them was Kilgore, the other Baldy Bates. Naked as babes newly born, they were now a crew to inspire awe. Without the benefit of rakish hats and tallheeled boots and vivid shirts, they resolved themselves into just naked human beings, and there were bow-legs and a fair set of knock-knees and two or three fat bellies.

" It's a nice warm night, boys," Rob Roy Morgan told them. " You won't catch cold, and maybe you can get yourselves some more clothes to-morrow. But you better start figuring right away where you're going to get 'em, and who's going in first to ask for 'em, and what you're going to use for money. Clothes, easy, sure; it won't take you long. But how long to grow a crop of hair!"

Steve Question for one, purple even in the moonlight with rage which seemed about to explode and blow him to pieces, strove to bite the hand that shaved his head.

Every man of them got a rough and ready head shave.

" How long's it take to grow a head of hair, Señor?" Smoke Keena asked politely of Señor Fontana. And Señor Fontana, for the first and last recorded time, snorted, and put his hand over his mouth so that his snort, divided between his fingers, sounded like a chorus of snorts. The truth is that Señor Fontana had been young once himself.

" They look kind of funny like that, don't they?" said Keena, appraising them critically.

" I was wondering," said Morgan, " what we're going to do with their saddles and bridles? They'll need their horses, poor devils, because it's long walking any place from here, especially barefooted. But take a look at those saddles and bridles. They're too good to throw away. Their boots, too; shucks, there's more'n one pair cost thirty-forty dollars. The hats ain't much, but there's some nice-looking shirts there, just needing soap and water and sunshine. Señor Fontana has a lot of Indians on his *rancho*; maybe they could use all this truck."

One saddle alone they did not remove; to it they lashed dead Slim Pickens to make the return journey with his new companions. As the new day flowered, the five naked, head-shaven bad men with their dead rode away from Hacienda Fontana.

" Me," muttered Smoke Keena, " I'm never going back to Twenty Mile as long as I live. I got a feeling in my bones it ain't going to be healthy."

Of course Red Barbee had slipped away to tell Barbara all that had happened—and Barbara rushed into Aldegonda's arms, and told her—and all the Fontana señoritas clustered about the two, and were told—and shrieked with unmaidenly laughter. And then they looked at their mamma, and lowered their eyes demurely and were ashamed—or should have been——

And Morgan in the dawn, while the others went for coffee, slipped away and went back to the bridge under the sycamore, and looked again up toward the waterfall.

And he saw what he had so little expectation of seeing, yet a thing that he meant to go on seeking until he found it; standing on the black rock by the mountain pool, looking down toward the house, was the girl of the gold pieces, the girl of the stolen blue dress and memorable cake.

Morgan crouched low among the shadows and moved with all possible stealth and silence up the slope toward her.

CHAPTER FIFTEEN

MORGAN realised that her attention was centred on the Fontana home; doubtless she had seen something of all that had just happened, perhaps had heard the pistol shots to begin with, but couldn't possibly know what it was all about. Now, if ever, he thought, was his one slim chance to take her by surprise. And he knew with absolute certainty that he would never be satisfied until he found out for himself, with his own eyes and ears, how much truth there was in all the tales, wild tales, he had heard of her—the Golden Tiger Lily, the White Tiger Lily, the Mountain Lily, just the Wild Girl. For one thing he was dead sure that she was not just a spirit, but a flesh-and-blood girl. Spirits, he felt instinctively without any first-hand knowledge, did not prowl about raiding a robber's cache, making themselves necklaces of gold twenties, stealing

K

blue dresses—and hurling messy cakes into people's faces, and then laughing at them.

He stole closer but only inch by inch, always careful to keep a screen of bushes, of leaves, between her and himself, so that at times he almost lost sight of her but never for more than a couple of seconds. He knew that if she saw him and ran, she could run up the slopes as she had before, not down into the open valley. So he kept close to the creek overflowing the pool, ready at any instant to leap across it and be after her the moment she broke into flight.

But this time, so did she concentrate her interest upon the Casa Fontana and what she could make of the goings-on down there, that she had no thought of being spied upon. And presently, with the day advancing, she began to make her retreat. She did so swiftly enough, but in no wild haste; it merely seemed that she couldn't move slowly even had she tried.

As he had expected, she turned upslope, going in the general direction she had taken before, and Morgan followed her with all caution, contented with barely keeping her in sight; he knew full well that if he called out to her, if he made a headlong dash in pursuit of her, she would vanish in the nearest thicket the way a deer or any wild woods thing vanishes, and there'd be no finding her. As it was, he was afraid at every moment of losing her.

She went swiftly and as far as he could see she left no track, no small sign of her passing. She trod lightly on the ground where it was hard and bare; where there was wiry mountain grass there were also stones, and she stepped from one stone to another, sometimes springing sure-footedly from stone to stone. He didn't see a twig that she had broken, not so much as a blade of grass crushed under foot.

Two or three times she stopped and turned and looked back, and he could see how she poised her head, listening, and he thought even that she put her head back to sniff at the little morning breeze as though she could smell pursuit when eyes and ears failed her; and each time her slim body was so still in the semi-dark, all but hidden entirely by a pine tree or a thicket which sheltered her, that it was hard for him to be sure that she was still there, that the wilderness had not quite absorbed her; and each time he himself crouched low and still in whatever shelter was at hand until at last she moved on again.

Straight ahead of her he glimpsed through the sparse scattering of timber a low cliff that was like a long rock wall; not over fifteen or twenty feet high, still it rose so steeply as to be virtually perpendicular, and it even seemed to beetle outward at the top, and he wondered which way she would turn now, right or left, to skirt this obstacle.

She did neither. She went straight up the side of the cliff as one might have run up a flight of stairs. And at the top she disappeared, running.

He ran, too, to the spot where she had climbed up. She had found handhold and toe grip, and where a girl could go Rob Roy Morgan swore he could follow. He saw a crevice here and a knobby handhold there, and started clawing his way up. But he could make no such easy work of it as she had done; for one thing, his boots hampered him so that, coming close to falling once, he wished he had had sense enough to pull them off. What she had done so easily and so swiftly required vastly more effort on his part and a considerably longer time, but in the end he clawed his way to the top. He found himself upon the rim of a strip of almost level tableland, grassy and dotted with pines and cedars. And he was barely in time to see the girl hurrying along, no longer turning to look back. And he witnessed another trick of hers, employed in making sure that she left behind her no sign of the way she had passed.

She caught the low limb of a pine in one hand, swung forward, caught another limb, swung again, caught a third limb, swung once more and dropped lightly to a flat rock. From this she leaped to another rock, from it, landing lightly, to the brown, dead leaves that carpeted the ground there. Then she sped on, running again.

" No man on earth could ever track her down," he told himself. " If once I let her out of my sight for as much as two minutes, good-bye."

She crossed the plateau, then skirted the steepening, rocky slope of the mountain that was in places stark and bare, at others thinly timbered. Her way led toward the far end of the plateau where a dusky, woodsy ravine made a dark slash across the bit of level land, and the air was filled with a pleasant murmur of running water. She went down into the ravine, headed upstream. And he followed, and began to draw closer, fearful of having her melt out of his sight in the dim light where the creek, so thick were the interlacing leaves overhead, seemed to be winding through a tortuous tunnel, where the ferns stood as high as her head.

And then the thing he had feared all along happened. She disappeared, simply vanished. Where there was a bend in the creek, where the leafy tunnel was darkest and the ferns stood tallest, she had for a moment passed out of sight. He hurried on to the bend in the creek—and there was no sign of her. And where on earth she could have gone in that brief time baffled him. Here he had come close to the upper end of the ravine, and here its walls were steep, and ahead were the cliffs, no low barrier of rock such as she had scaled a little while ago, but sheer and naked cliffs lifted a dizzy two or three hundred feet above the timber.

He paused briefly in a frowning uncertainty which swiftly became bewilderment. At first his eyes swept along the cliffs; not up there, for he would have seen her instantly. He moved forward again, eagle-eyed for some sign of her; here the ferns stood so thick and the grass and tall-stemmed flowers made so dense a pigmy forest, that not even she could have made a way through them without leaving her trail behind her.

He sought her sedulously a good half-hour, looking even as he thought, in all the impossible places, without coming upon so much as a broken blade of grass or a bruised fern or the hint of a track in what small patches of damp sand were at the sides of the stream. It was as though she had taken wings here and soared aloft. He gazed upward once more and thus, by the merest chance, made his startling discovery.

There was a straight-boled young poplar tree, thick with gently-stirring velvet-green leaves, a tree some thirty or forty feet high, standing close to the base of the cliff, so close that its branches brushed the rock in many places, and the largest ones, lowest down, had been forced to fan out on both sides of the trunk. And Rob Roy Morgan, with that fleeting upward glance of his saw something that you don't usually see on a poplar tree: it was a bright red blossom!

So that was it! No such blossom ever grew on a poplar,

but there were flowers like it all along the creek! This one wasn't even wilted yet. And he remembered how at the bridge, the night of the blue dress and the unforgettable cake, she had worn flowers in her hair!

He started climbing the tree; he caught a lower limb and swung up and found the climbing so easy that he could fancy her going up like a cat. How she could find any place, high up among the thickest of leaves, to hide, he couldn't make out, yet he began to think this girl could do just about anything she wanted to do and put her heart in. He climbed higher, still higher, seeking her all the while, keenly aware of the fact that she might be perched only a few feet above him, that she might have a rock in her hand ready to drop on his head; whereas the cake had been bad enough, a sizable stone right now was even less pleasant to think about. He kept on climbing; he got his feet on the limb where the red flower dangled; he leaned this way and that as far as he could without falling, peering into every leafy shadow even though it was not big enough to hide your hat in. And so he made sure that the girl was not in the tree.

" How the devil did that flower get up here?" Could she have climbed up the cliff somewhere after all, and had the flower fallen from up there?

He kept on climbing, to get a better look at the face of rock from this vantage. And so, when he had gone just about as high as he could, with the top of the tree beginning to sway with his weight, the mystery was explained. She had come this way, she had climbed this high—and then had kept right on going! Not sprouting wings and sailing heavenward. Simpler than that, as simple as climbing a ladder and stepping from it to a porch—provided only that you didn't go light-headed with dizziness, and were sure-footed along a very narrow path!

For there was a ledge along the cliff, not to be suspected from the ground below, and to the left as you faced it, it petered out within a dozen feet, but on the right it ran with a very slight upward slant for at least twice that distance; beyond that there was no telling from where Morgan clung to his perch, but the narrow, natural rock-trail led at least as far as what appeared to be a break or fissure in the face of the cliff.

Well, that was the way she had gone and that was the way he would follow! There was a moment of breathlessness as he leaned in toward the cliff and got a handhold—and pulled himself over, flat against the cliff and got his feet planted on the ledge. The treetop swayed back away from him; he stood rigidly where he was a moment, gripping with both hands.

Once he looked straight down; he made a face and shook his head and didn't look down again. He began making his way along, inching slowly with shuffling feet, clinging to what cracks or knobs or whatever handholds he could find, and so at last came to the fissure he had seen where his ledge was lost to sight, and found that the fissure was a great split in the rocks; he could look straight up and see the blue sky, an almost purple-blue from here. That rift in the rock, not wider than ten or fifteen feet at the top so high overhead, narrower where he stood, was no perfectly straight affair but angled to right and left so that at times he could see only a few feet ahead; it was floored with stones and harsh soil that had dribbled down from above during the ages, and sparse dry grass and harsh, arid-looking clumps of low brush grew precariously, and once in a while there was a tortured dwarf cedar.

He had never seen, never heard of, a mountain fairly cleft in two like this one and not only at every step did he wonder whether he was at last coming up with the elusive girl, but he wondered too into what strange sort of region this unique pathway led. He turned a sharp angle and came into a sort of pocket the size of an ordinary room but roughly rounded, where the accumulated soil seemed deeper and where there grew a clump of cedars higher than his head. He moved slowly through the cedars; no girl lurking here; and again followed the jagged fissure, narrower than before, filled with rumbled boulders. The way narrowed at places so that there was scarcely more room than he required for passage; at several spots, looking upward, he saw enormous blocks of stone that had dropped into this abyss from the clifftops, that had jammed between the walls of rock high overhead, that seemed ready at any moment, ready to break free and come crashing down. And then he came upon, with startling abruptness, a view that was like a glimpse of some secret, hidden corner of an earthly paradise. He had never seen

Yosemite Valley; very few men had. Had he ever seen it he would have thought of it now. Here was a tiny valley all ringed about with precipitous walls and spires and towers of granite that might almost have been the miniature model of the Yosemite.

Its grassy, flower-studded floor was only some four or six acres in extent; there was a scattering of lofty trees, both pines and cedars; he glimpsed through the trees two white-lacey waterfalls slithering down almost perpendicularly in the still air, and glimpsed a little winding creek—how the water escaped from this place without forming a lake he could not tell. There were just a couple of fern and flower-fringed pools . . .

" She's got to be in here somewhere! I don't believe there's any way out except the way I came!" And, man, what a hide-out!

All this he saw through an eerie twilight that was almost like a faintly greenish haze, for as yet no direct shaft of sunlight penetrated here; the sun would have to be high for that. And he picked other details: there were birds; a flock of mountain quail picked and fluffed at the edge of a thicket, and there were plump robins, and he heard the challenging call of a crested blue jay high in a pine—and he saw a small herd of deer browsing, and now and then a little bluish brush rabbit—and though it might be simple enough for the birds to make their way here, how about deer and rabbits?

And then, as his eyes roved everywhere, he discovered the girl.

She lay on a blanket or rug or something of the sort spread on the grass near the rim of one of the pools, the one near the centre of the little, cliff-locked valley. She lay very still, one arm thrown up over her face, the other lax at her side, fast asleep, as he judged.

And asleep she was. He found his way easily down to the floor of her valley, having but a few feet to descend. He walked as quietly as he could; he scarcely made the slightest sound. The deer lifted their heads and gazed at him; they seemed curious, mildly interested, not in the least afraid. They shook their short tails and paid him no further attention.

To take her utterly unawares was more than he had dreamed of, but he saw the wisdom of it if the thing were at all possible, as now it seemed to be. He had seen her in action when Steve Question got his hands on her! And if she jumped up and ran now—she might even have a gun handy; if she pilfered dresses and cakes and a highwayman's gold, why not weapons?

At last he stood over her, and still she slept! He looked down at her, strangely moved. For one thing, she was the loveliest girl he had ever seen. Her lashes lay long on her golden-brown cheeks; he wondered what colour her eyes were! She was slender and sweetly formed and gently rounded. Clad as when he had seen her before, in a scanty bit of a dress of deerskin, arms and legs were bare, her small feet were bare, too, as she had kicked off the pair of moccasins which lay near them. Her hair was in disorder, long sun-kissed bronze hair that partly framed her face, and in loose strands lay across her shoulder and breast.

When she awoke it was not as most human beings awake, gradually, with perhaps a yawn and a stretch and a twilight moment that hovers along the borders of sleeping and waking. She awoke in a flash, wide awake on the instant, her eyes wide open and alert; she awoke as wild forest things, dependent for their lives upon this instantaneous co-ordination of senses and muscles. She saw a man standing over her and leaped to her feet as though she had been shot erect by the sudden release of a single, powerful spring, and made her instant, wild bid for flight.

But he stood too close to her, he was too watchful, his legs were longer and he, too, was quick. As she started he leaped after her and his hand locked tight about her arm.

There was that naked knife hanging at her belt; he had not forgotten that! As her free hand flashed downward to it, he caught her wrist.

She struggled desperately, without a word but making little moaning sounds; she clawed at him, or strove to, but his greater strength held her helpless, and at that he was afraid several times that she was going to squirm and wriggle and writhe out of his grasp. For she had twice the strength he had supposed any girl ever to have.

She tried to bite him. Her mouth at which he had been looking just now while she was asleep, which had been so soft, almost smiling, was a different affair now. Her teeth were bared; they were small and white and he fancied they might prove mighty sharp. She did her level best to sink them into his arm.

He held her firmly, so firmly that he knew he must be hurting her. Then all of a sudden, from being a small fury, she grew perfectly relaxed and let her entire body grow limp. But Rob Roy Morgan, fearing a trick, kept his same grip on her. " I am going to take your knife away," he told her. " But you've got to understand that I am not going to hurt you. I want us to have a talk. Then after a while I will let you go, and I'll go, too. Now don't try any tricks while I get your knife."

He would have to free one of her hands—not the hand nearest the knife! Even the other hand? How that girl could writhe and twist, and how she could strike as swiftly as a snake! It remained that she was a small bit of a girl, that he was far taller, bigger, stronger. With an unexpected movement as quick as her own, he whipped her around so that her back was to him, and holding her arms behind her he snatched at her knife. It dangled from her belt in the noose of a slight thong; one jerk and the thong snapped and she was unarmed. He threw the weapon into the heart of the nearest clump of brush, and now he freed one of her hands, content with having one wrist imprisoned in his grip that ringed it like a bracelet of steel.

" Now," he said, " are you going to be good?"

And now for the first time he had his long deep look into her eyes. And those eyes of hers looked back up into his, wide open, softly bright, alert and watchful, as steady as his own. To him they were like still, shaded forest pools, their depth a mystery. They were large, intelligent eyes, softly luminous and beautiful. But there was no reading the thoughts hidden in their limpid depths. She was startled, frightened, angry—yes. Quick instinctive reactions. But she was thinking—thinking—thinking, and he could have no faintest inkling of her thoughts.

At last, for the first time she spoke, and even her manner of speech was distinctly her own, unlike that of any human being he had ever heard. Her voice was soft and low and musical, a singing voice. But her words sounded strange in his ear; queerly accented, oddly intoned. She spoke very slowly, spacing her words, a small frown of concentration puckering her brow from which, with a backward sweep of her free hand, she had swept her hair.

He watched her mouth, fascinated. Often her lips would shape the next word and would remain steady and soundless for a second or two, quite as though she almost, yet not quite, knew what the next word was to be or as though she had formed it within her consciousness yet remained uncertain exactly how to utter it. She might have been a foreigner but recently learning the language, no American girl at all. There was something haunting and charming in her inflections.

" Why," thought Morgan, of a sudden realising, " she never talks to anybody! She never has!"

She said, " You come—after me—to kill me! Oh, I know! . . . You are bad—every man is bad. . . . They kill. . . . But you can't kill me! I am no girl—like other girls! . . . I am a Spirit Girl! . . . And I can—kill you! I can let you take my knife—everything—and I can kill you easy!"

He stared at her: She struck him as believing herself every word she had said! Was the girl mad, then? Madness would explain a lot, her living alone in the wilderness as she did, a lot of the wild tales men told of her, far and wide.

" I don't want to have to hold you like this all day," he said. " But I don't want you to run away until we have a talk!"

Her eyes looked bigger than ever, and innocent. Too innocent by far, thought Morgan, as she said:

" I will not run. I make you my—my—promise."

He shook his head. A promise from her?

" No. But if you will go back to your rug and sit down, I'll stand close to you, so you'll have to scramble up before you can get started, and I'll nab you."

" Oh!" she said. And then, " I will do that. You hurt me."

She dropped down on her rug—it was a black bearskin—and curled up, making him think of a kitten. She tossed her hair back again, looked up at him where he stood watchfully, leaned on her elbow and appeared utterly relaxed, not in the least like a captive thing alert for the first slim chance to be once more in full flight.

And so he watched her all the more narrowly.

CHAPTER SIXTEEN

ROB ROY MORGAN rolled himself one of his slow, meditative cigarettes.

She lay motionless, looking up at him. She watched his slightest gesture, the pouring of the tobacco into the trough of his brown paper, the process of rolling, the sweep of a match along his thigh, the lighting, the first dribble of smoke from his lips. Her big, cool, deep eyes studied him with the frankness of a child of three, with detached interest. She took him in, slowly so as to miss no detail, from the crown of his hat to the soles and heels of his boots. He knew when she was concerned with his eyes, his nose, his mouth, his hands, the length of his lean body.

It made him vaguely uncomfortable to have her staring at him like that. He wished she would smile. He had heard her laugh—in mockery. He wondered whether she knew how to smile!

Well, anyhow she could talk! There had been a time when he had wondered about that!

And he was doggoned if he was to stand up all day. He squatted on his heels, nicely balanced, so close that he could have put out his hand and touched her.

" You've got a mighty pretty place here," he said. " It's the nicest I ever saw."

She listened to him, watching his eyes or the movement of his lips. Her expression did not change.

" I noticed your deer, the rabbits, too. They seem mighty tame."

She listened. That was all. He could tell that she listened, and that was all he could tell. He said:

" A man can't help wondering how the deer got in here. Even the rabbits. I saw a couple of tree squirrels; they and the birds could have made it; seems funny, though."

She continued to listen. And he had heard it said that there was no woman who could hold her tongue!

But then, he had just been telling her things; no answer

had been necessary if she felt taciturn. How about a direct question or two?

"I keep thinking about those deer," he said. "A deer can't climb a tree. How did they get here?"

She remained silent so long, studying him intently, he began to think she'd never speak. Finally:

"I brought them," she answered.

"You brought those deer in here? You tucked a deer under your arm—after you had caught it!—climbed a tree with it, and——" He snorted. Then he bethought him to tack on a question, trying to elicit any response from her without a question was like fishing without a hook. And by the way, a question mark did look like a hook, didn't it? So he asked, "That's the way you did it—is it? *Or is there some other way to get in here?*"

"I brought just two—the mamma and papa deer. I brought them when they were baby things."

"The rabbits, too, I suppose?"

She nodded.

"Maybe some of the birds?"

She nodded. Her expression had not once changed. She was still, as far as anything her eyes told him, the frankly interested child of three.

"Well," he said, "maybe. After all, if there was another, an easy way in, this would be a happy hunting ground for a timber wolf or a mountain lion. I haven't seen anything of that brand around."

No direct question, no answer.

"How did you catch your wild animals to start your menagerie?" he asked. "Run 'em down?"

Her brow, with already the shadow of a frown of concentration, puckered further.

"Men-ag-erie? she repeated. "What is that?"

He told her. Then she said:

"I make traps."

He came back to that other question: "Is there some other way to get into this valley?"

She was a long time making her reply. She stirred slightly, and instantly his muscles were corded, ready to snap into action. But she was merely reaching for a blade of grass; she put it between her strong, white teeth and nibbled at it. And he knew that she was just setting in the balance the two answers, one of which she would give him. She was trying to figure whether one answer would be more to her advantage somehow than the other. Whether she would give him the truth or a barefaced lie would depend on her judgment of values. He gave her time. After a while:

" There is only one way," she said.

" You are not very fond of talking, are you?"

" Sometimes."

" Who do you talk to?"

" To my own self. And to all my friends."

" You don't think I am a friend?"

" No."

" Who are the friends you talk to?"

" My deer and my rabbits and my squirrels and my different kinds of birds and my flowers."

" They listen? And understand? And they talk back to you?"

" Yes." It was as though she had gone on to say, " Of course! What do you suppose?"

He scratched his jaw and, like her, plucked a blade of grass and bit at it. So she was a Spirit Girl, was she? And she could commune with wild things, flowers included, and of course butterflies and bees; trout even, maybe! And she really believed all that? He couldn't tell. But he believed that she did believe!

" Then you never talk with other people? Girls like yourself, men and women?"

For the first time and, quickly, she responded to an observation he had made that was not a direct question. She said:

" No other girls are like me!"

He had to grin at her then, that good-humoured, humorous, infectious grin of Rob Roy Morgan's. Her face lost none of its gravity.

" I don't even know your name," he said. " Mine's Morgan, Rob Roy Morgan." Then his grin gave way before his chuckling laugh. " Does no good, just saying things to you, does it? What is your name?"

" I have many names. I give myself new names—when I think about them—and like them."

" What name do you like best?"

" My very first name."

" What is it?"

" It's Honey."

" Honey? Yes, that's a nice name. Who gave it to you?"

" They—did."

" They? Who?"

She didn't answer immediately. She didn't look at him now, but lowered her head, let her lashes lower too, until they lay close to her cheeks; he couldn't be sure, but possibly her eyes were closed.

He said again, " Who?"

" My mamma and my papa," she said, and her voice was very low.

" Where are they now?" he asked.

She gave no hint of having heard. He asked again more insistently: " Where are they now? Tell me."

" They—they——"

" You mean they're—dead?" said Morgan quite gently.

She nodded. He saw that her long lashes seemed suddenly trimmed with pearls. But he had set out to know all about her and asked her:

" What happened? How long ago?"

She shook her head. She did not want to talk about it. And still, deep down in her heart, perhaps she did! And perhaps she needed to talk about it. Rob Roy Morgan could not know that she had never spoken to any human being of the horror, the tragedy, the thing which set her all alone in a wilderness world, which had shaped her strange life.

At any rate, in the end she told him. And so almost in a flash he came to understand a great deal about this Robinson Crusoe of a girl named " Honey "!

She told him how happy they had been in their big wagons, coming west, her mother and father and big brother, and some friends, strong men with big black beards, and other children, too, two little girls not much older than she was, and some good boys, and they had some horses, and some cows, too, and even her mamma had brought a cage with some chickens in it, and it was all fun for the little children, but the big folks had to work pretty hard and didn't have enough to eat sometimes, and all the time were afraid of the

Indians. Oh, that was so long ago! And there had been more Indians then, bad ones, and they were ugly and had painted faces. Oh, not like these Indians here, they were tame Indians and fat and lazy and not so bad. And it was far, very far from here.

And finally she told, her voice hushed almost to a whisper, of the day when she had slipped out of camp without telling anybody, because she knew they would not let her go, and she had seen some pretty flowers along the creek where they had made their camp, and she kept going, farther and farther, picking flowers, running ahead for the always prettier one farther along. And she got tired and lay in the grass and rested, and maybe she went to sleep because all of a sudden she saw that it was late afternoon and she was hungry and her pretty flowers were beginning to wilt, so she gathered them up and started back . . .

And she heard the guns going bang, bang, bang! And she heard men yelling and she heard women and children scream, and she heard the Indians' terrible yells, too, but she kept on running, keeping close to the creek. And she saw what was happening, and she hid in the willows and peeked out and nearly died right then. There were a lot of Indians, and there were two bad white men with them. The white men were worse than the Indians because they just laughed. She saw her father shoot two or three Indians, and then when his gun was empty he killed another with a knife. She saw her father shot down—she hid her eyes, she looked again just at the wrong time—they slaughtered her mother and the big men with the black beards—the little girls tried to run—an Indian ran after them and—all the time the white men, sitting on their horses, were watching and laughing—yes, they shot, too, a few times. She saw the Indians taking scalps—she couldn't move; she lay in the willows a long time—she thought she was dying—she thought afterwards that she did die—when she knew anything again it was getting dark and the Indians and the bad white men were gone—and she didn't know what to do. After a long time she crept on toward camp—she called to her mamma and papa, and they didn't answer and she knew they never would—and she crept a little bit closer and . . .

She screamed and ran and ran and ran.

She was afraid of everything—of wild animals—most of all, men. Indians, even white men, because she remembered the two white men with the Indians. She hid, day and night. Summer had started. She was always hungry. She grew as skinny as a starving dog they had found one time. When she could find them she ate berries that were half-green and sometimes they made her sick. She ate watercress. She drank lots and lots of water, because she had gone higher up in the hills where there were forests and creeks. And her dress got torn, and so did her stockings, and her shoes began to wear out, and she cried all the time. She heard a man singing, a terrible song in a terrible voice. She knew now that he was drunk; she had seen drunk men since. And with his voice came a little breeze through the trees—and she smelled something good cooking, so good that the smell tied her tummy all up in knots. She was more afraid of the man than she would have been of a bear or a wolf or a lion or any wild animal— cowering down where she hid, she kept on sniffing.

After a while she saw smoke—she crept a little closer, crawling like a snake. She saw the little house through the trees, a little house of logs and rocks and dirt. She saw the man come out—he carried a gun and some steel traps, and he went away, not toward her, the other way. She waited a long time. She didn't hear any one else. She kept on smelling the good things to eat.

She crept close to the little house and peeked in through a crack between the logs. There was no one there. There was a stove, and a pot and pan on it.

She went in, leaving the door wide open, watching, listening. There was a pot, still warm, half-full of a stew that had meat and potatoes and other things. There was a pan of biscuits.

She took the pot of stew and the biscuits—she ran again, faster than ever before—not the way the man had gone—the other way.

Rob Roy Morgan held himself to be a hard man, tough like saddle leather; more than once his eyes were moistly bright. More than once his hands knotted into fists.

Through the years—surviving that first dreadful year because she had started with the beginning of the long summer, because she was the healthy, vigorous, courageous daughter of hardy pioneers. Hunger and cold—fear, too—going in rags, tatters, barefooted, at last almost naked. Learning every day. Learning to pass through the woods without leaving a trace of her passing—to find whatever food there was—to rob a lonely cabin now and then. Food, then, the most delicious food. And a knife—a blanket which she used both as blanket and as a dress. A gun, a little hatchet, another knife which she liked better. A cooking pot not too big. Matches.

Travelling with the sun, instinctively moving southward as the weather grew cold. Travelling south and southwest. Following the setting sun. Killing her first deer, and crying over it and cooking and eating some of it, and taking its skin for a better dress, and making moccasins. Oh, with the passing of the years!

Tiny backwoods settlements. Lights at night, candles or smoky lamps at the windows. Peering in at people's faces. Men, mostly, terrible men. She saw them quarrel and fight; she saw a man kill another with an axe and rob him of something he had in a buckskin pouch—gold, that's what it was.

Living alone through the summers and falls and winters and springs, happiest when spring was in the air. Always hiding, often bitterly cold, nearly always hungry—always afraid. Drawn to lonely camp-fires—afraid, yet drawn close in the dark—lying hidden, watching dark figures moving against the tongues of flame and the wavering shadow-shapes of wood smoke. Times of unutterable loneliness—then of some greater fear.

Learning how most successfully to commit her small robberies—as stealthy as any other wild forest thing that crept close to human beings at night when the men, and once in a great while women and children, were asleep. Cooked food whenever she could get it—another gun later, with cartridges—a strip of canvas, a bit of cloth. Listening to people talk.

Two or three times during a year or two, listening to people talk—*about her*! Some of them were afraid of her, too! They said the Indians were afraid! They said she was not like other girls, not like other men and women—she was a Spirit! She had been seen once or twice, or they lied about her—a man had seen her standing on a high place when the sun was just

L

coming up—he said she was a Spirit, too beautiful for any girl, and that she wore stars in her hair. And once some Indians saw her in the moonlight—she was on a high place, she loved the high places—and the Indians had run away before she could run! They were afraid! But one of them came a little way back—on an Indian blanket he left a pile of things for her—a bow and arrows, some dried meat, some parched corn—a great armful of fresh flowers! They, too, knew her for a Spirit; she was a goddess and they were afraid.

Still always moving westward until she had found this place and had made it the home she loved best. Oh, she had other homes, far and very far away, and sometimes went to them, but this one she liked best.

Only now she would have to go away! If Rob Roy Morgan did not kill her—and he had said that he would not—she would go far away. Her voice grew husky and she broke off.

He saw her breast rise to a long, sobbing intake of breath.

He asked her how she had found her secret valley in the first place; she answered him in a voice that was all but lifeless, her thoughts elsewhere and her present grief heavy upon her: She had seen a tree-squirrel run up the poplar tree, out to the end of a limb, and leap to the cliff, and disappear. She had waited a long time to see the squirrel again. When it did not come back, her curiosity led her to climb after it, and so her discovery was made.

" It was mine—all mine! " she said sorrowfully.

" It is yours right now! It is always going to be yours! "

She did not look at him; she shook her head slowly.

" I will have to go again—I will have to hide in one of my other far away homes."

" No! You are never to run and hide any more! "

He spoke so emphatically that he sounded stern. Again she was afraid of him.

Morgan stood up. " Suppose we take a little walk through this Garden of Eden of yours," he suggested.

She was quick to rise. " Garden of Eden?" she repeated after him, questioning him with her brows arching upward.

" You don't half know how much like Eve you are, do you? That would be another good name for you, just Eve." And he explained about the earthly paradise the best he could, which was quite sufficient unto the occasion.

" Oh!" Her forehead wrinkled, her eyes narrowed as she made her effort to see back through the mists of wavering half-memories. Her mother had told her so many stories, and even when she had listened so eagerly to them they remained a jumble of Bible tales and fairy stories. She could almost remember—there was an old, battered book—pictures in it, too; they must have been coloured pictures, else her childish imagination had coloured them——

" Yes!" she exclaimed. " There was a garden—like mine! And Eve lived there and—*and there was a big, bad snake!*"

" You've got it! A snake in every garden, they say."

" And you—in mine!"

" Dammit," snapped Rob Roy Morgan, " I'm no snake in anybody's garden. Now, let's have a look round. Only don't try to run away. If I have to grab you again I'll hold on to you. I'll grab you by the hair."

" I won't run," she promised, and sounded very docile, so docile that he watched her all the more narrowly and never let her beyond the sweep of his long arm. " Let's walk down your little creek, huh? I want to see how it ever gets out of here."

" It goes down a hole."

They followed the creek's merry, indolent way across the grassy floor of her park-like bit of valley until they came under the cliffs at the western rim, and Morgan saw how the water fanned out against the rocks, and found its escape. Any sign of a hole he did not see, and said so.

" I poked with a long stick," she told him. " There is a long, flat hole where the water squeezes through."

They strolled back across her small sylvan estate, and about its centre he came upon a surprise which, by now, might have been expected but which startled him. It was a small, fenced-in vegetable garden where grew corn, potatoes, squashes and he did not know what else. But he did know where the seed came from—without asking! Some lonely cabin raided by night for a potato, a handful of corn!

" Your full name ought to be Eve Crusoe!" he told her, and laughed.

He had to explain; she became greatly interested in Robinson Crusoe. She had heard about parrots, she did not know where. Maybe her mother had told her; she might have overheard the scrap of information when lying hidden by some pioneer camp where men told many tall tales and even true ones.

" It would be nice to have a bird talk to me," she said wistfully.

It was a crazy sort of fence with poles thrust down into the deep, moist, fat soil, with a weaving of willow withes between them, the willow work resembling a basket weave at the bottom. Thus she kept the deer out and some of her rabbits; the birds and squirrels didn't do much harm, and she chased them out and scolded them when she caught them interloping.

" I notice your creek and pools are full of trout," Morgan said as they moved along. " Were they here? Or did you bring them in too?"

" I caught them outside and brought them here. In my bucket."

" I'd love to see you climbing a tree with a bucket full of trout! And no use asking where you got the bucket, is there? In somebody's cabin?"

She nodded. Of course. Other people went to stores; she knew that. She went to their cabins.

Gradually the light was losing its eerie, greenish tinge as the sun climbed higher. Already the tallest of the western cliff-tops were bathed in the warm yellow sunlight, and here and there the light seemed to spill over and trickle down the faces of the cliffs. Soon the direct shafts of the sun would penetrate the little valley, filling it like a bowl with golden light, and, with the deep blue of the sky overhead, would bring about its daily, ineffable loveliness.

Small wonder this was " Honey Eve Crusoe's " best-loved home.

A young doe came up and nuzzled her, wanting to be scratched behind the ears. A rabbit sitting up directly in front of her refused to budge and she walked around it. They passed through the band of quail; none of the birds ran or flew; they moved to right and left and went on about their business. A quail hen was trying to take a dust bath.

" I know where your house is, now," said Morgan.

" How do you know? You can't see it, can you?"

" I see two rose bushes! I'll bet a man they're in front of your door."

And so they were, a red and a yellow rose, both in bloom —and he knew where the slips had come from! There were roses like that about the Fontana home.

The house itself—call it a house—so blended with its environment and was so sheltered that it was hard to make it out until you came very close. About it was a young grove of aspens, and at its back was the cliff. The small structure, casually irregular in shape and not much taller than the girl herself, had walls of upright poles set in the ground, other poles stretched horizontally, of willow withes interwoven somewhat after the fashion of portions of her garden fence, and a steeply sloping roof of the same order heaped high with the flat branches of firs and over-topped with ferns.

" Are you going to let me look inside?"

She didn't answer but went straight on to the door, between the two rose bushes as he had judged, and her glance as much as said, " You'll do what you want to anyhow."

He looked into a room which she had made amazingly cosy and homey. On the bare ground she had made a carpet of ferns a couple of inches thick, and on this carpet were two bearskins. There was a table of sorts in the middle of the room, contrived like fence and building of poles. There was even what went for a fireplace, flat rocks chinked with clay and a hole in the roof, like an Indian's chimney. There was a dresser—anyhow a sort of shelf with a small mirror over it and a comb and brush on it. In a corner hung two or three dresses—dresses like the ones you got in stores! There was a hatchet and there were a couple of pots and pans—two rifles in another corner—and a guitar with ribbons!

Rob Roy Morgan whistled softly. He thought, " Those poor Indians of Fontana's that he blames for swiping some little something once in a while!"

He said, " I'm sorry you had to waste that nice cake on me! I bet you hated to let it go! Well, I still have the little blue dress; I'll save it for you. I'll bring it along the next time I come out to see you."

She looked at him strangely; she didn't say anything.

He saw her bed, a bunk against the wall, with real blankets on it.

And he saw a book on her table! It was open. He glimpsed a coloured picture, a bright picture of a seacoast village, all white walls and red roofs and blue sea trimmed with white lace on the beach, and white sails against the sky. What on earth did she want with a book? Where had she ever been to school—except to the great school of the wilderness?

She was quick to catch a thought.

" I can almost read. I am learning. Someday I will learn to write, too. And I draw pretty pictures."

Her schooling? Her mother, pioneer woman that she was, was always reading whenever she had the chance. She had even taught her little daughter things like c-a-t.

" And you play the guitar?"

" I make nice noises on it. My deer like to listen. Sometimes the rabbits do, too."

" The sun will soon be in," said Morgan. " Let's walk back and meet it halfway——"

For the moment he had clean forgotten the main issue!

" What about Steve Question's gold?"

A sudden light shone in her eyes.

" Question? You call him Steve Question? He is the man—the man who caught me down by the waterfall—and you came—and you fought—you threw him in the water! *And you want his gold !* "

That was what she was thinking with all her might! Men were crazy for gold, oh, she knew that much about men! Wasn't that what most of them were always talking about when she listened under their windows or at their camp-fires? Wasn't that what they were forever quarrelling about, fighting over, killing one another for? And this man was just like all other men. Gold, gold, gold! Give them their gold and they had everything!

" I will trade with you, Man!"

" I told you my name; it's Rob Roy Morgan."

" I will trade with you, Rob Roy Morgan!"

He couldn't guess her thought; he said, " You have it here?"

" Yes. I brought it. And I have some more—some from Steve Question's other place."

That pleased him enormously. No wonder Steve Question was hell-bent to get his hands on her.

" I made a hole; I put it all in there," she told him.

" But some of it must have been paper money?"

She nodded. " I brought it, too—just to tease that man—just to make him mad!"

" Why tease Steve Question? You don't even know him, do you?"

Her face clouded, her eyes darkened.

" I—I don't know . . . It was so long ago . . . One of those bad white men with the Indians—this man looks like him!"

" And at that, it might be!" Morgan muttered. " I wouldn't put it beyond him!"

" I will give you all that gold, all that paper money, too, if you will go away—and never come back—and never, never tell where my place is!"

" Let's walk out to meet the sunshine," said Rob Roy Morgan.

" Don't you want to see the gold? All men love gold so much!"

" And you?"

" No. I played with some of the gold money—it was bright and pretty, and I sewed a sharp thing I got that was like a big iron needle—and wore the gold around my neck. But I don't want money—it isn't any good to me. There is nothing I would do with it—and you, oh, you would be a rich man!"

" Right now I want to watch the sunshine spilling down into this valley of yours."

" You don't even want to—you don't want to look at the gold, Morgan?" She was incredulous.

" Not now. Later maybe. You go out and get what you want, don't you, wherever you can find it! You spy on camps, on cabins, and take what you want? Gold or a gun, cake or a dress—and anything! And get away with it!"

" Sometimes," she said dreamily, " I don't get what I want. Only a little while ago—it was just when the hot days were going and the leaves were all turning yellow and red colours—there were some people. They had wagons and they had cows, too, the way we had—and there were men and women and—and little ones. *And there was a baby !* "

She clasped her hands. She lifted those big eyes of hers heavenwards. She snuggled her hands up to her breast as though cuddling something. " I creeped, oh, so still! It was in a box with a soft blanket. I picked it up while nobody

saw—it was just after dark—I started to run—A woman saw
me and she made terrible screamy noises—and a man jumped
up with a gun—and they saw me!—Oh, it was such a nice,
soft little baby thing! I had to put it down and run!—And I
heard the woman's ugly screamy noises—she said, ' It is that
Spirit woman—that blood-sucking devil woman! She is going
to eat my baby!'—and I just ran away—and that time I
didn't get what I wanted, Morgan.''

He pulled a long face.

" Were you going to eat it?" he asked

" You are a fool," said Honey Eve Crusoe.

Rob Roy Morgan didn't in the least suspect the fact at the
moment, but later he knew that he had come to a forking of
trails. She was looking at him; she saw how his eyes all of a
sudden were stormy.

" I don't want your gold," he said, and bit his words
short off. " Dig a hole, put it down deep, leave it there for all
of me. *I don't want it !* ''

" But—you—you came to get it!"

" I—don't—want—it! *Understand !* ''

" You scare me again!"

He caught her hand, but not making a prisoner of her.

" Let's run," he said. "Over there where the sun is."

The Kid from Virginia, Rob Roy Morgan, the Captain of
Adventure and all that, began to realise that he didn't know
anything after all. What a tremendous forward step! Right
now, running across the grassy floor of this secret park, he
was happy. He didn't exactly know why—it didn't seem to
matter. He thought, " I guess there are things I didn't
know about."

She had never smiled at him, never laughed with him, but
somehow, just running with her—into the sunshine— was like
light, bright laughter.

He threw himself down in the sunlight and let her go.

" Run away, if you want to, Honey," he said. " I'll
never stop you."

Again that amazed incredulity stood tall in her eyes.

" You—you will let me go?"

" Honey, I'm just going to lie here and think a little
while. Did you ever go and flop down on your back and
look up at the sky and—and anyhow try to think? Then I'm

going back down to the Fontanas, I'm going to saddle up and ride away. You stay here. I won't ever tell anybody. And some day I'll come back, just to see you."

" To the Fontanas?"

" You've seen the Fontanas. You get your cakes and dresses and red and yellow roses there! You've seen the Fontana girls—you're not afraid of them, are you? You know they wouldn't hurt you——"

" Did you kill Steve Question last night? I heard the guns go. I saw, early—early this morning, that you sent men away on horseback. They looked like naked men! I couldn't understand!"

" Another man was killed, not Steve Question. He did ride away naked, and his men with him. They tried to rob the Fontanas last night."

" And you stopped them, Morgan?"

" I did my part in it," said Morgan.

" Why didn't you kill them?"

" I don't know," said Morgan.

Instead of running away—now that she knew that she could!—she sat down in the grass beside him.

Neither of them spoke or moved for a long while. The purple-blue of the arc of sky turned a blue-bird blue, then a lighter blue, and the sun poured a golden flood of light down on them. Now and then he watched the curve of her cheek, the soft round of her throat, the play of her long lashes, the deep breaths she drew. She saw that there were curls in his hair, that his cheeks were tanned and hard and clean, that his hands were at once strong and sensitive.

" Do you want to eat, Morgan? I will feed you."

" You have fed me already, Honey," said Morgan.

She, too, lay back in the grass, she slid her slim little fingers through its blades as through tendrils of hair, Mother Earth's hair. She relaxed and threw her bare arm over her face. She put her other hand on her heart; it was throbbing strangely.

They let time slide past. Time has a way of doing that, but they became its accessories and accomplices. The sun stood high straight above them——

Then Morgan, suddenly grown restive, sat up and started to roll a cigarette—and saw Steve Question.

CHAPTER SEVENTEEN

STEVE QUESTION was standing at the mouth of the narrow cleft through the cliffs, looking into the little secret valley. Steve Question clothed, even to hat and boots, obviously not his own, and with his hands on his guns which, one might be sure, were loaded.

Thoughts ran through Morgan's mind like streaks of zigzag lightning: Steve Question, during these hours through which Rob Roy Morgan had loitered so steeped in the present that he had no thought to the past and future, had busied himself. Whether in Twenty Mile, whether at some nearby ranch-house or prospector's cabin, he had clothed and armed himself.

He was broke. Morgan had cleaned his pockets last night. Yet he had thousands of dollars hid away in the mountains— only that damned girl had stolen his gold! His hand was more or less forced; he had come back on the long chance that he might find her again and this time make sure he kept her.

She had left no track behind her. But Rob Roy Morgan, following her, had had never a thought about the trail he left in his pursuit of her, tracks on the bank of the creek, broken ferns, trampled grass. So here already was Steve Question. And not alone, for Morgan saw the narrow face of Kilgore at Steve's shoulder, and could not be sure that there were not other men backing them up.

Morgan flopped down on his back in the grass, and his arm bit into the girl's arm, forcing her down.

" It's Steve Question," he said. " Some of his gang with him. It's all my fault; they followed my tracks in here. Tell me, and tell me the truth: Is there any other way out of here?"

She understood his deadly earnestness. She shook her head.

" No. I told you the truth. Just the one way."

" Wriggle through the grass, like a snake," he told her. " You can do it, I know. Back to your house. Grab a rifle——"

" They are empty, Morgan. My bullets are all gone."

" I won't let them get you," he said. " See that big pine tree? I'm going to get behind it and then argue it out with Steve Question. You crawl off the other way. You'll know how to hide. If they're too many for me, well then, while I've got 'em busy, you make a break for the one way out—*and keep on going ! Don't ever let Steve Question get his paws on you !* "

He snaked his way the ten or fifteen feet to the big pine. She lay perfectly still. He got to his feet and looked out from his bulwark. Steve Question, still at the mouth of the giant fissure in the rock wall, was just about to make his way down the few feet into the valley. Morgan sighted carefully—and shot Steve's hat off.

He couldn't help that. It was bred in the bone. He had handled firearms since he was five years old; his daddy had schooled him; his daddy had taught him several things which he remembered. One was, " Don't ever shoot a settin' bird, Robbie. Give it a break. Throw a rock at it and then when it starts goin', you start shootin'. If it gets away, that's its good luck, and you ain't much of a shot. If you eat it for supper, that's the way it ought to be."

So he had to shoot Steve Question's hat off.

He didn't ignore Kilgore. He sent a second shot, hoping not only to drill Kilgore's hat but, with luck, just to scorch his skull. Somehow he didn't like that man Kilgore.

The two whipped back and out of sight in an instant.

And there was the girl at Morgan's side. She said eagerly:
" You have scared them away, Morgan!"

" No," he said glumly. " No such luck. Steve Question knows by now that this is your hide-out—that likely his money is right here—that I'm with you. That there's just the two of us. No. Like I said, it's all my fault they're here. I'll fight it out with them. If I'm real lucky I'll get 'em before they get me. If it works out the other way, you do what I told you: hide, and when they come poking down here looking for us, you somehow get the jump on them and dodge out through the pass—and keep on going!'

Somewhere, deep down in the girl's heart and human understanding, there occurred then what was like a minor explosion—it dawned on her that all men were not just the same after all—that what Rob Roy Morgan had said to her was the truth—he did not want to molest her—he did not even want the gold! And he was going to fight for her now, giving her one slim hope of escape! That moment, though neither of them had the smallest inkling of it at the time, was one of the great moments of her life.

Morgan said, hurried and emphatic, " You do what I tell you!" And then he forsook the shelter of his pine, and broke into a run, heading straight to the rock-bound passageway where Steve Question and Kilgore were making their plan. He meant to meet them at close range, to be ready when they were—maybe even the great split-second before. He had thrown his rock at the sitting birds—now it was up to them.

What words were passed between Steve Question and Kilgore, of course he could not hear. But, had he guessed at them, he would not have been far wrong.

" It's Morgan!" Steve Question gloated. " We've got him and the girl bottled up in here! Slow does it, Kilgore; no hurry now. I'm going to rip that kid's scalp off—and when he gets to the Happy Hunting Grounds he can tell 'em who skinned him!"

" Slow does it!" A very good even praiseworthy maxim at times, at most times. Not always. As for Rob Roy Morgan, he had forgotten that there was any such word as " slow " in the bright lexicon.

" I'll nab 'em in the alley!" was his quick thought. " There's hardly room for one man at a time in there!"

So he ran on and came to the short, rocky slope that led up to the mouth of the split in the cliff, and kept on going.

He came up into the narrow pass. And there, where they had withdrawn to the first sharp angle in the rock walls, were Steve Question and Kilgore, some thirty feet from him.

Morgan had a gun in each hand.

" Back up or take it!" he said.

Steve and Kilgore were crowded close together, Kilgore behind Steve. It was Kilgore who fired first, shoving the nose of his gun by Steve Question's side, and hitting the rocks close to Morgan, the glancing bullet burning through the slack of his shirt, some ten inches from his heart. Morgan fired next, not one shot only, but emptying the gun in his right hand, four shots. He shifted guns quickly, being better

by far with the right hand than with the left. Steve Question
was shooting, too, and Morgan felt the drive of a bullet, and
kept on with the second gun, and saw Steve Question
sinking down on knees that had turned to water, and felt
another bullet stab into him, and saw Kilgore's evil face
through the powder smoke, and blazed away at him. And
Kilgore sagged down, too—and so did Rob Roy Morgan.

Then there was the girl standing over him.

He wet his lips and spoke to her.

"Hold back a minute—there's just the two of them—
When I tell you, you just step over them—and keep going—
You're a great girl, Honey. The finest that ever was. Now,
dammit, step back around the corner out of range and keep
still!"

He was down, but had his back against the rock wall, and
still had control of his gun hand. Not perfect control, yet he
could manage. He squeezed the trigger. Both Steven
Question and Kilgore were down—alive and venomous, but
down.

"Got you, Steve," said Morgan, and had to clear his
throat, and that was hard work. Pick up your gun—if you
can."

Steve Question's hand groped for the gun he had dropped.
He couldn't seem to find it—his fingers were on it but he
didn't know. He sank even lower down and lay still.

Kilgore lifted his head, his freshly shaven head, and
brought his gun up over Steve Question's back. Morgan fired
first and Kilgore, his gun exploding aimlessly, fell back.

"Now," said Morgan. "Now—go! I'm getting dizzy—I
don't know—but now's your chance, Honey! Jump over 'em
—*run*!"

The girl ran!

She ran to where Steve Question and Kilgore lay. She
snatched up their guns, slipping her fingers, right and left
hand, through the trigger guards; she came running back to
Rob Roy Morgan who, inch by inch, was settling down.

She crouched down beside him and took his head on her
knees. His face was dead white and there was a smear of
blood across it. She could scarcely breathe for the heavy
powder smoke that filled the place. His eyes were shut. She
bent lower and lower over him. She ran her hand inside his

shirt, over his heart. His body was warm. His heart was beating.

She put her hand on her own heart. It was beating like an Indian drum!

" He is good! There is one good man! My papa was a good man—there are some good men in the world! Oh, God! He had been good to me. Let me help now! Help me, God, to help him! Please, God, don't let him—*don't let him die*!"

She put her arm around him and held him close, determined to hold him back from dying.

She took all the guns except one, which was left in Morgan's lax right hand, and ran back to her house. She snatched up a big tin dipper, whirled, ran back and, still running, scooped it full of cold water from her creek. She put cold water on Morgan's face, she wiped the blood away with her hand—there was no wound there! It was just that he had drawn his hand over his face, and there had been blood on his hand from one of his body wounds.

None of the three men had moved. For an instant, a terrible, black moment, she thought that all three were already dead. Again she slipped her hand inside his shirt. His heart was beating. Slow—strong—steady.

She put the dipper to his mouth and Morgan gulped the cold water down, gulped without knowing, without opening his eyes. She tore his shirt open all the way down to his belt; she saw his three wounds, one in the shoulder, two in the side. His blood was pouring out.

She leaped up and looked at Steve Question and Kilgore; they lay still, white-faced—dead? She didn't know. She didn't wait to see. She ran back to her house. She caught down one of her prettiest dresses from her wardrobe—at least she thought it one of her prettiest dresses, never guessing that it was Señorita Aldegonda Fontana's nicest nightgown—and was tearing it into strips as she ran back to Morgan.

She washed his wounds the best she could in cold water, and tied strips of the clean white cloth about him. She tried to make the wounds stop pouring his blood out. And she put more water on his forehead, and she again put the dipper to his lips, and he drank.

This time he opened his eyes.

He sat straight up, shaking his head, he saw her bending over him, and frowned. He thought she had gone long ago. He remembered Steve Question and Kilgore, and fumbled for his gun, and she helped him get his grip on it.

"Please, Morgan," she whispered, "be good. Be still. Don't move. You are hurt so bad. Those two men, you shot them both. Maybe already they are dead. If they come alive and try to do anything, I can shoot, Morgan. I will kill them. I won't let them come near you. Please, Morgan." She ran her arm about him, squeezing him close to her breast. "Be good and lie still. You won't die. I won't let you!"

He tried to smile up at her. Not much of a smile.

He said, "Just the two of them? No one else behind them?"

"No one. And you shot both of them down. We are safe now, Morgan. Just you be very still—and—and get well! Oh, Morgan! Oh, please don't die and leave me all alone!" And she began to cry. Her heart was so full, it felt like bursting.

"Shush," said Morgan. "I'm all right. I can tell. I've never died yet, have I? And don't intend to now. Only, I told you to go while the trail was open."

"I won't," said Honey Eve Crusoe.

And that seemed to settle that point.

"I've messed things up pretty bad for you," said Morgan. "I was so busy following you, I didn't even think of somebody on my trail. I ought to have remembered Steve Question."

"It's all right, Morgan——"

"No. It's all wrong." He began lifting himself up. "But somehow I'm going to make it all right yet."

"What are you going to try to do?"

"I'll find out if they're both dead, Steve and Kilgore. If they are, I'll get 'em away from here somehow—I'll cover all tracks coming in here—you can go on living here and nobody'll ever find you—unless you go hanging red flowers in the tops of poplar trees!"

He made his slow way, a hand on the rock wall to steady him, to where Steve Question and Kilgore lay.

"Their guns—they're gone!"

"I got their guns."

He squatted down. Both men looked to be in pretty bad

shape. He had shot Steve Question through the upper body, maybe elsewhere too. There was a shallow groove along Kilgore's shaved pate, nothing particularly serious, from the look of it; another body wound for Kilgore that looked bad. But it remained that both men were still alive.

" I ought to shove a gun between their eyes, and get done with it," Morgan muttered. " But it goes against the grain somehow. Wonder why?"

" Morgan! You're killing yourself! You ought to be lying down, not letting your blood run out like that. You ought to be resting—lying down—letting your wounds start to get well."

" I've got to get 'em out of here. Have you got some rope at your place? A piece long enough so that I can lower them down the cliff where they climbed up after us?"

" Yes, I have. Then what?"

" Their horses won't be far off. I'll haul 'em off some-where——"

" Oh, but you can't! *You can't!* They—they've nearly killed you, too. *I won't let you!* "

" I got you into this mess, I tell you. I'm going to get you out. Go get me your rope. And you might bring back another dipper of water."

She sped away, snatching up the dipper as she ran, and in a very few minutes was back again, a coil of rope in one hand, the dipper in the other slopping water out as she hurried. And she found a very quiescent trio, Steve Question and Kilgore as she had left them, Rob Roy Morgan seeming to have made up with them—since his head was on Steve Question's knee, and Morgan looked like a man sound asleep or dead.

How many times had her sensitive hand listened for his heartbeat? Yes, it still drummed—strong, steady—but slow, a laboured drumming.

She moved him so that his head was on her lap, not Steve's, and again she bathed his face and temples, and again gave him water to drink. And he drank it as before, thirstily. His eyes opened, clouded, studied her, cleared. Again the tears stung her eyes as he tried to smile up at her.

" I don't know what to do with you," she said. " You are hurt bad. But I won't let you die. *Where is your horse?*"

" I left it down at Fontanas'. Why?"

" They are your friends? You have other friends there, too?"

He wondered about Smoke Keena and Red Barbee: they'd come in mighty handy right now. Gone, hours ago, no doubt.

" I am going to the Fontanas'! I will find your friends. They will come and help."

" No!" he roared it at her, and she dropped down at his side again. " We do this my way," said Morgan. " Come, help me."

She helped him and they dragged the two unconscious men, Kilgore first because he was on the farthest side of Steve Question, then Steve, too, to the outer opening of the cleft through the cliff. Morgan, fighting his faintness and dizziness, made a loop about Kilgore's body, under the armpits, braced himself and slowly let Kilgore down the thirty feet or so—and all the while the girl was holding the rope with him paying it out slowly.

" One man down," said Morgan, and pretended to grin. He sat down on the ledge. " Will you run down your stair-step poplar tree, and get the rope free? Then we'll let Steve down."

She obeyed docilely—because she had already made up her mind what to do. In no time at all she was back, the coil of rope in her hand. And then they lowered Steve Question to lie cheek by jowl with his playmate, Kilgore.

" And now," said Morgan. " Now—I've got to sit down a minute——"

She ran the rope about his body, as he had done for the other men, making a trustworthy knot; she dragged him close to the cliff edge; she lay flat on her back with her feet braced against the rock; she made sure that she could do it; she moved one foot and gently shoved him nearer the edge. She felt his body slipping over, and she lay back again to brace both feet—and prayed between her clenched teeth—and slowly, slowly paid the rope out. And so after what seemed a long time and was only a couple of minutes, she deposited the all but lifeless form of Mr. Rob Roy Morgan with the inert bodies of Steve Question and Kilgore.

She peeked over; she jumped up and ran again. Back to her house. She tore down the pretty dresses. For the first time in her life—the first time since life really began, those ten years ago—she was going to see people! Men and women. The Fontanas! And she had to wear a Fontana dress!

She didn't have any shoes. Shoes, time and again, she had pilfered, but always they hurt her feet and she had thrown them away. She had to wear her moccasins. For a dress, she chose one she had stolen a couple of years ago; maybe they had forgotten it! She didn't think about arranging her hair; it was floating down in a glorious cascade over her shoulders, down below her waist, when she raced down her poplar tree.

She took time to look at Morgan again, to take the rope off him and toss it far away into the bushes. She had brought his gun, just one; she put it in his hand. She strove to make him lie comfortably. He shook his head, opened his eyes——

" Your gun is in your hand, Morgan," she told him, her lips close to his ear. " I will be back quick." And her lips brushed his forehead. Then she was away like an arrow.

Much had happened since dawn. It was only high noon now. And the Fontanas, from Señor Fontana and Señora Fontana, all the way down to the littlest Fontana, almost jumped out of their skins.

Señor Fontana, smoking in the patio, had seen her first, and exclaimed," Here comes a girl, running! A strange girl!"

She came into the patio—oh, she had been there many a time, but always in the deep of night, when the household slept!—and, with her heart in her throat, walked straight to Señor Fontana.

" Is any one here," she asked simply, " who is a good friend to Rob Roy Morgan!"

" But we are all his good friends, Señorita!" cried Fontana. And then the patio filled; there was the Señora, there were the girls, their big eyes bigger than ever before—there was Mentor and Benito—and Smoke Keena and Red Barbee. For these two, with Morgan vanished, had lingered on, fearing some trouble had caught him, fearing some back fire from the raging men with the shaven heads.

There were many exclamations. " Oh, who is she?" cried Zayda. " Oh, what a little beauty!" cried Aldegonda. " It is that girl——" began Don Benito. And a small voice, with a hand quickly pressed over ripe lips, was gasping: " My dress! The one that disappeared two years ago!"

" Who here—which men—are the best friends of Rob Roy Morgan's? He is in trouble; he is hurt; he needs help. And his horse. And I want a horse, too!"

Smoke Keena hurried to her. " Me, I'm with you, Miss. I'll get the horses. How far from here?"

" Not far. Just up there." She pointed to the mountain slope. " Hurry!"

Red Barbee hurried with him. The two headed for the barn and the horses. She ran after them.

" Look at her hair!" whispered Anita. " It is like a wild pony's! Oh, it is lovely and as long as I am high, almost!"

" It is the Tiger Lily girl!" said Don Benito, his voice hushed. " I saw her once before. I know."

" It is my—my dress!" said Teresita. " And I thought Josefa, that fat Indian girl, stole it—and I slapped her!"

" Be still, be still, little ones," said Fontana. " There are things we don't understand. There is trouble in the air."

CHAPTER EIGHTEEN

When Rob Roy Morgan dragged his eyes open and tried to figure out where he was and what had happened, and all that, he looked up into a face vaguely familiar.

He said, puzzled and short-tempered, " Who the devil are you?"

Then he knew. It was Doc Bones. That meant Twenty Mile, and the last thing Morgan remembered was the edge of Eden, a long way from Twenty Mile. He tried to rear up.

" Lay flat," said Doc Bones, " or I'll put you down with a tack hammer. How'n hell can I fix up all these gouges in you if you keep hopping around?"

Morgan, through sheer weariness lay flat and hardly winced as Doc Bones went about his business. The Doc was whistling through his teeth. He was in a hurry. In the back room Morgan heard, as from a great distance, the clink of bottle and glass, the riffle of cards, the clink of coins. Seemed as though there was always a game running in Doc Bone's back room.

" You see, Doctor? He'll be good. Won't you Morgan?"

It was a soft, caressing voice, the loveliest voice he had ever heard. He knew who it was without looking at her. But look up at her he did, through the sheer joy of it.

" But you shouldn't——"

That was as far as he got. Soft fingers on his lips hushed him. He was quite willing, in this new mood of his, to lie still, to let the reins slip out of his hands. Of course she shouldn't be here—but here she was—and he was glad.

Doc Bones fixed him up. They got a piece of canvas, spread a blanket on top of it, and carried him out; they were Smoke Keena and Red Barbee, Big Mouth Altoona Jackson and Tony, using one hand, and Buck Braddock and Charlie Duff, six of them carrying him so as to make it gentle for him—and two girls hovering and helping, and the two girls were Barbara and the Wild Girl!

They bore him, stepping carefully, to his own place, his own room, and put him into his bed—and the men went out and left Barbara and Honey Eve Crusoe to tuck him in and take care of him.

They didn't tell Morgan everything he might have wanted to know for several days. He was too close to the edge of things, a man not to be troubled, a man to rest and sleep and save what little strength had not already been drained out of him.

He asked once how he got here. Before he was answered he asked, " What about Steve Question? And Kilgore?" When he insisted, and he didn't do much insisting, his mind wandered loosely, they answered. It was always Smoke Keena or Barbee—or Barbara or the Girl of Secret Eden Valley, who answered. Putting him off all that they could— Doc Bones' orders were not to get him worked up—they answered his questions.

Steve Question was alive. So was Kilgore. Matters would have been simplified if both had died. Doc Bones, damning them up hill and down dale for bothering him when there was a fat jack pot coming up—and by the way he stayed at his guns long enough to see the jack pot go into other hands than his, which did not gladden him any, though he still whistled through his teeth—patched up both Steve and Kilgore and said, " Pole cats are hard to kill. If a cat has nine lives, how many has a pole cat? Ever notice, if you kill a snake the damn thing won't die until sundown?"

. . . There was a buzzing in Rob Roy Morgan's ears. A heavy booming sound as of drums far off, coming nearer. He shook his head, trying to get the noise out of his ears. It persisted. He squinched his eyes tight, batted them wide open.

" What's all that racket?" he demanded, his voice faint and rough.

" Please, Morgan, lie still."

" Oh, it's you?" said Morgan. " How come you're here? You've got mighty pretty hair, Honey. And you've got a real dress on."

" I bought it at the store—the first dress I ever bought in my life! And I took some of your money——"

" I keep hearing things. Like an army marching. Am I crazy? Or is it just the blood pumping back through me? It goes, boom—boom—boom—boom——"

Her hand was soft and warm on his brow.

" Boom," she said. " That's what they call it, Morgan. A big gold strike just at the edge of town—hundreds of men have been pouring in—they say a boom has hit Twenty Mile."

" I said so," said Morgan. " I told them that a boom— Your hand is so——"

He went to sleep, muttering, " Boom—boom—*Boom*!"

He didn't know that she had stayed with him day and night. He had his two rooms; she had pre-emptied the outer one and would not budge. She had not the faintest inkling of that time-honoured trite phrase," What will people say?" Where in all her life could she have heard such empty-headed chatter? And if she had heard it, she would not have cared. He had been good to her. And she loved him. And she knew it.

At night, Barbara, knowing, stayed with her, or Barbara's mother. She thought that was just because they wanted to help.

She did not know that Smoke Keena fell in love with her the first minute, and so did Big Mouth Altoona Jackson, and

so did Buck Braddock and Charlie Duff—as did Don Benito
and Señor Fontana who hastened to look in on the wounded
man, each loving her in his own way. She was such a lovely,
lovable little thing, they swore she was the first real girl,
utterly unspoiled, just a natural dear girl, that ever lived.
Señor Fontana, going home, raved about her to such an
extent that Señora Fontana sniffed and said she would go, too,
to Twenty Mile to see what she could do for their young
friend—and all the Fontana girls wanted to go, too.

The girl who had lived alone since she was six years old
now burst into a new world. And it seemed that her starved
heart was big enough to take the whole world into it. She
couldn't tell Morgan about the two Old Men—when she wasn't
with him she was with them. At first every one, taking Doc
Bones' word for it, said that neither of them could live more
than a few hours.

" Oh, I love them so!" she said. " There are so many
good men—and I didn't know!"

" Boom—boom—boom!" Rob Roy Morgan, through the
mists of weakness and the throb of his own blood tides, heard
it. The little town was filled to overflowing with men, all
sorts and conditions of men. But they were men alike in one
thing, they wanted to fill their hands with gold. This was
California, wasn't it? And wasn't young California a
beautiful, golden-haired, blue-eyed virgin, still awaiting the
strong hand of the conqueror? California, the bountiful,
California holding in her hands everything a man wanted,
ready to give, to surrender, to enrich.

And so the days thrummed by. There were a lot of things
which Morgan did not know: he did not know what a glory
the girl of the hidden ways, the lonely trail, had found the
world to be. He did not know that for several days the two
Old Men were near death because Steve Question and Kilgore,
led along by Slim Pickens, now of fading memory, had told
them of the two old men: That they were old misers who,
along with their dried lizards and salubrious red dirt and
withered weeds, had also a lot of gold money hidden somewhere; how Steve and Kilgore and Slim, not to make too
much noise when they broke in to rob the old men, hadn't
found it necessary to shoot them, but had beat them halfway
to death with their gun-barrels. But old Luke Christmas and

Gran'pa Jonathan had weathered the storm. Tough old boys, they were, and kept on living after Doc Bones as good as wrote their obits—and, incidentally, lived a good ten years after Doc Bones was gathered to his fathers.

None of these things did Morgan know. He knew that Steve Question and Kilgore were alive and on the road to recovery—like himself. But he did not know what awaited them. Nor did they.

But he was worried, knowing them alive. One night, feeling his oats, thinking he ought to get up and get dressed and go find out a lot of things for himself, he looked up into the girl's eyes, nearly always just above him, like stars. He said:

" Tell me. I'm all right now. In the morning I'm up and around. Tell me this: has Steve Question told everybody where your hide-out is? Will you have to leave it?"

She squeezed his hand.

" No, Morgan. He——"

" Don't call me Morgan," he said irritably. " That's what all the men folks call me, all but Nancy Keena, and the big fool calls me Virginia, for which some day I'll kill him and take his hide. My name is Rob Roy Morgan. My dad called me Royal, just to be funny; my mother called me Robbie——"

" I like that. Robbie! No, Robbie, Steve Question hasn't said a word. You see, he thinks that maybe I've got all his gold hid up there, and he doesn't want anybody to get there before he does. So he is keeping his mouth shut. And——"

She didn't tell him the rest. A boom town was a mad town. Men surged in from all ports of the world—ships with billowing sails still came into San Francisco Bay, and men deserted, as men had before, and poured into the mines, and right now many of them came, hell-bent to Twenty Mile. Hard men they were, or they would not be here, men who flowed along in a heady, tumultuous tide. They heard enough of the Steve Question crowd in the first hour to make them yearn to use a good stout rope and the first tree. Just for what they had done to Luke Christmas and old Jonathan, if for nothing else——

And so Morgan got, at last, to hear of what happened to the two old men.

He got rousing, raving mad.

" Those two old boys that wouldn't hurt a grasshopper, that are just the finest two old boys that ever happened—and between them they haven't got two dollars. Let me up! Dammit——"

And the next day they did let him up; there was no holding him down any longer. Once up, he groped for a chair and sat down in a hurry, like a man whose bones had turned to water. Smoke Keena said, " Hold it, Virginia! " and dashed off to his room for a bottle of whisky.

" I guess I'll go slow for a day or two, Nancy," said Morgan. " The old grey mare ain't what she used to be. But, Nancy, do this for me: soon as you can, round up all the boys and bring 'em in here. I want to make 'em a speech."

It was a soft-spoken speech that he made them. He sat at his table in his front room; he was haggard, gaunt, a spectre of a man, and yet there was the same bright fire in his eyes.

Even the two Old Men came in. Luke Christmas had a bandage round his head, and Jonathan showed a healing scar from above his right eyebrow down across his thin cheek, all the way to his chin.

" I don't see Slim Pickens and Baldy and Skinner," Morgan said. Then he scratched his jaw. " Sure, Slim got killed, playing around with Steve Question's gang. How about Baldy and Shorty Skinner?"

" Nobody can find hide nor hair of them two, Virginia," said Keena. " Maybe they've gone somewhere else."

Morgan nodded, understanding. He said, " I've done me a mite of thinking, boys, and I've changed my mind about a thing or two. I did some pretty damn big talking the other day, saying I'd cut you boys in on something big. Hell with it. I don't see it that way any longer.—Now keep your shirts on! I know where Steve Question's cache is—I can grab it for maybe forty, fifty, maybe a hundred thousand dollars. And I'm going to—Just watch me do it! And I'm going to give every damn cent of it back where it belongs! Sabe? It's easy to find out who shipped the money by stage —it's still theirs—and I don't want any part of it!

" Now shut up and listen to me! I've changed my mind about two-three things, maybe more. Stick with me, if you want to, and you'll still ride easy. But not the way I started out. There's a boom on in Twenty Mile. Picks and shovels are dirt cheap over at McWilliams' store. I've got a notion for once in my life that I want the cream scooped off the top of the pan—but, by the Lord, I want to do the skimming myself. I don't need some low-life like Steve Question to go out and make me my money. I want a great big ranch, like Fontana's, and I'm going to have it; but I don't need to steal the damn thing. California is wide open, and a man can have anything he wants—and I want mine. And I'm going to get it—my way!

" Now, shut up, I told you! I said I was going to make a speech, didn't I? Here's a damn good speech: I'll whack up with you boys on everything I've snagged in so far, because I said I would."

" It ain't any speech—it's a damn sermon," said Big Mouth Altoona.

" Shut your trap, Big Mouth," snapped Morgan, " if you can. Steve Question is a dirty dog, and you can tell him I said so. I don't want anything his paws have been on. I can make my own way. I'm always going to make my own. And—I'm going to do it—*in my own way! Sabe, hombres?* If you don't like my way, say so, and get the hell out of here. If you want to stick with me—that's different and it's your business."   He dragged a buckskin pouch up out of his pocket and slammed it down on the table. " There's money there; split it up, Nancy. Leave me out of it, and deal all the other boys their share."

The Blind Man joggled the Old Man in the ribs with a lean elbow. He put his hand over his mouth to whisper:

" Like we said. Just a pup he is, just growing up. He'll make the grade all right—give him plenty time!"

The two Old Men stepped out together, holding hands. They felt pretty shaky, but could still navigate under their own power. They saw the many strangers milling along the street. One of them saw, the other felt, and was told what the crowd looked like, young and tough and harum-scarum, milling around like a scared herd of cattle. They went straight to the store, McWilliams' store.

There was McWilliams in the rear, hunched over his table behind the counter, going through papers, his hair on end, chewing at his lead pencil and achieving little else. There was Barbara, ready to wait on customers, a pale, distrait, Barbara red-eyed from weeping, but doing her best to be brave. They went straight to her.

"Miss Barbara," said the Old Man, Luke Christmas, "me and Johnny want to talk to you."

"You two old dears!" She hugged both their hands in her little ones. "I'm all right, boys."

"Your daddy went and lost that last four hundred dollars, didn't he?" said Gran'pa Jonathan.

She nodded, then remembered that he couldn't see, and said faintly, "Yes, he did. He's terribly sorry, though, and——"

"Miss Barbie," said Luke Christmas, "will you come along with me and Johnny a few minutes? It's awful important; you can help us a lot. And your old man can run the shop for ten minutes. Will you, Miss Barbie?"

"Why, of course I will! I'll do anything in the world you ask me to, and you know it."

She called to McWilliams that she was going out for a few minutes; he let her go, hardly lifting his head.

The three, with Barbara in the middle and holding their hands, went along the crowded sidewalk.

"Seems as though," said the Blind Man, "there's heaps of folks in town. Hm. They might be wanting to buy a lot of things out'n the store, Barbie."

Barbara's lips trembled. "Yes," she said, and the little word was all but lost in her deep sigh. She squeezed their hands tighter. "You two are such darlings! You know, don't you, that we're through? Dad can't go on with it—he is broke, he can't pay what he owes and——"

The Blind Man said sharply, "Hey, Luke! What's going on across the road? Sounds like big doings."

"We're right straight across the road from the Pay Dirt Saloon, Johnny. There's a crowd busting in at the doors, a tough-looking crowd of Johnny-come-Latelys. There's a great big man sort of herding 'em in—he's a sailor man, you can tell by the way he walks—looks like he hadn't walked on land much since he was born. Sort of waddles, Johnny; you know——"

"What are they up to, Luke?"

" I dunno," said Luke. " Fellers sort of like a thunderstorm."

" Where are we going?" Barbara asked.

" Not far," said Luke Christmas. " Just to our place."

Rob Roy Morgan was sitting on a bench in the sun at their front door. And the Girl from Hidden Valley was standing near him, lovely in her pretty new dress—and wearing shoes. Barbara had picked them out for her, and they had pretty tall heels—and if they were a wee bit stiff on her feet and hurt a little, she didn't mind. She kept looking down at them. They were nice. They made her feel very much like a lady. She had never thought about them before —a lady!

" Morgan, if you can walk a few steps, will you come along with us?" said Luke. " You, too, Miss. Just to Johnny's and my room."

Morgan cocked up his brows, wondering what was up. He said, " Sure, Luke," and put his hands down on the bench to heave himself up. In an instant there were two girls at his sides, helping him. He looked shame-faced, saying, " Aw, shucks, I can make it," but they conveyed him along.

In the two Old Men's room the visitors stood and wondered. The place was still pretty much upset, things scattered all over. But both Luke Christmas and old Jonathan were grinning.

" Steve Question and that man Kilgore and Slim Pickens busted in on us here," said Luke. " They sort of messed things up. Slim, we reckon, had a pretty fair guess, but he didn't know how smart me and Johnny had got to be, 'cause we had to. And they missed a trick. Looky here."

He picked up an old rusty tin can that had been kicked across the room, a can overflowing with dried lizards. Another old, battered can with dried brown weeds on top, then dirt. A broken cigar box, falling apart, with dried " yarbs " and a couple of rattlesnake's appendages trimming the top.

" Got all three cans, Luke?" asked old Jonathan.

" Yep." He put them into Jonathan's thin old hands. " Feel 'em, Johnny, then pour 'em out on top the bunk. We got damn nigh four thousand dollars there, ain't we?"

" We got," said old Jonathan, " three thousand *and* nine

hundred *and* seventy-two dollars, *and* forty cents. Count 'em and see if I'm a liar."

" Spill it!" said Luke.

Jonathan spilled it, spread it widely across the bunk. There were gold pieces, mostly twenties, a few silver dollars, a wad of greenbacks.

" Count it, anybody that wants to," said Luke. " Jonathan, he always knows; he says it's three thousand *and* nine hundred *and* seventy-two dollars *and* forty cents. And he knows."

They stared at old Jonathan, who had poured all this wealth out; he was scrabbling around with his lean fingers, stacking twenties, feeling the silver dollars, smoothing out wadded paper money. They stared at Luke Christmas.

Luke pulled at his lower lip.

" Me and Johnny sort of believe in the future of Twenty Mile," he said. " So we're going in business here. And we got to have a pardner, since me and Johnny ain't so spry as we used to be, and don't like to stay up late nights counting what we made, so we're taking Miss Barbara in as pardner, and she's going to take over the store in her own name, and pay off what debts there is, and the store is going to be in her name, so me and Johnny won't be responsible for nothing, and——"

Barbara, tears running down her face, hugged them close, one after the other. She tried to say something—she couldn't. Not a word.

" Don't you go waste all that money, Barbie," said Luke. " Me and Johnny has been saving it up for nigh on forty year——"

" Thirty-eight year, come October," said the Blind Man. " You hang tight to it, Barbie. And your dad—Hell's bells, little girl, he'd make a fine clerk for you."

Morgan, as weak as he was, stepped over and hugged the two Old Men. He said, " I knew all the time you boys had it in you, that you were real folks." Then he pulled up, glared around him and said, " Me, I'm going across the street to see what's all the fuss about.—And you better look out, Miss Barbara, these two old four-flushers don't take all you got."

He walked, wide leggedly to keep his balance, over to the

Pay Dirt Saloon. He balanced on his heels, letting other men have the right of way; it was just about all he could do to keep going. He squeezed in when he saw his clear chance.

The place was overcrowded. And the crowd was like a swarm of bees, buzzing, hunting a place to settle, or so it seemed to him. A man, a very big man, as big as a barn door and as solid as oak, caught him by the arm, slung him around and grabbed his hat off. Then the big man laughed, clapped the hat back and said genially:

" No harm meant, mate. We're just looking for fellers with their heads shaved. Every damned man of 'em is going to hang, long before come daylight again. Lucky for you you got a mane of hair like an old tom lion. Hey, kid! What's gone wrong? You look sort of sick! I didn't do you no harm, did I?"

The bartender let out a yell that pierced through the buzz and noise of the saloon like a clean knife.

" Hey, you, you sea-going jackass, lay off! That's Morgan. He's just been shot up by Steve Question and Kilgore. Can't you see, you damn fool, he can't hardly stand up?"

" The hell I can't," said Morgan, and shook himself loose from the sailor's relaxing grip. He got back to the wall, at the side of the door. He needed something to lean against.

He got his hands, not altogether steady, though his teeth were set and he was putting every ounce of power he had left into the moment, on both guns. He seemed to smell powder smoke even before the first finger found the trigger.

At the far end of the bar he saw Steve Question and Kilgore. Their hats were off and you couldn't miss their shaven heads. And they were unarmed, and men were laughing at them. And a man stood close to them, a coil of rope in his hands.

" So you're Morgan," said the big sailor. " I've heard a lot about you, matey; so has the whole damn town of Twenty Mile. There are a couple of friends of yours, those bald-headed boys. We're buying 'em a few drinks, old-timer, then we're taking 'em out and hanging 'em high to the first tree. Want to come to the party? It won't last long, but——"

Then there came a diversion. Morgan saw them as they came in through the swinging doors, Baldy Bates and Shorty Skinner, those two followers in the footsteps of the recently dead Slim Pickens, and there were with them three other men he had met—three of the Steve Question crowd who had taken him to the old barn to rob him and, perhaps, in order to make a clean job of it, so that he couldn't babble, to cut his throat. Other men didn't note their entrance as quickly as he did.

The five went straight to Steve Question and Kilgore— and shoved guns into their hands. So now there was a compact crowd of seven men, with a leaping hope blazing high in Steve Question's eyes. And Steve Question, hate like poison in his veins, yelled, and sounded gleeful and at last triumphant:

" Got you, Morgan! Everybody else stand back!"

Steve Question fired the first shot. The big sailor ducked, squatted down on the floor, and reached for his gun. After all he wasn't a sailor by trade, just a pick-and-shovel man from Hang Town, who one night, with gold in his sack, had dropped down to San Francisco for a time, and had got himself shanghaied on the rolicsome, frolicsome, utterly lawless Barbary Coast.

Rob Roy Morgan, intuitively warned, blazed away with both guns. Bullets whined all about him. Other men chipped in, men who were out to-night, most of them warm with liquor, to hang the Steve Question gang. Morgan caught a bullet in the leg and sat down and kept on shooting. He saw Baldy Bates clutch at his side and drop his gun, saw him fumbling on the floor for it.

A man at the far end of the bar lifted a whisky bottle high—a bottle almost full—and broke it over Shorty Skinner's head—and Shorty's hat came off, revealing his hairless pate, and Shorty went down, flat on his back. The bottle broke, wasting nearly a quart of whisky—very, very bad whisky, however.

The bartender ran down to the end of the bar—he had a " persuader " in his hand, a leathern thing like a long, slim sausage, loaded with buckshot. He crowned a staggering, bleeding Steve Question with it, and ducked down behind his bar, listening to bullets whizzing like hornets.

Then Honey Eve Crusoe came running! She hadn't the vaguest idea that nice girls didn't go into saloons. How could she know? She had watched Morgan weave his way across the road and into the place, she had heard the shots——

And there she was, hovering over him as he sat on the floor and kept on shooting. A bullet snipped off one of her curls; she just tossed her hair back and knelt down by Morgan.

A yell went up from the crowd, a truly magnificent yell. They all knew her, though she hadn't any way of knowing that during these last few days every man in Twenty Mile was looking at her as she went back and forth between Morgan's place and the store. As Smoke Keena and Big Mouth Altoona and the Fontanas, men and girls, and even the Señora, were in love with her—in their various ways—so was all Twenty Mile.

It didn't last long. Out of the seven of the Steve Question gang, four were left with enough life in them to hang. Nor did the final ceremony take long.

Rob Roy Morgan stood up and held on to the bar with both hands, his guns in their leathers again, and had his drink. And every man in the place took his hat off as Morgan went out—but that was not for Morgan. It was for the girl with an arm about him, steadying him, helping him home.

CHAPTER NINETEEN

ABOUT a week later, this is what happened:

It was a lovely, soft, warm summer evening trimmed with stars.

Morgan said, his hand finding hers, " Let's go back to your valley. Let's live there the way you did. Nobody knows where it is."

She said, " Oh, yes, Robbie! Let's go!"

He spoke shyly, " How about getting married first, Honey? Will you?"

She didn't exactly know what marriage was all about. So Rob Roy Morgan had to do the best he could toward explaining. And when he finished, she asked simply:

" What good will all that do you?"

He didn't quite know, but he did know that it was one of those things that were imperative. He said, "Well, you would belong just to me, you'd be mine as long as we live, and the other way 'round, me, I'd just belong to you."

"We'd be like that anyhow, Morgan—I mean, Robbie——"

"Will you, Honey? Do you want to?"

"Yes! And let's get married quick, right now, so we can be there to-night! I want you to see my stars shining down into our valley!"

THE END